You are cordially invited to Blythe Gifford's

Royal Weddings

A hint of scandal this way comes!

Anne of Stamford and Lady Cecily
serve two of the highest ladies in the land. And
with their close proximity to the royal family
they are privy to some of the greatest scandals
the royal court has ever known!

As Anne and Cecily's worlds threaten to come
crashing down two men enter their lives—
dashing, gorgeous, and bringing with them
more danger than ever before. Suddenly these
two strong women must face a new challenge:
resisting the power of seduction!

Follow Anne of Stamford's story in
Secrets at Court
Already available

And read Cecily, Countess of Losford's story in
Whispers at Court
June 2015

AUTHOR NOTE

Historically, for most children of royal birth, the course of true love not only 'never did run smooth', it was not expected to run at all. A royal wedding was typically more like the signing of a treaty than a celebration of love.

But King Edward III, who ruled England for most of the fourteenth century, had a soft spot in his heart for his oldest daughter. And her romance with a French prisoner of war—or hostage—is one of the most astonishing love stories of the medieval era.

Today, the very word 'hostage' brings shivers of fear. But during the medieval war between England and France an elaborate set of rules—both economic and chivalric—guided the taking of prisoners in battle. A hostage was held until a ransom was paid, but he was treated according to his noble station and expected to conduct himself accordingly. In return, some of the French knights held in the court of the English King were entertained (dare I say?) 'royally'.

Cecily, Countess of Losford, has no sympathy for the French hostages—men she blames for her father's death—and she disapproves of the Princess's flirtation with one of them. In an effort to stop 'whispers at Court', she forms an unlikely alliance with Marc de Marcel, a French hostage who learned long ago that for too many of his fellows, 'honour' is no more than a word. As Cecily and Marc try to keep the English Princess and the French Lord apart the two of them become dangerously close—until finally each must choose between the demands of honour and the desires of the heart.

WHISPERS
AT COURT

Blythe Gifford

MILLS
BOON

Published in Great Britain 2015
by Mills & Boon, an imprint of Harlequin (UK) Limited,
Eton House, 18-24 Paradise Road, Richmond, Surrey, TW9 1SR

© 2015 Wendy B. Gifford

ISBN: 978-0-263-24786-2

Harlequin (UK) Limited's policy is to use papers that are natural,
renewable and recyclable products and made from wood grown in
sustainable forests. The logging and manufacturing processes conform
to the legal environmental regulations of the country of origin.

Printed and bound in Spain
by CPI, Barcelona

After many years in public relations, advertising and marketing, **Blythe Gifford** started writing seriously after a corporate lay-off. Ten years later she became an overnight success when she sold her RWA Golden Heart finalist manuscript to Mills & Boon. Her books, set primarily in medieval England or early Tudor Scotland, usually feature a direct connection to historical royalty.

She loves to have visitors at blythegifford.com, 'likes' at facebook.com/BlytheGifford and Tweets at twitter.com/BlytheGifford

Books by Blythe Gifford

Mills & Boon® Historical Romance

Royal Weddings

Secrets at Court
Whispers at Court

The Brunson Clan

Return of the Border Warrior
Captive of the Border Lord
Taken by the Border Rebel

Linked by Character

The Harlot's Daughter
In the Master's Bed

Stand-Alone Novels

The Knave and the Maiden
Innocence Unveiled
His Border Bride

Visit the author profile page at millsandboon.co.uk

For my readers, with all my thanks.

A special wave to the Chicago Divas,
who happily listened to me whine, and to Keena Kincaid,
Terri Brisbin, Amanda Berry, Robin Owens
and Kim Law, whose brainstorming triggered a solution.

Chapter One

Mon Dieu, this island is cold.

Frigid English wind whipped Marc de Marcel's hair from his forehead, then slithered beneath the chainmail circling his neck. He peered at the knights at the other end of the field, wondering which would be his opponent and which would face his fellow Frenchman.

Well, it mattered not. 'One pass,' he muttered, 'and I'll unhorse either one.'

'The code of chivalry calls for three runs with the lance,' Lord de Coucy said, 'followed by three blows with the sword. Only then can a winner be declared.'

Marc sighed. It was a shame that jousts had become such tame affairs. He would have welcomed the opportunity to kill another *goddam*

Anglais. 'A waste of the horse's strength. And mine.'

'Best not offend someone when you are at their mercy, *mon ami*. Cooperation with our captors will make our time here much more tolerable.'

'We are hostages. Nothing can make that tolerable.'

'Ah, the ladies can.' De Coucy nodded towards the stands. 'They are *très jolie*.'

He glanced at them. Women stretched to King Edward's right, near impossible to distinguish. The queen must be the one gowned in ermine-trimmed purple, but the rest were a blur of matching tan and violet.

Except for one. Her dark hair was graced with a gold circlet and she glared in his direction of the field with crossed arms and a frown. Even at this distance, he could read a loathing that matched his own, as if she despised them all.

Well, the feeling was mutual. *Les femmes Anglaise* were not his concern. Two visiting kings sat beside the English Edward today, overlooking the tournament field. 'It is *les rois* I would impress, not the ladies.'

'Ah, a chevalier always strives to impress the ladies,' his dark-haired friend said, with a smile. 'It is the best way to impress their men.'

It amazed him, this ability the younger man,

Enguerrand, Lord de Coucy, had to cut down a foe with an axe one day and warble a *chanson* with the ladies the next. Marc had taught him much of the first and nothing of the second.

'How do you do it?' Marc asked. 'How do you nod and smile at your captors?'

'To uphold the honour of French chivalry, *mon ami.*'

What he meant was to preserve the pretence that Christian knights lived their lives according to the principles of chivalry.

And that, as Marc well knew, was a lie.

Men spoke allegiance to the code, then did as they pleased.

'French honour died at Poitiers.' Poitiers, when cowardly French commanders, even the king's oldest son, had fled the field, leaving the king to fight alone.

Enguerrand shook his head. 'We do not fight that war today.'

But Marc did. He fought it still, though the battles were over and the truce had been signed. He was a hostage of *les Anglais*, trapped in this frozen, foreign place, and resentment near strangled him.

The herald interrupted his thoughts to give them their order and their opponents. De Coucy would ride first, against the larger, brutish man. A foe worth fighting, at least.

The one left to him? No more than a boy. One he might kill by accident if he were not careful.

How careful did he feel today?

By the saints it is cold.

Shivering, Lady Cecily, Countess of Losford, saw her breath turn to fog in the frigid air as she gazed over the frozen tournament field. Red, blue, gold, silver—colour ran rampant before her eyes—decorating flags and banners, spilling across surcoats that shielded armour and draped the horses. A splendid display for visiting royalty. And King Edward, third of that name, reigned over it all, triumphant after his victory in France.

She lifted her chin, struggling to keep her countenance worthy of her rank.

It is your duty.

Her parents' words, their voices alive only in her memory now.

'Is that not so, Cecily?'

She turned to the king's daughter, Isabella, and wondered what she had missed. Six other ladies also attended the princess and, sometimes, Cecily's attention strayed. 'I'm certain you are right, my lady.' That was always a good answer.

'Really?' The princess smiled. 'I thought you did not care for the French.'

She sighed. Isabella loved to tease her when

her thoughts wandered. 'I'm afraid I was not listening.'

'I said the Frenchman looks fierce.'

Lady Cecily followed her gaze. At the far end of the field, two Frenchmen had mounted their destriers, but not yet donned their helmets. One of them, a knight she had not seen before, was tall, sharp and blond. Like a leopard. A beast who could kill in a single leap.

'He is handsome, is he not?'

Cecily frowned, ashamed that Lady Isabella had caught her staring at a French hostage. 'I do not care for fair-haired men.'

Her lady did not bother to hide her smile. 'I meant the dark one.'

Ah, the one she had barely looked at. Yet it did not matter which the princess meant. Cecily despised them both. Despite the conventions of chivalry, she could not understand why the king allowed the French hostages to take to the tournament field. They were, after all, little better than prisoners and should be denied such privileges. 'Both of them will be handsomer when they are unhorsed and covered in mud.'

That sent Isabella and the other ladies into peals of laughter until a frown from Queen Philippa forced them to stifle their mirth.

Cecily smiled, relieved she had saved the moment with a jest. Yet she had been deadly serious. In fact, it was a shame that the joust had become so tame and ceremonial. She would not have minded seeing a bit of French blood spilled.

'I wonder,' the princess said, 'which one rides against Gilbert?'

Cecily looked to the other end of the field where Gilbert, now properly Sir Gilbert, sat tall and straight and hopeful on his horse. Her favour, a violet silk scarf, fluttered expectantly on his lance.

Opposite him, covered in chainmail and plate armour, the blond French knight on his battle-tested mount looked even more imposing. She was no expert at war, but the way he sat on the horse and held his lance bespoke a confidence, a sureness, that she could see through the armour. 'I am certain,' she said, not certain at all, 'that Gilbert can unseat either man.'

Isabella flashed a sceptical expression. 'Don't be gooseish. This is Gilbert's first tournament. He'll be blessed if he doesn't drop his lance. Why ever did you give him your favour?'

Cecily sighed. 'He looked so forlorn.'

A quick frown deepened the lines between Isabella's brows. 'You are not thinking of him as a husband.'

'Gilbert?' Cecily laughed. 'He is too much like a brother.' He had come to her father as a young squire, just a couple of years older than she. And when the king selected her husband, he would not choose a lowly knight, but a man powerful, and trustworthy enough to hold the key to England.

But who?

Frowning, Cecily leaned closer to Isabella and whispered, 'Has your father said anything more of my marriage?'

Since her father had died, Cecily had become a very eligible heiress. She was now near twenty and it was time, past time, that she and Losford Castle be delivered to a man of the king's choosing.

The princess shook her head. 'His royal guests have consumed his attention. The King of Cyprus, Jerusalem, and whatever else he styles himself is urging my father to go on Crusade.' She rolled her eyes. 'At his age! It is bad enough he plans to lead the final charge in the tournament today.'

At least he is alive to do so, Cecily wanted to say, but held her tongue.

'Besides—' Isabella squeezed Cecily's cold fingers '—I don't want you snatched away so soon.'

But it was not 'soon'. It had been three years since her father had been cut down by the French. And the first annual death mass for her mother was barely two months away. The time to mourn was over. And yet...

She smiled at Isabella. 'You just want a companion for your revels.'

Isabella was an astonishing thirty-one years old and unmarried, with an abundance of time and money for all the pleasures of the court.

'You've been in mourning too long. You should enjoy yourself before you wed.'

Trumpets blared, signalling the next joust, and as the herald announced the rules for the single combat, Cecily could summon no joy. She frowned at the French chevaliers. God should not have let them live when her father had not.

De Coucy's red, white and blue banner snapped briskly in the breeze. He smiled at Marc, eager to ride. 'A glorious day! The king thinks to impress us! He is the one who will be impressed, *n'est pas*?'

Marc grinned. So many times, they had ridden side by side. Memories of successful battles quickened his blood. 'Will you take him in one pass or two?'

Enguerrand put on his helm and lifted his mailed glove in a brief salute. And three fingers.

Marc laughed. Ever the perfect knight, de Coucy, unlike too many of his fellow Frenchmen.

Yet as his friend rode, Marc watched each move, as if his attention could ensure the outcome. He still looked on the younger man as a novice, though de Coucy had long ago assumed his title, his lands and his rightful place as a leader of men.

On the first pass, his friend's lance hit the opponent's shield squarely. On the second, he allowed his opponent a touch, but with a last-minute twist, made certain it was only a glancing blow, one that scored poorly.

Matchless skill, to fight so that the poor English knight might actually believe he had landed a blow.

Finally, on the third pass, Enguerrand returned with a perfectly placed hit and knocked the other man's lance out of his grip and halfway across the field.

The squires rushed out to help them dismount and hand them their swords for the next phase of combat. Again, de Coucy made the contest look like an intricate dance. The first blow clean, but leaving his opponent standing. The second, he took himself, yet in such a way that it was inconsequential. With the third, he knocked his opponent's sword out of his hand, forcing him to concede the match.

Cheers rose from the stands, approval more generous than Marc had expected from their captors.

De Coucy strode back, helmet off, smile on. Three passes he had declared. Three it had been.

'Well done, my friend,' Marc said. 'Although that last blow was a little off.'

Enguerrand laughed. 'Only if I had intended to kill him.'

Marc looked down the field at the young knight who would face him. Marc's match, dwarfed by his armour, looked as if he had just earned his spurs.

'They insult me, to make me fight a boy.' At the other end of the field, a brave little purple scarf drooped from the knight's lance. 'You wanted me to impress the ladies. Do you think his lady will be impressed when her favour is trampled by the horses?'

'Behave yourself, *mon ami*.'

Marc sighed. He was expected to fight as de Coucy did: well enough to bring honour on himself, his colleague and his country, but not so well as to harm the *Anglais*. That was what the code of chivalry said.

For a moment, he pondered taking pity on the young man. He had a few crumbs of chivalry left in his trencher. A very few.

He could ride the requisite three passes with a gentle touch and allow his opponent to leave the field with his pride intact.

But men said one thing and did another. They gave an oath of fealty, then deserted their posts at battle. They swore to protect women and then raped them instead.

They cared nothing for honour, only the pretence of it. Some days, it seemed as if life was only a giant disguising with everyone pretending to be what they were not.

He was tired of pretending.

Today he would protest the only way he had left. Not to kill the young man, no. But embarrass him? That, he could do. That, he would enjoy.

His destrier shifted beneath him, stamping cold, hard ground that did not yield. He looked to the side, the starter gave the sign and he kicked his horse to ride.

Cecily refused to applaud the first Frenchman's victory until Isabella nudged her in the ribs. 'The dark-haired Frenchman fought masterfully, don't you think?'

Forced into clapping, she did so without enthusiasm. 'How can you say anything good about a Frenchman?'

'You talk as if he were an infidel. You forget my father's French blood.'

Yes, it was French blood flowing through the royal veins that had entitled King Edward to claim the throne of France. Cecily felt no such tie. Men like these, perhaps even these men, had killed her father. And then after his death had come her mother's...

She sighed, chastened by Isabella, and gazed back out on the field. With a helmet covering his face, the blond warrior in the blue-and-gold surcoat looked even more threatening, as if he were not human at all. She could only hope he would not wound Gilbert. Of course, this was not war. No one died in a tournament.

At least, not very often.

The herald gave the sign, she sent up a prayer for Gilbert's safety and braced for another drawn-out contest with lance and sword.

The horses charged, hooves pounding the turf, blue and gold galloping towards green and white. Atop his horse, Gilbert sat off-centre, unsteady, while the Frenchman rode as solid and immovable as Windsor's walls. She held her breath, as if that would make a difference. They were going too fast, what if the Frenchman really—?

Lances clattered on steel. Something flew across the field. A lance tip? A glove? Gilbert's horse reared.

Then, Gilbert lay flat on his back, his green-and-white surcoat covering the earth like spring grass.

She jumped to her feet. Was he wounded? Or worse? Not another loss, please...

The Frenchman backed his horse away, so the

beast would not accidentally trample the boy. As Gilbert's squire scampered on to the field, Gilbert sat up unaided and removed his helmet. Without the protection of his armour, shadowed by the man towering over him on the horse, he looked as young and thin and untried as he was.

But, thank God, unhurt.

Isabella arched her brows. 'I fear your scarf is a lost cause.'

'It was hardly a fair match. And since it was not, the French knight should have been chivalrous enough to spare the boy.'

'I don't think that one cares for courtesies. His friend, however…'

And as Isabella spoke, the French knight, the warrior Cecily had wanted to see toppled, turned his horse and left the field.

This time, there was no applause.

Westminster Palace—that night

Cecily scanned the cavernous Hall of Westminster Palace from the edge of the dais as servants bearing flambeaux wandered among the crowd. Torchlight flickered, casting shadows over the faces, and she studied each one, searching for her future.

Would the tall earl from the West Country be chosen as her husband? Or perhaps the stout baron from Sussex who had recently buried his wife?

Yet French hostages dotted the crowd as well, marring her mood. She was not inclined to feign politeness to more of her father's killers. At least, surely, the one who bested Gilbert would dare not show himself tonight.

Determined to impress the visiting kings with the full power and glory of his court, King Edward defied the darkness of the night. The high table was crowded with bronze candlesticks and dozens of twinkling flames.

Yet, for Cecily, memories lurked in the shadows. When her father was alive, he sat at the king's table. When her mother was alive, they whispered their judgements of the ladies' gowns. The scarlet that Lady Jane was wearing, her mother would have admired—

'Cecily? Did you hear me?'

She leaned forward to catch Isabella's whisper. 'I'm sorry. What is it?'

A frown creased Isabella's face. 'Attend. Father has had good news about Scotland. He's in a bounteous mood and not as clear-headed as usual,' Isabella whispered. 'You may find yourself promised to the nearest available lord before the night is over.'

Cecily looked around the hall, steeling herself. 'Has he mentioned anyone in particular?'

Isabelle shook her head. 'Not to me.'

She did not know who she would marry, yet she knew he would be an Englishman, loyal and strong. A man the king could trust as implicitly as he had trusted her father, for Losford Castle, Guardian of the Channel, was the most important bulwark in all of England, the one that could keep England's enemies away from her shores.

It could only go to a man for whom duty was all.

As it was for her.

She had grown up knowing this would be her lot, always. She was the only child of the Earl of Losford and sole holder of the lands and title. She would marry as her parents, and the king, decided.

'Do you think about him?' Isabella's question brought her back.

'I think about my father every day.' Not that she had seen him every day while he lived. Like all men, he had spent much of his life at war in France.

'I meant your husband. Who he might be.'

Strange question to come from a woman long unmarried. Yet Cecily's father had not hurried her marriage, either. Even as she passed an age to be wed, her world had remained her parents, their castle and the court.

She's not ready, her mother had whispered to her father.

But the death of her parents had rent her world so thoroughly that she wondered whether even a husband could make it whole again. 'I think only that I will accept the king's choice.' As was her duty.

'Well, Father demands that a man acquit himself well on the tournament field,' Isabella said, 'and he was more impressed with those hostages today than with any of our men.'

Resentment wrestled with relief. At least a hostage would not be a prospective husband. 'The dark one I can understand,' she admitted, grudgingly. 'He conducted himself according to the rules of chivalry, but the fair-haired Frenchman was a disgrace.'

'Perhaps, but Father said he would be a useful man to have on your side in the midst of a battle.'

A surprising admission, for a king who modelled himself and his court on the ideals of King Arthur's Round Table.

'Look,' Isabella said. 'Over there. There he is.'

'Who?' Relieved at Isabella's wandering attention, Cecily followed her gaze. 'Where?'

'The French knight. The dark one. There by the fire.'

The man was standing comfortably beside his blond friend before one of the hearths, halfway down the hall, as if they were lounging in their own hall instead of the king's.

'It is time we met,' the princess said. 'Go. Bring him to me. I would congratulate him on today's joust.'

'I refuse to speak to that man,' she said, thinking of the blond one. What was his name? Somehow in the noise and chatter of the tournament, neither she nor Isabella had heard either of the knights announced. 'After the way he treated Gilbert...'

Isabella twisted her mouth.

Cecily's frown twitched.

And then, they both gave in to laughter. 'Poor Gilbert.'

After initially appearing uninjured, Gilbert had developed blossoming bruises and left the hall early, limping. At least Cecily would be spared the need to feign an interest in a detailed account of his embarrassing performance.

'Send one of the other ladies,' she said, after she stopped laughing. 'Or a page.' That would be a proper insult to the man.

Isabella shook her head. 'Speak to the man or snub him as you choose. Just bring me his friend.'

Sighing, Cecily stepped off the dais and started down the Hall. And as she made her way through the crowd, her resentment grew.

She lived in England, under an English king and in an English court, yet French music surrounded her. When she danced, French steps guided her feet. Even the words on her tongue were French. No wonder the hostages looked so comfortable. But for sleeping on this side of the Channel, they might as well be at home.

Isabella was right. They shared culture, language and even, in some cases, blood. Yet all that had not been enough to keep them from killing each other.

Just as she reached the two men, the dark one slipped away. She paused, thinking to escape, but she had moved with too much purpose. The fair-haired knight looked up and met her gaze.

Now, she could not turn aside.

He leaned against the wall, seemingly at ease, but when she came closer, she could see that despite the sweet music and laughter all around him, he seemed coiled and ready for battle.

Cecily paused, waiting for him to acknowledge her and bow. Instead, he looked down at her, silent.

'It is customary,' she began, through gritted teeth, 'for a knight to acknowledge a lady.'

He shrugged.

Could nothing stir this quiet barbarian? 'I am attached to the royal household.'

'So am I to bow not only to the English royals, but also to those who serve them?'

'I am no serving girl,' she snapped at the demeaning suggestion. But he could not have mistaken a woman wearing velvet for a serving girl. He wanted to make her furious, that was clear. Worse, he was succeeding. She unclenched her fingers and forced a shrug to match his own. 'You have proven again that French chivalry is vastly overrated.'

He stood straight, then, as if her words had been the blow she'd intended. 'Chevalier Marc de Marcel at your service.' A slight inclination of his head, its very perfection a mockery.

'Chivalry is more than courtly manners. A chivalrous knight would have allowed an untried opponent to hold his honour on the field.'

He glanced at her violet gown and an expression she could not decipher rippled across his face. 'The favour he carried. It was yours.' Something in the timbre of his voice reached inside her, implying that she and Gilbert…

But it didn't mean what you think. 'I would have said the same even if it was not.' Pinned by his expression, she had trouble taking a breath. The anger in his eyes matched her own. Or was it something besides anger? Something more like hunger…

He smiled. Slowly and without mirth. 'You

would have frowned at me the same way if I had been the one unhorsed.'

True, and she blushed with shame to be thought as rude as he. A countess should be above such weakness. Assuming the disguise of polite interest, she reached for her noble demeanour. 'You are newly come?'

The scowl returned to his face. 'Weeks that seem like years. The Compte d'Oise pined for home. Before your king allowed him to leave, he demanded a substitute. *C'est moi*. Now you have your answer. You may leave.'

'The king's daughter would like to meet you.' A lie, but one that would explain her presence.

'She takes a lively interest in her father's prisoners.'

Only the handsome ones, Cecily thought, but held her tongue and turned, praying he would follow.

He did.

Lady Isabella suppressed a smile as they approached and Cecily could only hope she would be spared the humiliation of being teased for returning with the man she had sworn to snub. 'The Chevalier Marc de Marcel, my lady. He has come only recently.'

His bow to the king's daughter showed little more deference than the one he had made to

Cecily. 'May a hostage be presented to his captor, my lady?'

An edge to his words. As if they had two meanings. Well, Isabella would enjoy that. Her lady was always ready for laughter, and if it held a suggestive edge, all the better. All for show, of course. A princess, and a countess, must live above reproach. Still, Isabella's light talk and her constant stream of diversions had kept Cecily from being devoured by despair.

But strangely, the man was not looking at Isabella. He was looking at Cecily.

'Yes,' Isabella said, drawing his eyes to her. 'In fact, it is required. And your friend...' she inclined her head, regally, in the direction of the other knight, who had reappeared in the hall '...has not yet been presented. And he, I believe, has been in England much longer than you have.'

As if he had heard her request, the dark one approached. As if he had expected this. As if this was what the two of them had been planning when they put their heads together.

And when he arrived before the king's daughter, he did not wait for permissions or introductions. 'Enguerrand, Lord de Coucy.' No explanation. As if his name and title were enough.

Well, they were. The de Coucy family was

well known, even on this side of the Channel. Once, the family had even held lands here.

Silent, Isabella inclined her head to acknowledge him. She did not need to tell him who she was. Everyone knew she was the king's oldest, and favourite, daughter.

The minstrels' horns signalled the beginning of a new dance. Isabella rose and held out her hand to de Coucy, forcing him to lead her to the floor. He did not look reluctant.

Cecily searched the room, hoping for rescue. She should join the dance with a partner who might become a husband, not with a hostage.

And the hostage did not offer his hand.

Well, then, if she were trapped, she would attempt to be gracious. She pursed her lips. 'You are from the Oise Valley?'

A frown, as if the reminder of home had angered him. 'Yes.'

'And do they dance there?'

'On occasion. When *les goddams* give us a pause from battle.'

She blinked. 'The what?'

He smiled. 'It is what we call the *Anglais*.'

'Why?' Did they wish to curse the English with every name?

'Because every sentence they utter contains the phrase.'

She stifled a smile. Her father, indeed, had

been known to swear on occasion. She could imagine that he would have had many more occasions in the midst of battle.

But she held out her hand, as imperious as the princess could be. 'If you can dance, then show me.'

'Is this part of a hostage's punishment?'

'No,' she retorted. 'It is one of his privileges.'

'Then, pray, demoiselle, tell me your name, so I may know my partner.'

He shamed her with the reminder. Anger had stolen all her senses. She was acting like a common serving girl. 'Lady Cecily, Countess of Losford.'

The surprise on his face was gratifying. He looked at her uncovered hair and then glanced behind her, as if expecting an earl to be hovering close behind.

'I hold the title.' Both a matter of pride and sadness. She held it because the rest of her family was gone. Held it in trust for a husband she did not yet know.

His nod was curt, yet he held out a hand, without hesitation now, as if that had been his intention from the first.

Surprise, or something deeper, unfamiliar, stirred when she put her fingers in his. She had expected his hands to be soft, as so many of the knights' had become now that war was over.

Instead, his palm was calloused; his knuckles scraped. Wounds from today's joust, she thought at first, but in the passing torchlight, she saw he carried scars of long standing.

They joined the carol circle. On the other side, de Coucy and Isabella smiled and whispered to each other as if the evening had been prepared for their amusement. That man showed not a whit of resentment at his captivity, while beside her, de Marcel glowered, stubbornly silent as the music began.

They could not have been more unlike, these two.

Carol dancing, with its ever-moving ring of dancers holding hands, did not lend itself to talk. And he moved as he spoke, with precision, without excess, doing only what was necessary.

She wondered whether this man enjoyed anything at all.

Certainly he did not enjoy her. When the dance was done, he dropped her hand quickly and she let go a breath, suddenly realising how tense she had been at his touch.

He stood, silent, looking around the Hall as if searching for an escape. And yet this hostage, this enemy could, if he wanted, lift a goblet of the king's good wine, fill his belly with the king's meat and his ears with sweet music played by the king's minstrels, all the while alive and comfortable while her father lay dead in his grave.

'What did you do,' she asked, 'to earn the honour of substituting for the other hostage?'

'Honour?'

'You were defeated in battle, you killed my... countrymen, yet the king welcomes you to his court where you have food and wine aplenty and nothing to do. It seems a generous punishment for defeat.'

'A prison with tapestries is no less a prison.'

'But you are safe. You may do as you please.'

'And if it please me to go home?'

And yet her father would come home no more. 'You must pay some penalty. We conquered you!'

As the words escaped, she saw his expression change.

'No! Not conquered. Never conquered. We were betrayed by cowards. Lord de Coucy and I were not among them. We would have fought until the last *goddam* was dead.'

This time, it was a curse he hurled.

'So you hate the English,' she said. Blunt words, but he was a blunt man.

'As much as you the French,' he answered.

'I doubt that,' she said, sheer will keeping her voice steady. 'But since you detest us and disdain the king's hospitality, I hope your time here will be short.'

He bowed then, the gesture a mockery. 'In that, my lady, we are in accord.'

Chapter Two

Marc watched the countess walk away, his eyes lingering on her swaying hips longer than he intended.

De Coucy, relieved of his attendance on the king's daughter, rejoined him and followed his gaze. 'Ah, she is lovely, is she not, *le belle dame de* Losford? The way her head balances on her slender neck, that cloud of dark hair…' His voice trailed off to delights unseen.

Marc had a momentary vision of sweeping the woman into his arms for a kiss, erasing the frown that turned her lips when she'd looked his way, even before they had met.

She would think even less of his honour then. Of course, if she knew all he had done, and all he was willing to do, she would think nothing of it at all.

Marc forced his gaze away from Lady Cecily's retreating form and shrugged. 'I've no interest in *les goddams*, men or women.' Yet he lied. The countess, by turns ice and fire—he had an interest in her. An interest of the wrong kind.

Enguerrand shook his head. 'Your voice would curdle milk, *mon ami.*'

'How can you stomach this?' Yes, the English king was hospitable, and their detention truly a *prison courtoise* as Lady Cecily implied, created by a shared sense of honour that required a hostage to submit, according to the rules of chivalry, rules which all pretended to follow.

Yet Marc resented the disguise.

His friend looked puzzled. *'Pardon?'*

Marc sighed. It was a question too large. 'How can you be so gracious to your captors?' De Coucy had been here for three years. Perhaps he had become accustomed to it.

'Better to get along with all men when you can.'

'And women, too?'

'Bien sûr. Avec les femmes most of all.' His friend laughed.

So easy for de Coucy to do as he was expected, to cloak his warrior's sins with the charm of a courtier. And so hard for Marc, though that was the way of the world. Chivalry said one thing. Chivalrous men did something different and all the while, the code winked and smiled.

Enguerrand lowered his voice. 'Sometimes, a

more subtle assault can obtain the objective when a frontal attack cannot.'

'What do you mean?'

Now Marc saw the smile with a plan behind it. 'If I…befriend the Lady Isabella, she might persuade her father to restore my lands, *n'est-ce pas*?'

He had heard Enguerrand speak of the English lands, soil he had never seen in places with strange names like Cumberland and Westmorland. Northerly lands, near to Scotland, where a de Coucy great-grandmother had gone as a bride. The holdings had been forfeited to the English crown years before.

'Why would King Edward relinquish holdings to a hostage?'

A shrug and a smile. 'How do I know if I do not try? In the meantime, the months grow long. I've been told the princess creates gay entertainments for those of her circle. Better that we enjoy more nights such as this than moulder in the draughty tower, eh?'

Ah, that was his friend, still viewing himself as a guest instead of a prisoner. 'I want to spend no more time with the court.'

'Not even with the lovely countess?'

'Particularly not with her.' Yet, unbidden, he searched the room, catching sight of her purple gown, and let his gaze linger. She had stirred a dangerous mix of anger and desire. One to be avoided.

He turned his back on the hall. 'You do not need me for _this_ campaign.'

'Not tonight, _mon ami_. But soon, there will come a time. And when I do…?' A raised eyebrow. Waiting.

Duty. Honour. Little more than empty words. But loyalty? A man was nothing without that. 'When you do, you need only ask.'

'Now come.' Enguerrand rested a hand on Marc's shoulder and turned him towards the crowded hall. 'Sing. Dance. Make merry. Make friends.'

'I leave that to you, _mon ami_.'

With a wave and a laugh, Enguerrand left to do just that. He moved through the Hall with a nod and a smile, as gracious as if he were at home in the Château de Coucy.

And why should he not? De Coucy and the other French hostages all lived in certainty that some day, the ransom would be raised, money exchanged and they would go back to a castle very much like this one to sing and dance.

He did not.

The Compte d'Oise had promised to return, or send the ransom, or send a substitute, by Easter. Marc would have to stay in _Angleterre_ only six months. Less if the Count could make arrangements more quickly.

But in retrospect, replaying the conversation, the man had not met his eyes when he described his promises and plans. Options and timing had been vague.

So why had he come? Why had he chosen to put himself in enemy hands? The debt of fealty. The chance to see his old friend, who had been held by the English for three years.

His own foolish attempt at honour?

But tonight, the only person in the hall whose bitterness seemed to match his own was the Countess of Losford.

Gilbert, Cecily was pleased to see, had rallied by the next day, walking stiffly, but all of a piece. Feeling guilty for her laughter with Isabella, she approached him after the morning mass, but he refused to meet her eyes.

'I am sorry I did not uphold the honour you bestowed on me,' he said, as they walked from the Abbey back to the Palace. His head held slightly down, a shock of brown hair almost in his eyes, he looked as young as a squire, though he was two years older than she.

And yet, in making that hard admission, he took a step towards being a man, a man who regretted not his own humiliation, but that he had disappointed her.

'The fault was not yours, but de Marcel's,' she said. 'I've never seen such a violation of the rules of the tournament.'

Uneasy, she refrained from telling him she had danced with the man the previous evening. His hand on hers had been rough, but sure. Implacable.

The warmth of the memory touched her cheeks and she searched for the dignity of her title.

Gilbert, fighting his own disappointment, did not notice. 'I was ill prepared. A good lesson.'

'Are you not angry?' She was. Easier, better, to channel sorrow into anger. Anger had righteous power. Grief was an open wound.

'At myself,' he said. A hard confession. 'I will do better next time.'

She shook her head. 'Think of him no more.' She certainly wouldn't.

In the coming days, as the tournament celebrations ended, the hostages were returned to their quarters and preparations began for the court to move to Windsor for the Christmas season.

Cecily put the rude Frenchman out of her thoughts.

Well, perhaps she thought of him once or

twice, but only because Gilbert replayed the entire joust in great detail every time she saw him, each time suggesting what he might do differently, should he ever face de Marcel again.

And if she, once or twice, replayed her own private joust with the man, it was only to scold herself, as her mother would have done, for losing her temper and her dignity. She would not see him again, of course, but she vowed to maintain her calm the next time she was confronted with any of the hostages.

A week later, as she watched the tailor unpack Isabella's Christmas gown, she had more immediate concerns.

Although her family had spent Christmas with the court for as long as she could remember, her mother had always been the one to make the plans. Cecily had helped, of course, but now the season loomed before her, only three weeks away.

She must make the preparations, alone. She must demonstrate that she was not only an eligible heiress but would be a competent wife. The problem was, she was not quite certain what she should be doing.

'Isn't it beautiful?' Isabella held up her new dress, so heavy with ermine she could barely lift it.

The train piled on the floor of the princess's

chamber, nearly as high as her knees. 'Fit for a queen,' Cecily answered.

'Not quite,' Isabella said, handing it to the tailor who spread it carefully across the bed. 'Mother's has ermine on the sleeves as well.' She smoothed the dress, her fingers caressing the fabric. 'But this one is paid for by Father's purse.'

Cecily bit her lip against the sudden reminder. She had no father, now, to dote on her and shower her with gifts. No mother to advise her on which gown was most flattering. Yet sometimes she would hear the door open and think she heard her father's step or her mother's voice—

'Cecily, attend!' Isabella's voice, jolting her back to the present.

'Yes, my lady.'

'What are you wearing?'

Ah, that was one of the things she should have done. 'I...don't know. I have nothing new.' Deep in mourning, she had ordered no new Christmas clothes except for the matching gowns she shared with the other court ladies. 'Perhaps no one will notice.'

'Don't be a fool! You must look ready for a wedding, not a funeral.'

She looked down. While she had not put on widow's garb, she had chosen colours dark and subdued since her mother's death unless she was wearing the royal colours. 'I could recut one of

Mother's gowns. The green one, perhaps. Mother liked me in green.'

'That shade is too strong for the current fashion.' Isabella shook her head. 'I thought this might happen.' She waved to the tailor. 'So I had something made for you.'

Eyes wide, Cecily watched him lay out a fur-trimmed sideless surcoat. Worn over her current gowns, it would make them look new. 'I don't know what to say.'

Isabella laughed. 'Just try it on, you silly goose.'

And with the help of the tailor and the maid, she pulled it over her head. It fitted loosely, with a large, curved opening from shoulder to hip, revealing the dress beneath and the curve of her waist and hip.

She slipped her hands beneath the surcoat, where the soft, sable lining tickled her fingers, and tried not to tally the cost. Isabella never did, which was why she regularly exceeded her household allowance. The king grumbled, but always covered his daughter's debts. 'My lady, how can I thank you?'

Isabella waved the servants out of hearing. 'This is your last Christmas season as an unmarried woman! You can thank me by enjoying it!'

Last as an unmarried woman and the first without her mother.

Her father had been gone for three years; her mother not yet a year. The loss was still new, raw. Still, she must convince the court that she was ready to look to the future and her duty instead of wallowing in her grief. There must be no tears this season.

She lifted her chin and twirled, making her skirt sway. 'So you would have me sing and dance and smile at all the men from now until Twelfth Night!' The light words, the forced smile were an ill-fitting mask.

Yet, Isabella laughed and clapped in approval. 'Yes! By then, every man at court will hope to be the king's choice as the new guardian of Losford. Even the hostages!'

Cecily stumbled at the memory of de Marcel's eyes. Angry. Hungry. 'What?'

'Father has invited some of them to Windsor.' Isabella's smile, normally so bright and open, turned shy. 'Including Lord de Coucy.'

Cecily bit her lip. How was she to smile when her father's murderers could dance and sing beside her?

But Isabella did not notice. 'Lord de Coucy is a very good dancer. And handsome, don't you think?'

'I think of the French as little as possible.' And it was not the dark-haired hostage Cecily thought of now. She turned away, hoping Isabella would not see her blush. 'Will there be other hostages there, as well?'

'Other Frenchmen, you mean?'

'Have we any other hostages?'

'Have you an interest in any one in particular? His fair-haired friend, perhaps? What is his name?'

'Marc de Marcel, and, no, I have not,' she answered, dismayed. Could Isabella see her thoughts?

'De Marcel, yes! A delightful distraction for you.'

'No!'

But Isabella was not listening. 'The perfect answer. One for each of us.'

'Totally unsuitable!'

'Exactly! That's why they are the right companions for the season. To be enjoyed, to make your suitors jealous, and then, tossed aside.' Laughing, she plucked a riband from a pile, tied it in a bow, then tossed it the air and let it fall to the ground, where she kicked it away. 'Like that! In the meantime, for a few weeks, Lord de Coucy's attention can be devoted to me alone. And de Marcel's to you.'

The words *Marcel* and *alone* made Cecily shiver. Even in a crowded hall, his eyes had near devoured her. What would happen if she were close, day after day, to a man who had told her clearly he cared nothing for honour.

'My lady, Lord de Coucy appears to be a man of the code while de Marcel has proven quite the opposite. What if your trust is misplaced? What if...?' To finish the question would be an insult.

And the expression on Isabella's face proved it. She was suddenly the princess again, her haughty frown as regal as her father's. 'Do not mistake my meaning. I would permit nothing unseemly.'

Cecily nodded. 'Of course not, my lady.'

There could be no suggestion, ever, that either of them had been less than chaste. By deciding to remain unwed, Isabella had chosen a life of chastity as pure as a nun's. And as for Cecily, her title was not the only gift a husband would expect. He would demand her purity, as well.

Isabella's stern frown dissolved. 'We will both be quite safe, Cecily. And a little romance will be guaranteed to lift your spirits. I will make certain Marc de Marcel is also invited to Windsor.'

'Invite him if you must, but do not expect me to waste my time with him.'

No. Marc de Marcel was the last person she wanted to see this season.

Suddenly awake, Marc blinked, peered out the window of the Tower of London at the frigid London morning and shivered. Their gaolers were not ones to squander money on firewood to warm French hostages.

'Arise, *mon ami*! Did you hear what I said?'

Marc rubbed his eyes and turned to look at his friend. 'You're doing what?' He must have misheard. It was too early in the morning for anyone to be awake and so talkative. 'What did you say?'

'We have been invited to join the court as guests of the king. We shall celebrate *Noël* at Windsor Castle!'

The words made no more sense the second time. He sat up and looked at his friend. 'Are you mad?'

'I would be *fou* indeed to refuse the invitation of a princess.'

Ah, the princess that de Coucy saw as the key to the restoration of his lands.

A vision not of the princess, but of the countess drifted into his sleep-fogged brain, as if she were a leftover dream. Her dark hair, her square jaw.

The hatred in her eyes.

His friend was *fou* indeed. But it was none of Marc's affair. 'Then accept and leave me out of it.'

'Ah, but she specifically asked me to bring you.'

Strange. Certainly the Lady Cecily had no desire to see him again. Why would the princess? *'Pourquoi?'*

De Coucy shrugged. 'Perhaps she wants to be certain I am not *isolé*.'

Marc laughed. The thought of his gregarious friend being lonely was absurd. 'You do not need me to press your cause with the Lady Isabella.'

'It is no sin to find some joy in our captivity.'

Perhaps not, but the one joy Marc had found in England was the chance to be reunited with his long-time friend. Other men had wives and families. Marc had only Enguerrand. 'If I did not know you so well, I would think you cared for nothing but pleasure.' His friend was a man of extremes. Dancing or fighting, he would do both with all that was within him. And the time for fighting was over. For now.

'And you do not care *enough* for pleasure.'

Marc had never been a man accustomed to soft comforts and pleasure seemed even more discordant in the face of defeat. To dance and sing seemed to imply that the deaths in battle had been only an illusion and that the dead would rise and join the carol ring. 'I do not celebrate my enemy's victory.'

'No, you celebrate *Noël*. You will feast on English mutton and drink Gascon wine and, for a few weeks, they will pay the cost.'

It was the final insult. Every day he ate and drank in England would be added to the required ransom, as if he had to pay for the privilege of being held hostage. 'Tempting, my friend, but English food sours my stomach.'

'Would you rather sit in this cold tower and chew tough meat?'

With so many hostages to be housed, the city gates and the Abbey were full, so he and Enguerrand had been given quarters in the grim and impregnable Tower of London. And as the winter cold crept through the stones, the vision of *Noël* without even Enguerrand beside him seemed bleak.

But not bleak enough that he could force himself to smile with cheer at *les goddams*. To say yes would make him sound ungrateful. And yet... 'Yes. I would.'

Enguerrand sighed, clearly exasperated. 'The princess will be *désolée*.'

'All the better for you to console her.' He turned over and pulled the covers up. *'Joyeux Noël, mon ami.'*

There would be three masses on Christmas Day. He might even arise in time for one of them.

And if the guards decided to celebrate too heartily, perhaps a prisoner might roam the halls freely and unnoticed.

Perhaps, he might roam even further.

Cecily should have paused when she heard the soft laughter beyond Isabella's door, but she was

hurried and distracted and had important news,
so she knocked and opened quickly, as she had
so many times before, only to see Isabella standing close to Lord de Coucy.

Too close.

For a moment, they looked at her, guilt gild-
ing the silence.

Cecily looked away and scanned the room.
Alone. The two of them had been alone. Smiling,
relaxed, and standing so close they could have—

She opened her mouth, but could summon no
words.

'Ah, the beautiful countess,' de Coucy said,
bowing so smoothly that before she blinked, he
had moved a safe distance from the princess.
'A reminder I have overstayed my welcome, my
lady. The guards will wonder where I am.'

He took his leave with all the proper deference, then paused before Cecily with a knee bent
slightly less deeply than the one for the princess.
Another bow, a smile, an exit. As if nothing were
wrong. As if a young, French hostage had every
right to stand too close to the king's daughter and
whisper *bon mots*.

Cecily looked at Isabella, a hint of accusation in her gaze. To dance and laugh together in
public, that was allowed. When the music and
the wine flowed, many a couple kissed and em-
braced, a moment's passion, but always in a place
too public for true indiscretion.

But to be alone with a man opened up other dangers.

At least, that was what Cecily's mother had told her.

In the silence, Isabella did not rebuke her or ask why she had come, but moved with the regal assurance of one whose behaviour was never questioned. 'I'm afraid you will have to enjoy the season without your growling Frenchman,' Isabella said, as the door closed behind de Coucy.

'Pardon?'

'Lord de Coucy came to tell me he would attend, but his friend won't.'

'Is he ill?' The thought did not displease her.

'No.' She shrugged. 'He refused.'

Irrationally, Cecily felt a twinge of insult. No matter that she had not wanted him invited—no one refused the king. 'How could he?'

'No matter,' Isabella said, without a touch of indignation. It had been only de Coucy the princess cared to see. 'You'll find someone much more pleasant to dally with for the Yuletide.'

Cecily made a non-committal humming sound. Isabella persisted in thinking male company was essential for enjoyment of the season. But Cecily must be mindful that prospective suitors were watching. She should not be seen laughing and smiling and standing too close to a captive chevalier.

Yet the insult of de Marcel's refusal soured her mood, like wine kept too long in the air.

And then she remembered what had driven her here. 'There is news. The King of France is returning to England.'

Isabella's eyes widened. 'My father's message must have succeeded.' She smiled. 'It was quite pointed. Something about kings must have honour.'

'Even if their sons do not?' When King Jean had been allowed to return to France, several nobles were sent to England in his place, including two of his sons. After less than a year, one of the sons had escaped captivity and fled home to France.

So like a Frenchman, her father would have said. De Marcel, she was certain, was no better.

'Did you hear when he would arrive? Will he be here in time for the Yule celebrations?'

Yet another Frenchman to entertain? Cecily stifled a groan. 'I don't know. Why?'

'If so, we must entertain him according to his station. Lord de Coucy will be so pleased. Ah, what a Christmas this will be!'

De Coucy again. Cecily frowned as Isabella chattered on. Surely there was no cause to worry about the princess and the hostage.

But Cecily worried anyway.

Chapter Three

'Marc! *Ecoute*! I have news!'

Marc weighed the last bunch of faggots he was holding in his hand and momentarily thought of heaving it at Enguerrand's head instead of into the dwindling fire.

For the last week, his friend had talked of nothing but the progress of his campaign to convince the princess to support the restoration of the de Coucy lands in England. Marc was now counting the days until Enguerrand would set off for Windsor and leave him in peace. 'Spare me, my friend. I have heard all I care to.'

'No. You have not heard this.'

The tone of voice, the shock on Enguerrand's face—no, this was something different. 'What's wrong?'

'King Jean. He comes to England *encore*.'

Marc shook his head, certain he had misheard. 'What?'

His friend slumped on the bench at Marc's side, staring into the flames. 'The king. He will cross the Channel and deliver himself back into King Edward's hands until the ransom has been paid.'

'Why?'

'To redeem the honour his son defiled.'

Marc shook his head. Honour, and the treaties negotiated after Poitiers, dictated that the king remain a hostage until the ransom of three million crowns was paid. The amount was more than double the yearly income of the entire country, or so the whispers said.

There had been negotiations, many of them, before Marc had even come to England. Finally, the king was allowed to return to France to help raise the ransom, but four dukes of France, including two of King Jean's sons, had been forced to come in his stead.

Marc himself had questioned the honour of the Duke d'Anjou when the man ran home to his wife, but for the king to surrender to the enemy again? It was folly. There was no reason for it.

None but honour.

Ah, yes. Here was the king Marc had seen on the field at Poitiers, fighting even when the rest had fled. 'It is like him.' One man, at least. One man upheld honour, still.

'King Jean sent these words to King Ed-

ward,' Enguerrand said. '"That were good faith
and honour banished from the rest of the world,
such virtues ought still to find their place on the
lips and in the breasts of princes."'

Good faith. Honour. The things that made a
hostage's imprisonment a sacred duty. For they
were held captive not for the ransom alone, but
for a promise made, one knight to another.

And with that thought came the larger realisation. Lord de Coucy, one of the most eminent
lords of the land, was one of the forty royal and
noble hostages held surety for the king himself.
If the king returned to England, even if part of
the ransom remained unpaid...

'This will mean you can go home.' Marc felt
envy's bite. England would be a colder place
without Enguerrand.

His friend nodded, silent, his face a mix of
perplexity and wonder. 'Yes. Home.'

Marc stifled a moment's envy. He had known
no other home but de Coucy's.

'Was there any word about the rest of us?'
Marc was not one of the treaty hostages, but a
poor and partial substitute for the Compte d'Oise,
taken captive by another English knight who
had sold his interest in the ransom to the king, a
man better equipped to wait years for full payment.

Enguerrand shook his head. 'Only the king.'

But the king had proven that honour must rule all things. Marc had brought partial payment for the count's ransom with him. His presence here was to ensure the Count would pay the rest. By Easter, the man had promised. At the latest.

Until now, uncertain, restless, Marc had thought of escape, perhaps during the lax days of Christmas when the king's own son had disappeared. But with this news, his doubts and plans seemed shameful. He could not dishonour his own vow and have the king, the one shining example of chivalry he knew, arrive to hear the name of Marc de Marcel covered in shame.

'When does he come?'

'He celebrates Christmas in Paris, then crosses the Channel.'

So King Jean would be here at the end of the year. Surely, the honour of the Compte d'Oise would match his king's. Surely he would send the remainder of his ransom with the king's party. Or return himself, as his sovereign had. It did not matter which. Marc would be free.

Enguerrand rose and headed for the door. 'So soon. There is much to do to prepare.'

Marc threw the faggot into the fire, shivering. He was beginning to regret having turned down the opportunity to go to Windsor. It was going to be a long, cold, *Noël*.

* * *

'I shall need a new dress,' Isabella said. 'To greet King Jean.'

'Do you think he remembers the one he last saw you wear?' Cecily smiled, wishing that Anne of Stamford were still at court. Despite their differences in station, they had exchanged knowing smiles when the princess and the Countess of Kent had engaged in wars of the wardrobe.

She wondered what had happened to Anne. The last Cecily had heard, Anne had retired to a small priory. Probably for the best. Life was difficult for a lame girl.

'The fashion has changed since then,' Isabella said, 'as well you know. And there isn't much time to organise a royal welcome.'

Cecily's familiar resentment boiled. 'For a hostage?'

'For a king,' Isabella said, spine straight with all the shared solidarity of royalty.

A good reminder. Though the king's daughter might sometimes seem frivolous and *volage*, she, like Cecily, would never forget her position and her duty.

'I spoke to Enguerrand,' Isabella said, 'and he thinks that the king will want to go to Canterbury first, before he comes to court. So we decided...'

Enguerrand. We. 'We?'

'Enguerrand and I. Since he will be at Windsor I asked him to help arrange a proper royal welcome.'

Wrong to hear the princess sharing decisions with anyone, worst of all with a hostage. She was royal and unmarried. The only people who could gainsay her were the King and Queen of England. 'Can we not plan a king's welcome without the help of a hostage?' It was one thing to invite him and de Marcel to Christmas at Windsor. It was quite another to allow him to plan a royal ceremony.

'He is Lord de Coucy,' the princess said, in her stern, royal tone. 'He deserves the treatment accorded his station.'

As, yes, even among hostages, rank mattered. De Coucy was one of the greatest lords of France. Of course he would not be treated as if he were no more than a simple chevalier.

He would not be treated as though he were Marc de Marcel.

And yet…

'But are you not concerned that such access might become…?' She dared not insult the princess again. 'That it might raise his hopes?'

'Hopes of what?' Said with a raised eyebrow.

Cecily blushed. It was his lust that must not be raised. Men aroused were hard to control. And so were women. Or so her mother had told her.

'What I mean is, if you spend too much time together, might he not become too bold?'

A wave of dismissal. 'Have no fear. Enguerrand is as chivalrous as a knight can be.'

De Marcel had proven that chivalry was in short supply among the French. Such a man might not stop at a bow or a dance. Or a kiss. 'Still, to treat him as you would an Englishman does not seem...wise.'

Isabella answered with a merry laugh. 'It is the Yuletide season. Why should one be wise?'

To prevent disaster.

Isabella was extravagant and headstrong, and her dalliances had been many, but, as far as Cecily knew, none of them had gone beyond hidden kisses and a passionate embrace. None of them had put her at risk. Each had been easily cast aside.

Yet the way she spoke of this Frenchman, the excuses she created to keep him near, were troubling.

They would have three weeks at court, full of Yuletide cheer. It was a time when fools ruled, when the proper order of things was deliberately turned upside down. What if things went further? What if things went too far?

Cecily could raise no more questions without angering Isabella, but she must be vigilant. She herself must stand guard, silently, to make certain nothing unbecoming happened. Yet, what could she alone do? And who else would be in a position to help?

Marc de Marcel.

She fought the idea, but as unlikely as it seemed, they might have a common purpose. The chevalier had no more love for the English than she for the French. Surely he would hate to find his friend in a tryst with an English princess.

But he had refused to come to Windsor.

'Well, if the king needs a royal welcome,' Cecily said, as if it were of no consequence, 'de Coucy will need company of his own kind. Perhaps his friend *should* be forced to come as well.'

Isabella's smile broadened. 'You scold me for my interest in Lord de Coucy, yet you've come around to my suggestion at last. But the man has refused our invitation.'

No. He could not refuse. She would not allow it. 'Then I must persuade him.'

'I saw him do little but growl, your leopard. Does he do anything else?'

Cecily gritted her teeth. 'I will have time to discover that, won't I?'

All she had to do was make him understand the urgency of the matter without casting any aspersions on the princess.

That meant she must convince him that Lord de Coucy was to blame.

* * *

Cecily plotted for a week, then, when the princess was busy, had de Marcel brought to her at Westminster.

Isabella was right, she thought, as he stood before her, as menacing as a beast about to pounce on the prey. Nothing about him was soft or easy. Nothing of his face was gentle. Everywhere a hollow, a sharp corner, an unexpected turn, a scar earned. And yet, taken together, a face that drew her eye...

'Why am I here? Why have you had me dragged before you with no more courtesy than if I were a prisoner to be executed?'

She fought a twinge of guilt. 'You *are* a prisoner.'

And the pain that flashed across his face near made her ask the guards to let him free.

Instead, she motioned them to stand outside.

Did his gaze become more fierce when the door shut? Did she have trouble catching her breath? He had warned her what kind of man he was. Yet here she was, alone with him, just as Isabella and Enguerrand had been.

As she must be. Her fears for the princess were not for other ears.

She straightened her shoulders and lifted her chin. 'Lord de Coucy has been much at court in recent weeks.'

'He is as skilled a courtier as he is a chevalier.'

'And you are not?'

A shrug. A frown. But he did not argue.

Looking down at her clasped hands, she took a few steps, summoning her composure before she faced his eyes again. 'Lord de Coucy has spent much time with Lady Isabella. And I fear that they…' No. She must not involve the princess. 'That Lord de Coucy may have developed…feelings. I mean a…' What did she mean?

'Tendresse,' he said, in a tone that conveyed no tenderness at all.

'Yes. Exactly.' What did she say now? That she was afraid Isabella might… No.

She must not let this man upset her. *You are a countess. He is a chevalier and a hostage. He must bow to your will.*

She raised her head. De Marcel seemed disinclined to bow to anyone. Yet his lips carried the hint of a smile. And *that* made her angry. 'I am sure you like it no more than I do.'

'Moins.'

She raised her brows. 'Oh, I don't think you could possibly like it any less.'

Now, he smiled in truth. 'But it is all according to the laws of courtly love, *n'est-ce pas*? Nothing serious.'

As if de Coucy should not be honoured that the second-greatest lady of the land had deigned to honour him with her attention. 'It is *she* who is not serious. And yet, they have...' what could she say? '...spent much time together.'

'You worry overmuch.'

Did she? The games Isabella was willing to play with the hostage angered her. But to think the Frenchman did not take the honour Isabella bestowed on him seriously made Cecily furious. 'She is a royal princess! To disport herself with a...a...'

'The de Coucy family is one of the most respected in France.'

Now she had made *him* angry and an angry man would not agree to help her. She took a deep breath. 'Forgive me,' she hated to say it. 'I see that we both are loyal to our friends. But there is more. Last week, I found them...them alone and...close.'

So, finally. The shock on his face mirrored hers. *'Imbécile!'*

She nodded, afraid to ask whether he was referring to de Coucy or the princess. 'Exactly. We must do something.'

'We?'

'We do share the same goal, do we not? You can see how foolish he is acting. And how bad it would be for him if...' Now she must say the words. 'And why I need your help.'

His jaw sagged a bit and he blinked. *'Pardon?'*

'*Votre aide,*' she said, more loudly. '*Assistance.*'

'I know what it means,' he said. 'And I am not deaf.' Yet he glowered as if the last thing on earth he would do would be to help her.

'So will you?' She held her breath.

He glared at her, then his eyes became thoughtful, as if he were seeing her as a person for the first time, trying to assess who she was aside from simply a *femme Anglaise*.

'What would you have me do?' he asked, finally.

He had not agreed, she could tell that. 'I want you to accept the invitation to Windsor for Yuletide.'

Something flashed across his face. Disappointment? Calculation? 'Why? What good would that do?'

'If we work together, we may be able to keep them apart. There will be more than a fortnight of Yuletide festivities. Celebrations, the upside-down time of year. Opportunities for...' His eyes did not leave hers. Her cheeks flushed.

She fell silent, unable to speak the words.

His smile carried no trace of chivalry. 'Opportunities for what?'

And suddenly, she saw not Isabella and Enguerrand, but herself with Marc, in a dark corner, in an embrace...

'For trouble, chevalier,' she said, sharply. 'Opportunities for trouble.'

'But she is a king's daughter.' At least, the idea had surprised him.

'Exactly.' And so she must make it clear the fault would be his friend's. 'Which presents special dangers if Lord de Coucy is not a careful man.'

He stood still, unbending, as if considering all she had said. But he did not say *yes*.

Cecily glanced at the door. They had been alone too long as it was. Stepping closer, she raised her eyes and lowered her voice. A command would not sway this man. A plea might. 'Please. Say you'll come. To help your friend.'

Regret flashed across his face. Ah, so friendship was something he understood. Something that meant something.

He sighed. 'You are as relentless as some of the knights I faced on the field.'

A strange compliment to give a woman. And yet, a glow of pride touched her. Only because he complimented her countrymen. Not because he approved of her.

'And what,' he asked, in a tone devoid of approval, 'do I gain from this bargain?'

He did not pull away. Worse, he moved closer.

She refused to step back, refused to look down, but his very gaze seemed an assault. All the risk of this course shimmered between them. In helping Isabella, she might jeopardise herself at a time when all would be watching her, waiting to see the man the king would choose.

'You gain the satisfaction of saving your friend from disaster!' Now she could put distance between them. Now she could breathe again. 'Is that not enough?' If it were not, she was at a loss, for she could think of nothing she could offer this man except what she must not give.

He took a step closer and again something— desire—emanated in a wave, washing through her, hot and sweet. Oh, if Isabella felt this for de Coucy, they were all doomed.

'No, Countess. It is not enough. I live as your prisoner and now you want me to dance like your puppet?'

His anger broke the spell. Relieved, she could match it with her own. Anger was permitted to a countess. Fear was not. 'I am helping you to accomplish something you also want and cannot get alone. Do not expect too many *mercis*!'

'I expect,' he said, 'that if I do this, you will help me return to France.'

She was glad she had not faced this man when he carried a sword in battle. 'How can I do that? Treaties and ransoms are in the hands of the king.'

'When the time comes, I will tell you.'

What could that mean? She was promising to do…she didn't even know. But that was in some distant future. The celebrations at Windsor were an immediate threat. 'When the time comes, then, I will do my best.' Not exactly a promise.

He stared, silent, as if trying to read her face. Did he believe her? Should he?

'Even our kings have called a truce,' she said. 'Can't we?'

She refrained from saying it was a truce only because her king had bested his. And yet, Jean, not Edward, was King of France. The thought gave her pause.

'D'accord,' he said, finally, as if they had shaken hands on a battle plan.

It was as close to a truce as they would get.

But as she called the guards and they led him away, she wondered what she had promised. To help him return to France? But that, after all, was the ideal solution. Send both men back, and quickly. Yet by treaty, a hostage returned home when his ransom was paid or a substitute sent. She could not change that. There was no other way.

Except the dishonourable path the French king's son had taken.

Tucking her hands inside her fur-lined surcoat,

she gritted her teeth against the chill. Surely de Marcel did not expect her to help him escape.

She would see him freeze in hell first.

'So I will come to Windsor after all,' Marc told Enguerrand that evening as they sat across the chessboard before a dying fire.

His friend looked up, brows lifted. 'I'm not sure which surprises me more. That you changed your mind or that you found a way to change your refusal.'

Marc shrugged and pushed his pawn to the next square.

'You can't just say that without telling me more,' Enguerrand said, sitting back and folding his arms. 'I know the Lady Isabella did not press you to come.'

He knew, Marc thought, much too much about the Lady Isabella and her plans. 'No. But her friend the countess did.'

'The countess? I did not think you impressed her so highly the other night.'

'I didn't. But you did.'

'Moi?'

'She is worried that you have developed a *tendresse* for the Lady Isabella.' He watched for Enguerrand's reaction, for any hint that the Lady Cecily might be right.

'Ah, then my plan is working.'

'Working well enough that she fears the Lady Isabella might not be safe in your company.'

'Safe? From de Coucy?' The shocked look was undercut by his wink. 'How can she worry?'

How indeed? But Marc had not realised until today how serious this was to the Lady Cecily. Here was a woman as loyal to her friend as he. 'She is worried enough that she begged me to come to Windsor and help her keep you and the princess apart.'

And now, a wicked grin. 'Which is exactly what you will do, *mon ami, bien sûr*.'

They shared a smile that held the trust of years. A smile which meant Marc would do no such thing. He was glad to help his friend, and yet... 'You know that I am no good at subterfuge. I may do you more harm than good.'

'You will do me a great deal of good just by keeping the Lady Cecily entertained.'

Marc groaned. 'How do I do that? I have no more use for the woman than she for me.'

'You'll find a way. Just don't let her know I seek Lady Isabella's influence, not her virtue. I can do the rest. Once I get my lands back, the countess will find all her worries disappear.'

His own, Marc was certain, had just begun.

Chapter Four

Windsor Castle—December 1363

On a blustery December afternoon, Cecily left London for Windsor Castle, fighting memories. Last year, her mother had been with her. This year, she was alone.

Yet Gilbert rode beside her and she was grateful for his company, though all his thoughts were on how he might redeem himself for his tournament disgrace.

'You were sitting near the king,' Gilbert said, as Windsor came into sight. 'What did he say about me?'

She swallowed. There was no disguising the truth. 'I'm afraid the king was disappointed.'

He nodded, as if the answer were exactly what he had expected. 'I don't blame him. Those men, they were hardened during war. I've done nothing.'

'You served my father in France! You were…' The words would not come. *You were there when he died.*

'But only as a squire. I was never in battle as a warrior. Now all I have is this pretend fighting. I want something that matters. Something of life and death.'

His very eagerness clutched her heart. 'The war is over now. You can stay safe.'

He looked at her as if she were a babe. Or a woman who lacked all wit. 'I don't want to be safe. I want to prove myself. The King of Cyprus is recruiting knights for a Crusade. Perhaps I will join him.'

'So you, too, can die in battle?' A question more sharp than she intended.

He looked at her, some sort of realisation in his eyes. 'You have not buried your father.'

She turned away from him and looked to the Castle. 'Of course I did.' She remembered it all. They had brought the body home in a sealed, stone coffin. The funeral mass was said on a bright summer day, with the sea breeze wafting into the church and ruffling the black cloth covering the bier. 'You were there.'

'But his effigy is unfinished.'

A stark accusation of what she had left undone. She winced. She had allowed grief to in-

terfere with her duty. *You have not buried him.*
She had not buried either of them.

There should be a carved image of her father
and her mother, side by side, as if they had been
turned to stone in death. It was her duty to see
it completed.

To honour them both.

Her mother had begun work on her father's
effigy, soon after he died. She chose the stone,
had it shipped all the way from the Tutbury
quarry, and selected a sculptor, one of the best
alabaster men from Nottingham.

And when the man arrived, her mother had
spread his sketches on the table, but Cecily could
barely see them through her tears.

Her mother sighed. *I can see you are not yet
ready.* Her tone, sharp. *Go. I will look at them
first.*

And so, while Cecily stared at the sea and took
long walks along the cliffs, her mother was left
to sort through the choices so she could give the
sculptor approval to begin.

Peter the Mason was a careful man. The work
proceeded slowly, or so her mother said. Cecily
refused to look.

And then, early in this year, nearly three years
after her father's death, her mother said the carving was all but complete. Shortly after, she had
ridden on a boar hunt again for the first time

since the earl's death. Left with the rest of the court, smiling again at last.

And never came back.

The grief that had just begun to ebb smothered Cecily again, worse this time. She, who had been expected to take command, to make decisions, could not face the cold stone. She put aside the sculptor's sketches of her mother's effigy. She had not picked them up again.

Disgraceful weakness. Unworthy of a Countess of Losford.

But that was not the excuse she gave to Gilbert. 'The king needed the sculptor. You know that.' Indeed, for the last several years, there had scarcely been a stone cutter or a carpenter to be found beyond Windsor's walls. The king had called them all to work on the renovations and punished any man who sought to pay the workmen enough for them to leave their work on the palace. 'I loaned the sculptor to the king.'

No need to explain that the king would have made an exception to let the man continue to work on the tomb of his old friend.

'It has been three years,' Gilbert said.

'It's been less than a year since Mother died.'

He raised an eyebrow. 'Waiting won't bring her back.'

'I know.' Yet she felt as if to cast them in stone would be to admit they were truly gone.

They passed through the gate to Windsor and she was spared the need to answer as servants converged to take care of horses and trunks. A welcome to the Christmas season the same as every year, and yet, this year, different.

You will be the countess some day, my dear. The honour of the name will rest in your care.

And yet, she had failed to uphold the simplest duty, to complete their tomb. Now, she must prove that that she was ready, willing, able to take up the mantle of Losford with the man of the king's choosing.

Leaving the chests for the servants, she and Gilbert ran for the shelter of the castle and the warmth of a fire. Inside, she took a breath, glad not to be fighting the cold. And as she soaked in the heat and loosened her mantle, she put a hand on Gilbert's sleeve.

'I will ask if the sculptor can be released,' she said.

He did not simply smile, as she had expected. 'When?'

Ah, and with that question, Gilbert proved he was no longer the youth she remembered. Now, he spoke as a man who would hold her to her word. Yet she could forgive the lack of deference in his question, for he had loved them, too.

'Soon. Before Twelfth Night.'

And with the completion of the effigies, her

mother, and her father, would finally be laid to rest.

Her feelings about the men who killed him, men like de Marcel, would never be.

Marc rode beside his friend, surrounded by the king's knights, as the walls of Windsor Castle emerged in the distance. He had seen castles across the whole of his own country, beginning with the stronghold of the de Coucy family, one of the strongest châteaux in France. He did not expect to be impressed by anything *les goddams* had to show him.

But he was.

'Well sited,' Enguerrand noted, as the walls rose before them.

Impregnable was the word Marc would have used.

Like the Château de Coucy, Windsor perched atop a hill above a river, the steep approach making an assault nearly impossible. Parts of the walls seemed hundreds of years old, as if they must have been built when the Norman-French bastard had crossed the Channel to become England's ruler.

Yet as they rode inside, Marc saw handsome buildings of freshly cut stone flanking the inner walls. This king was a builder, he thought, with grudging admiration, though he suspected French crowns had paid for most of it.

He had not expected a royal welcome, but the Lady Isabella herself received them graciously, as if the castle were solely hers. And Enguerrand greeted her as if he were the most honoured guest attending.

Marc gave his horse into the care of the stable master, then stood a safe distance from the couple, giving them time to exchange whispers and smiles. And when he looked around, he saw the countess wrapped in a mantle against the cold, watching them as well.

She shifted her weight and took a step, as if to interrupt their greeting. A sharp wind swept over the walls, sending her mantle flapping. He stepped in front of her, blocking her view, and tried to pull the edges close again.

She looked up, surprise parting her lips.

Tempting. *The way her head balances on her neck...*

Dark hair set off her fair skin and her square jaw drew his attention to her slender neck, now hidden by layers of wool.

Meeting her eyes again, he tugged the cloak closed and let his hands fall to his sides. He must be careful of his hands around the countess, careful they did not come too close, or be too bold. 'Your island is the coldest place I have ever been.'

She shivered. 'Truly, it is the worst winter I can remember. Frost came in September and has not left us since.'

'So we agree on the miserable weather of *Angleterre*.'

She smiled. 'Do you blame us for the cold?'

He wanted to blame them for everything, but standing this close to her, he was warmed by unwelcome desire. *Mon Dieu*. Did he not have obstacles enough?

Trying to speak, he had to clear his throat first. 'Even a king cannot control what God sends.'

His words seemed to summon some private grief, but she quickly looked away, peering over his shoulder, trying to see what was going on behind his back. 'You must move. I cannot see what are they doing.'

Instead of giving her clear sight, he moved to block her view. This was why he had come. Not to help her, but to keep her at a distance. 'You cannot make your intentions so plain.'

She sighed. 'I know, but the princess—'

'Cecily!' And there was her voice. 'Attend!'

'Come,' she said and he let her turn him to see. 'The princess herself is taking you to your quarters.'

Cecily walked quickly, no doubt intending to catch up with the couple and interrupt their private conversation. Marc deliberately slowed his stride, so that when she turned to see where he was, Enguerrand and Isabella pulled ahead, disappearing inside the great tower in the centre of the castle grounds.

Lady Cecily was forced to wait for him at the door.

Together, they stepped inside the stone gatehouse, blessedly away from the cold wind, and started up a long, enclosed stairway, climbing steeply up the mound to the tower. The walls sheltered him from the wind, but they also felt as close as his prison in London.

'Are you taking us to guest quarters or to gaol?'

'If it were not for me, you would still be in the Tower of London. These were the royal quarters until recently. You should be honoured.'

'You are always telling me I should feel honoured at things that honour me not at all.'

Ahead of them, out of earshot, the princess and Enguerrand had their heads together. Then, a feminine laugh echoed off the stone walls.

His friend was having success already. He could see why the Lady Cecily might be worried. But he was there to keep her occupied so that Enguerrand would be free to win the princess's support for regaining his lands. At the same time, he must make her *think* he was working with her to keep them apart.

He sighed, wishing instead to be leading a battle against an enemy of overwhelming force. It would be simpler.

He put a hand on her arm to slow her. As in battle, he must delay the enemy's arrival to give Enguerrand as much time to advance as possible.

She frowned. 'We are falling behind.'

Unfortunately, he could not take the forthright approach and physically hold her back. He must be subtle.

And Marc de Marcel was not a subtle man.

'We cannot simply force them apart,' he said. 'We need a plan, just as if we were in a battle.'

She frowned again. 'The plan is for you to keep your friend away from the Lady Isabella. That is why I brought you here.'

He gritted his teeth, wishing that he was back in London. 'In order to do that, I must know something about her.'

Still watching the couple mounting the stairs far above them, she sighed, exasperated. 'She is the king's oldest and favourite daughter, generous and loving to her friends and family and to the poor. She enjoys all manner of entertainment and gaiety.'

The princess sounded no different from any other noble man or woman he had known. 'Why is she not yet wed?' He had not wondered at it before, but now that he did, the question was

baffling. He was not a man privy to the plots of
kings, but such a woman would be an important chess piece. The right marriage, to the right
ruler, could have secured an unbreakable alliance. From what he knew of Edward, he was not
a man to let such an advantage go unclaimed.

Cecily slowed her steps and dropped her voice.
'There were many suggested. I don't even know
them all. And finally, there was a Gascon noble
she wanted to marry.'

'She chose her own husband?'

She nodded.

He looked back up the stairs. Enguerrand and
the Lady Isabella were no longer in sight. 'I did
not know she was a widow.' That could change
many things. A woman who had already known
a man's touch...

'She isn't. The king consented and all the arrangements were made, but when she went to
board the ships, she...could not.'

'She refused?' He could not comprehend such
a thing. The court of *le roi Anglais* was truly a
strange place. 'The king allowed that?'

'The man had been her choice. So her father
allowed her to change her mind.' A rueful smile
touched her lips. 'The Lady Isabella is accustomed to getting her way in all things. No one
tells her no.'

'Not even the king?' He knew little of women,

but in his experience, they did as they were told. Perhaps *les femmes Anglaise* were different.

She shook her head. 'She has a loving father and mother. They have given her everything she needed. Or wanted.' Her words were wistful.

'So she has everything she desires.'

Cecily shrugged.

'And you, Countess? Did your parents give you everything you desired?'

She nodded, her smile quick but sad. 'Until they died.'

He should not have reminded her of her loss, yet he felt a moment's regret. He had lost his family years ago. Had he loved them? He could not remember.

'Yet you have not wed either.' Suddenly, he wanted to know why.

'Only because the king has not yet selected my husband. I expect the man to be named by the end of the Christmas season.'

I hold the title, she had said, the first night they met. She, and her title, would be a prize for some nobleman. One far above a humble chevalier. He wondered, with a thought he refused to call jealousy, who the man would be.

'So now,' Lady Cecily said, in a tone that he now thought of as her 'countess voice', 'I've told you about Lady Isabella. What is your plan?'

He must convince this woman he was doing

something. 'She sounds wilful and capricious.' And thus, perhaps more dangerous than de Coucy had suspected. 'Perhaps knowing that will cool his ardour.'

'You shall not disparage her! Would you have me tell the princess vile tales about Lord de Coucy?'

'You would find none. He is admired even by his enemies.'

'The Lady Isabella has no enemies!' As if there were nothing more to say. 'She is the daughter of the king.'

'If you will not let me speak ill of her, how am I to dampen his ardour?'

They had reached the top of the stairs and, ahead, saw Enguerrand enter a room. The princess followed.

Cecily gripped his sleeve. 'We must do something.' She looked towards the open door, then bit her lip. Suddenly, she smiled. 'I know! While you are here, you will entertain the princess.'

'What?'

'That way, she will find it difficult to spend too much time with Lord de Coucy.'

Already, the plan had gone awry. 'The princess may be content to while away her hours with one of the mightiest lords in France. She will not feel the same way about a landless chevalier.'

'Ah, but that is the way it is practised in the

French courts of love! The landless knight inspired by the high-born lady. That is what Isabella told me.'

Landless knight. Did she know how true that was? 'And you? Will you then distract Lord de Coucy?'

'Of course not.' Her voice dripped with disdain. 'I am to be betrothed soon. I cannot be seen too much in the company of a French hostage.'

The Lady Isabella emerged from the room, looked over her shoulder with a smile and waved to de Coucy unseen, still inside.

Marc raised his eyebrows and looked back at Lady Cecily. 'You blame de Coucy for this folly,' he whispered, as the princess approached. From what he knew of women, this one seemed as eager as his friend. Or more. 'I think Lady Isabella shares the fault.'

'How can you say such a thing?' She gestured towards the room and then raised her voice so that the princess would hear. 'You will share quarters with Lord de Coucy.'

Then, putting on her countess posture, she joined the princess, who smiled in his general direction, though he could not be sure she actually saw him. The Lady Isabella, he was certain, had already chosen her courtly lover for the season.

Now, he faced three weeks of Yuletide cel-

ebrations pretending to interfere with Enguerrand's plans in order to support them. He sighed.
This *Noël* would be anything but *joyeux*.

Chapter Five

With the hostages settled, Cecily left the tower to give her deference to Queen Philippa.

Isabella had said renovations were complete, but as Cecily entered the new wing in the upper ward, glassmakers, painters and carpenters still littered the corridors.

'I thought the work was done,' she said, rising from her curtsy. Yet it obviously continued. The sculptor would still be needed and she could not possibly ask for him to be released.

Despite her promise to Gilbert, she felt a sense of relief.

The queen dismissed the workmen still painting the walls of her receiving chamber. 'Their work on the outer walls and the Hall is complete. My quarters are near finished, as are the king's, but your guest quarters are still wanting, I'm afraid. Edward plans two more wings…' She waved her hand in the direction of the outer walls. 'But until those are built our guests are still crowded, I'm afraid.'

Cecily swallowed a grimace. They would not be so crowded if rooms had not been sacrificed to de Coucy and de Marcel.

'But come,' the queen said. 'Let me show you my chambers.'

She led Cecily through rooms for praying, for sleeping and for dressing, pointing out the details, including the glass windows, each embedded with the royal coat of arms, which quartered the lilies of France with the leopards of England.

As if de Marcel and his kind had invaded the most private heart of England. As if she could escape him nowhere.

'And this,' the queen said, when they reached the final chamber, 'is for dancing.'

Cecily looked around in wonder. 'Mother would have loved this. She loved to dance...' She bit her lip.

A countess does not cry. Not even when her husband is killed.

The queen paused. 'This is your first Christmas without her.'

The queen's compassion made Cecily feel like a child again. How many Christmases had she spent with the royal family and her own? And now, only her royal family remained.

'I also miss my son Edward this year,' the queen said.

'Yet you will see him again, some day.' The queen's son was absent, but still on this earth. The prince and his bride, Joan, the Countess of Kent, had left for Aquitaine in July, one corner of France, at least, where an Englishman still ruled. She wondered how far that was from Marc's home.

'But not the others. I will not see the others.'

'Forgive me, Your Grace.' How could she complain of her own loss when the queen had lost six of the twelve children she had borne? Yet the king's wife, plump and motherly, was full of sympathy that made it easy to forget her station. 'I should not have spoken so.'

The queen reached for her hand and squeezed. Forgiveness. 'Your parents did not expect you to mourn for the rest of your life.'

Cecily's parents, she knew, would have been appalled to see her languishing as if diseased. Neither had any patience with ill moods, tantrums or tears. Yet despite her struggle against her grief, the last three years seemed to have disappeared in a fog of loss. 'I know, Your Grace.'

They expected me to put emotions aside. And she had failed, utterly.

'You remind me of your mother.'

Cecily mumbled her thanks, forcing her lips

to curve upwards, knowing it was far from true. 'I am proud that you think so.'

'The last few years have been difficult, my dear,' Queen Philippa said, 'but life must go on. We must see you settled.' She pursed her lips. 'I fear in the past we have been too lenient. There are risks, dangers, for a woman alone.'

Cecily blinked. The scandal surrounding the prince's marriage must have made the queen more sensitive to behaviours at the court. 'I assure you, Your Grace, you have nothing to fear.'

'Yes, I know that you would do nothing that would disappoint your parents.'

Cecily stiffened. 'Out of doubt!' Surely the queen did not fear for her chastity. 'No more than Isabella would disappoint you and the king.'

Queen Philippa's smile was fleeting. 'The king has been preoccupied with state matters, but he is now considering the question of your husband.'

'I am ready, Your Grace, to wed the man of the king's choosing.' She donned a determined, hopeful face. And yet, her hopes were that the man would be one who, when he died from war, or illness, or accident, she could release without mourning.

She could face no more losses.

Queen Philippa studied her, silent. 'What do you think,' she said, finally, 'of Lord de Coucy?'

Cecily considered the question with horror. Surely the king would not consider de Coucy, or any Frenchman, as her husband and custodian of the most important stronghold in the kingdom. Yet she must choose her words carefully, uncertain why the queen asked. 'He seems skilled and chivalrous at the joust.'

Even if his friend did not.

The queen sighed. 'Isabella has been urging Edward to restore his English lands.'

'Should a Frenchman be given soil my father died to protect?' Isabella had said nothing of this to her, perhaps because she knew Cecily would be aghast.

The queen put a hand on hers. 'Sometimes, we must hide our feelings, my dear. Sometimes, we must even forgive.'

Ah, the queen, whose tender heart had spared more than one man who deserved her husband's wrath. 'Yes. Of course, Your Grace.' Cecily renewed her vow to suppress her tears. But she would not forgive. Ever.

'Cecily, I would like you to keep close company with Isabella this season.'

Ah, now it became clear. The queen's true concern was not Cecily's behaviour, but her own daughter's.

Had Isabella's folly become so obvious? If she were advocating for de Coucy to receive English lands, the situation was even worse than Cecily had feared. In that case, her desperate plea to de Marcel was justified.

'I intend to, Your Grace.' She smiled, as if casting off all care. 'She is determined that I enjoy all the giddiness of the season before I marry.'

'We have been selfish, I fear, keeping her close.'

'She is glad of it. I know she is, Your Grace.'

'Still, she is alone.'

There was no answer to that.

In the silence that followed, the queen seemed to be lost in thought. Perhaps she was thinking of the lost alliances, lost opportunities. If Isabella had married the King of Castile or the Count of Flanders or the King of Bohemia, perhaps King Edward would hold the French throne, as well as French gold.

But when next the queen spoke, the moment had passed. 'Come. Let me show you the Rose Tower. The paintings are not yet complete, but it will be exquisite.'

She did not speak of Isabella again.

Yet later, as she left the queen, Cecily knew she had been right to be concerned. Now, she must not only protect Isabella from the Frenchman and her own foolishness, she must protect the queen from worrying about her daughter.

And more, she must ensure that de Coucy never was given sway over even an inch of English dirt.

Had Marc de Marcel been privy to this plan all along? Did he truly share her goal to keep the princess and de Coucy apart? Or was his real objective to undermine her efforts?

Determined to know, she searched the castle and found him, finally, talking to the keeper of the hunting dogs. A deep breath first, before she entered the kennel. Everything about the hunt seemed a cruel reminder of her mother's death.

The boar charged your mother's horse and she fell to the ground. It was all too fast. There was nothing we could do.

De Marcel rose when he saw her, and the huntsman bowed and backed away.

'We must talk,' she said, when they were alone with the hounds. 'Your friend. De Coucy. He seeks control of English lands.'

His face turned dark and grim. 'The lands belonged to his family. They are rightfully his.'

'So you knew.'

'It is no crime.'

'Do you also think to gain by stealth what you could not earn in battle?'

'I fought for my own country and king. I want no part of yours.'

'And yet, you killed my father!'

But instead of the shame or guilt she had hoped to see on his face, there was only shock.

At her shout, the dogs started to bark and she flinched. The hounds must have bayed so, just before they found her mother.

Their keeper rushed in, quieting them with a few stern words. He threw a puzzled glance their way and she motioned de Marcel to follow her outside.

'What did you mean?' he said, when they stood just beyond the door. The walls sheltered them from the worst of the wind.

She cleared her throat, trying to swallow her fury and bring her voice back to its proper tone. 'I said, you fought long enough to kill my father.' It sounded absurd, to repeat such a thing.

'The earl?'

She lifted her head, proud still to claim him. 'His colours were gules and or. With three lozenges on the shield.'

He frowned, as if trying to remember, then shook his head. 'I never met him in battle.'

How could he not understand? 'He was killed by a Frenchman.' He must have been, for he died in war.

'From where? I am of the Oise Valley.'

'What difference does that make?'

'The men of Bourgogne are different from the men of Picardy or Normandy.'

'Not to me. He was killed by one of you.'

'But not by me.'

What difference did that make? 'You are French.'

'And so, he claims, is your king. Your king who insisted on taking France from its rightful ruler!' He shouted now, having caught her fury. 'If you want to know who killed your father, look to him! To his greed! To his lust for power!'

'I will not listen to such slander. You know nothing of the king.'

He must have heard himself shout, recognised his anger. He clenched his fists and his jaw and took a breath. But lost none of the intensity. 'I do not need to know him. It is thus with all men. Kings, peasants. Even those who boast of chivalry. They are brutal and cruel and seek only for themselves.'

'And are you the same?'

A stricken look on his face, and then the edge of yearning, as if he had glimpsed something he wanted and lost it. 'Do not ever doubt it, Lady Cecily.'

She did not.

All her life, Cecily had been surrounded by expectations of honour and duty. This man violated every code she knew. If he himself had not killed her father, he had, she had no doubt, killed other men just as cruelly. He was no better than a wild beast.

'So you knew that de Coucy wanted the princess to help him gain his lands.'

'Is that a sin equal to the rest you accuse me of?'

'A man willing to violate the code in small things cannot be trusted in large ones.'

'So we are quit of our bargain?'

She wanted to say yes, turn her back and never see or speak to him again.

Yet the queen had asked for her help and this man, this man she did not like or trust, seemed her only ally.

'No,' she said. 'We are not. I must not allow...'

He did not argue, or question, but his eyes did not leave hers. Waiting. Demanding. Somehow full of a passion and pain she could not imagine.

But nothing filled the silence but falling snow.

She cleared her throat, searching for breath. He had not admitted whether he had known de Coucy's purpose, but it did not matter, after all, what de Coucy wanted. It was Isabella's desires that concerned the queen.

'Does the thought of de Coucy and the Lady Isabella truly aggrieve you?'

'Yes.' Said without hesitation. Or doubt.

'Then we are bound by that purpose.' The words, after she said them, sounded uncomfortably like a vow.

'And by only that,' he answered.

Behind them, dogs barked and she stilled at the sound. But the dogs did not chase the boar today. They had only been released from their cages for daily exercise. She glanced at the hounds' keeper, relieved he did not look their way. She had been too long in de Marcel's company.

'Until tonight, then.' She nodded, a gesture of dismissal, and walked towards the Round Tower, not looking back.

Marc watched her walk away, reining in his fury. At her, he wanted to think, but it was not. It was his own behaviour that rankled.

Are you the same?

He was. Which was why he knew.

One of the hounds jumped on him with snow-covered paws, holding a stick in his mouth. He smiled, then hurled the stick across the ward, waved to the dog-keeper, and headed indoors.

No, he had not killed this woman's father, but he had killed other men. What else was a warrior in battle to do? Yet those men no doubt had wives and mothers and daughters who mourned them.

Had he thought of that at the time? If so, he had buried it. But now, looking into her face was like looking into the face of all he had done and wondering.

Once, he had harboured illusions, too. Perhaps he still did.

Did he have regrets? No. No chevalier could regret what duty required.

A man willing to violate the code in small things cannot be trusted in large ones.

How little the Lady Cecily knew of men at war. The rules they touted were a story told to cloak the truth, honoured on the surface, betrayed without consequence. And when faced with enemies who were not of the noble class, honoured not at all.

But she would know nothing of that. Wrapped in velvet and music and tales told by kings, Lady Cecily would have heard only the stories fit to be told in the hearing of the ladies of the court. So she would know the code forbade violation of a noblewoman's virtue, unaware that such protections did not extend to a serf's wife.

Marc knew better.

When he and Enguerrand had ridden side by side to suppress the Jacquerie uprising, Marc had seen the sins of knights and of rebellious peasants. Sins that still haunted his dreams.

Yes, he had been knighted, but he owned little more than his horse and armour, and some days, he came near to understanding the wrath of a peasant forced to give up his pig to pay the ransom for an overlord who would only come back to demand the piglets.

Still, that did not excuse the rebel who had seized a knight and roasted him alive in full view of his family. But did that man's brutal act also justify de Coucy's slaughter of one, ten, twenty thousand ploughmen who owned not one sword to lift in their own defence?

No, he had seen the worst that men could do and he had little hope for any of them. Including himself. For even if he had only witnessed, and not committed, every act, he was tainted by all he had seen.

And now, he found himself forced to lie to protect a lying friend. A friend with one of the most chivalrous reputations on the Continent.

And one who seemed never to doubt.

No, de Coucy knew the game well and so, Marc suspected, did the Lady Isabella. No doubt she dangled the hope of restoring his lands like a sweet to keep him in attendance. By the season's end, their dalliance would end, leaving a honeyed taste on the tongue but no regrets.

His task was to prevent the meddling countess from learning the truth and disrupting the game before its completion. Was it a dishonourable violation of his knightly vows? If so, one that hardly deserved confession.

Yet this time, it seemed peace might hold dangers he had never imagined.

In Isabella's company, Cecily approached the Great Hall cautiously that evening, uncertain whether Marc would truly do as they had agreed. He had come here reluctantly, dour at the prospect, and after their fight today, her plan seemed more foolhardy than ever.

This night, the king and queen were absent and the Hall was left to the princess and the younger guests. The gathering was informal, as the most exalted guests had not yet arrived, but Isabella had prepared as carefully as if three kings were attending. She had donned, and discarded, three gowns before returning, finally, to the indigo blue after she asked Cecily and five more of her ladies whether the colour flattered her.

Yes, it seemed as if the princess had more than the usual interest in Lord de Coucy. Tonight, Cecily must be watchful and hope for de Marcel's help, all the while presenting herself as a woman who had emerged from her time of mourning ready to do her duty.

This was Cecily's first visit to Windsor's Great Hall since the king's rebuilding had been completed and before she stepped inside, she paused.

Last Christmas, her mother had been here.

And for every Christmas as she grew, she had
come with her parents to celebrate with the king.
Some of the minstrels had been here year after
year. She had watched the princess's fool grow
old before her eyes. And now, this year…

This year, she was the countess and would act
accordingly.

She stepped into the Hall, ready to battle a
wave of memories.

The space was large, powerful, vast. It made
her speechless, but with wonder, not with grief.
Yes, the rituals of the season held memories, but
this new and unfamiliar Hall did not.

She could see it as if she were a stranger. As
de Marcel might. It was the creation of her king,
the most powerful in Christendom, and it made
her proud, all over again, to be English. The vast
height of the ceiling. A line of leaded windows,
more than ten, evenly lining the wall, offering
a view on to the inner ward. It was a beautiful
room where she had never been before. Where
she could create new memories with her own
husband and her own children.

'Do you see him?' Lady Isabella whispered.

No need to ask who she meant.

Cecily brought her attention from the room to
those who filled it. 'No, my lady.'

A brief sigh, then a fixed smile and the Lady
Isabella moved into the room, looking fully royal.

Duty. That was her parents' true legacy. She vowed again to honour it.

As Isabella moved across the Hall, the two Frenchmen entered. De Coucy, at ease among nobility, walked immediately into the crowd and mingled easily, but de Marcel slipped to the side and hovered near the windows, wearing an uncertain frown and looking as if he would be more comfortable on a battlefield.

With a sigh, she made her way towards him. How was this stern-faced man to amuse the sociable princess? There was no gaiety in his expression as he watched Cecily approach and she feared another battle of words, but as she came closer, he bowed. A stiff and shallow effort, but at least he was trying.

'Are you ready to begin?' she said, smiling, as if they spoke of other things.

He shrugged, without eagerness.

She tried again. 'What did Lord de Coucy say? About the princess?'

'The man does not babble of women to me.'

A shock, to be reminded how little she knew of the world of men, of warriors. With her mother, and with Isabella, she could spend hours in laughter and gossip, examining the clothes, manners and motives of everyone at court, looking for things a man, apparently, could not see.

And if she told him that Isabella had changed

her dress three times, de Marcel would assume it was because the first two didn't fit.

'I think,' he said, 'you worry overmuch.'

Then so does the queen. But she could not tell him that.

'Let me try to show you, then. You see her? Over there?'

Marc raised his head, alert again, as if he must prepare for battle.

'Now watch. Do you see how she glances around the room, even as she speaks to the guest?'

A brief nod said he did.

'She is looking for him.'

And at that moment, de Coucy crossed her line of sight.

Only because they were watching did they notice when the princess met his glance and see her start working her way towards him.

'Our plan,' she whispered. 'You promised.'

But de Marcel had shifted his attention already. He didn't even glance at Cecily as he started to move. 'Stay right there.'

Before the princess could reach de Coucy, de Marcel had joined his friend. Heads together, he whispered something. They both looked back at Cecily. De Coucy smiled, too broadly, and nodded.

The next thing she knew, he had joined her and was charming her with some witty story, so that when the music started he was too far from the princess to join the dance with her.

Instead, Marc approached Isabella, bowed, and the next thing she knew, they had joined the carolling ring, leaving her alone with Lord de Coucy.

It was, astonishingly, exactly according to her plan. Yet as Cecily watched Marc dance beside Isabella, she found herself battling an unfamiliar feeling. He had not bent as graciously when he danced with her, nor smiled the way he was now.

It could not be jealousy. No. It must be relief that he had done as she asked.

'He is *un bel homme, n'est-ce pas*?'

Her cheeks turned hot to think de Coucy had noticed her wandering gaze. Of course, it was Isabella she was looking at, not de Marcel, but she didn't want to draw his attention to the princess. 'I had not noticed.'

But she had, of course. She had noticed and wondered that he appeared more comfortable with the princess than he ever had with her.

'But he is not a man at ease with this.' The gesture, some combination of the lift of the shoulders and a nod of the head, took in everything—England, the court, the abundance of the celebration.

Everything that had surrounded her all her life.

'Why is that?' If he spoke of Marc, de Coucy

would, at least, not be thinking of Isabella. That was the only reason she asked.

'Why is any man the way he is? Because of his birth? His life? Why are you as you are, lovely Cecily? A woman *très belle* and yet unwed.'

Ah, she could see how the man's charm would draw Isabella. He had at once smoothly refused to betray a friend and turned his flattery on her. 'The king has had more important matters on his mind.' She would not confide in this man, no matter how chivalrous. 'You know him well, though.'

'Almost since birth. He came to de Coucy when he was seven and I was barely two.'

A few innocent questions. He would have to be polite and answer and perhaps forget about Isabella for a while. 'So he was fostered by your father?'

He shook his head. 'My father died the same year Marc came. My uncle, who was my guardian, was far away. Marc was more like an older brother.' He nodded. 'He had no parents living.'

She steeled herself against unwelcome sympathy. She wanted no kinship of feeling with de Marcel, or any of the French. But this small, shared grief, knowing he had suffered the same loss as she, suddenly transformed him from an enemy to a person.

'How could he bear it? Losing them both?'

He nodded towards the other end of the Hall. *'On fait ce qu'on doit.'*

One does what one must. That was a code she knew.

The dance ended. Lord de Coucy slipped away from her side with such ease and grace that she could only watch as he made a straight course to Isabella.

As de Marcel rejoined her, she nearly opened her mouth and let a word of sympathy escape for a sorrow so old he must have forgotten it by now. But when she turned to speak, the pleasant smile he had shared with Isabella was gone, replaced by the frown she had thought permanently etched upon his brow.

She let the words go.

'In all my time with your princess,' he said, 'she wanted only to speak of Enguerrand.'

And the chill she felt from this realisation was only partially from the winter cold.

Because in all her time with Enguerrand, Cecily had spoken only of Marc.

Chapter Six

Rejoining Cecily after his turn with the princess, Marc watched a dwarf, one of the court fools, prance around Windsor's Great Hall, acting for all the world as if he were in charge.

And, as it was the season of *Noël*, he soon might be.

As Enguerrand had promised, the king's fire burned brighter than their chilly hearth. Certainly his table would be more bountiful, as well. He had a moment's feeling of well-being. What would it be like, to have a hearth of his own? For seventeen years, he had borrowed the homes of other men.

Across the room, de Coucy and the princess stood next to each other before the fire, heads close. He had told his friend of Cecily's 'plan', so at discreet intervals, Enguerrand would take Marc's place by Cecily's side. All done so smoothly that she would not notice that Marc actually spent little time with the princess, who had other duties. De Coucy was deprived of little time with Isabella and Marc was not required to dance attendance in his stead.

And after his obligatory interlude with the countess, his friend was free to work his wiles on Isabella, though he was careful to spread his smiles among the guests so that his preference for the princess was not obvious.

Marc did not have that skill. As a consequence, he spoke with as few people as possible.

'They do not even bother with the pretence of chess,' Cecily muttered, beside him, without taking her eyes off the princess. 'They simply gaze at each other across the board as if no one else is in the room.'

She leaned close to Marc as she whispered, her breath soft against his cheek. He turned, so close that he could see her lashes framing eyes of some mysterious shade of green and full of worry and distress.

What would happen if he took her lips? Would her gaze turn soft and sensuous?

He gritted his teeth, cutting off the impulse abruptly as if he pulled a visor over his eyes, and stared at Enguerrand, who had just moved a chess piece that exposed his knight to capture by Lady Isabella's queen.

A foolish move? Or a wise one?

Knowing his friend, the latter.

'You care for him, don't you?'

'What?' Now when he looked at Lady Cecily, she was studying him instead of the couple at the chess board. When did she turn her attention to him?

'Lord de Coucy. You have been close to him for many years. You care for him, as I care for Lady Isabella.'

He did, he supposed, or he would not be going through with this ruse, but her question suggested tangled emotion instead of loyalty's due. 'His behaviour reflects on me.'

'Because you are French?'

'Because I taught him.' A sin, perhaps, to be so proud, but de Coucy was renowned for his skill with lance and sword.

'I do not see you dancing as gracefully or singing as sweetly.'

'Taught him the arts of war, not of courtly graces.' Nor of courtly deception. War was so much easier. Your goal clear. Your enemies obvious. Usually. 'Enguerrand has a facility for pleasing people.'

'And you do not.' She did not make it a question.

True. And he did not try to do so. Yet, he flinched at her words. She had judged him; found him wanting. It should not matter. They loathed each other. Heartily. He should simply drink the king's good wine, distract Cecily from interfering with Enguerrand's plans and enjoy these few weeks, warm and well fed.

He cared nothing of what any of *les goddams* thought of him. Especially this one.

And yet, her scent teased his nose and tempted his brain. The princess, when he danced with her, had smelled of something heavy and sweet and cloying and rich. Cecily smelled of spring flowers after a rain on a cliff by the sea. She promised sadness and strength, haughtiness and caring in an impossible and dangerous mixture.

'I do not,' he said, finally. 'I am a man of battle.'

Across the room, Isabella waved the fool to her side and leaned down to whisper in his ear. The dwarf was wrinkled, as though his skin had been made for a taller man.

Marc leaned to Cecily. 'Are all the royal fools so old?' This one looked as if he had served the king for near as long as Marc had been alive.

She frowned. 'He's sharp and spry, despite his age.'

'In my country, fools can talk back to kings.'

'So fools are revered in France?'

He looked at her, sharply. 'Not in the way you mean.'

She looked down, with an abashed expression. 'I did not say it with spite. But this is not the king's fool.'

'No?'

She shook her head. 'The king wants no one contradicting him.'

It sounded like an apology. He smiled, an acceptance.

Apparently given instructions, the fool left Isabella and she smiled, shyly, at Enguerrand.

Next to him, Cecily gave a quick intake of breath. 'That does not bode well.'

'What do you mean?' His concentration had been on Lady Cecily; hers on the couple before them.

Before she could answer, the fool scampered atop the table atop the dais and waved to the tabor player to pound upon his instrument. The rest of the minstrels struck a chord and the room quieted, knowing something was to come.

Lady Isabella stepped forward and clapped her hands. 'Let the games begin! The fool is now in charge! And he is to be obeyed as you would the king!'

Titters, but no one protested, for the fool acted with royal blessing. It was all part of the expected Yuletide fun.

'But if it is Isabella's fool…' Marc's eyes met hers and widened in understanding.

She nodded, lips pursed, grim. 'This…' she

waved her hand '…is not the fool's idea. It is Isabella's. The commands will be hers.'

Isabella's way of funnelling her desires through a channel that would leave no hint of responsibility on her. Enguerrand would enjoy that.

And, he thought, looking at Lady Cecily with a smile, so would he. Realisation touched her face. Her eyes met his, widened, revealing hesitation and desire.

Or was that only what he wanted to see?

'Now,' the fool continued, his high voice cracked with age, 'take the lady next to you in your arms.'

General laughter.

Yes, the fool had read his mind. And not only his. Across the room, Isabella and Enguerrand, happily ordered into each other's arms, complied quickly.

'We must play the moment's jest,' Cecily whispered. 'Isabella will remark on us if we don't.'

Marc was not certain that Isabella would look at them at all, wrapped close to Lord de Coucy, but it didn't matter. He wrapped his arms around Cecily's waist, pulled her snug against him and hoped her dress would buffer the throbbing below his waist.

Fortunately, her face was not turned, temptingly, to his. She was not looking at him at all. Instead, she was craning her neck, looking over her shoulder at the crowded room. And as she did so, her breasts brushed against his chest and he gritted his teeth, wishing he were wearing armour.

Cecily was stiff in his arms. 'Can you see them?' she whispered.

Taller than she, he looked over the crowd, but in a room full of couples holding each other, he could see little. He shook his head.

She sighed. 'You must hate this even more than I.'

He nodded, vaguely, yet with this *femme Anglaise* in his arms, hate was not in his mind. In fact, nothing was in his mind. It was his body that spoke, that wanted, that did not care whether the woman was Valois or Plantagenet, but knew she was desirable. And if she had been another woman, he would have kissed her. Or wanted to.

'Turn around so I can see the room,' she whispered.

But when he obliged, the fool's voice interrupted. 'No one move! No one move!'

She looked up at him then. 'Can you see anything? Do you think—?'

The fool had scampered up on a table 'Now move!'

He let go a breath and stepped away, but too quickly, the fool called out again, 'Now stand back to back and lock elbows!'

He recognised Enguerrand's laughter, mingled

with that of the princess. As the couples broke, he could see Enguerrand, pressing her back to his, reaching for her arms.

Curse the man for his smiles.

Before he turned, he looked down into Cecily's upturned face. Her jaw was square and stubborn. But her eyes, wide-set, with strong, arched brows, swallowed the rest of her face. Her narrowed lips were pressed together with frustration, but then, she parted them, just for a moment...

He turned his back, relieved to be deprived of temptation.

Behind him, she turned and pressed her back against his. He reached for her arms. All around him, men and women stood with shoulders back and chests forward. Even though he could not see her, he could imagine how Cecily would look, her breasts in proud relief...

'Now, jump up and down!'

Instinctively, they both hesitated, then, without plan, jumped in unison.

Most couples did not. Some tottered on unsteady feet. Others stumbled, tripped over each other and fell to the hard floor, to roars of laughter.

His heart pounded, no doubt from the jump.

'Stop! Now, gentlemen, your heads to the left!'

He turned, now catching a glimpse over her

shoulder of the bare skin below her throat, disappearing beneath her gown into curves he could nearly see...

'Ladies, turn your heads to the right!'

And just like that, his lips were close to her temple, close enough that he could have kissed her, close enough...

All around them, laughter, some delighted, others nervous. He clamped his jaw shut.

Her lips, he saw, were just as tight.

'Is it not enough,' he muttered, 'that we must be defeated in battle? Must you humiliate us as well?'

'I do not see the humiliation being directed at you alone,' she whispered. 'The pain is fully shared.'

'Now, gentlemen, whisper a secret into your lady's ear.'

For one mad moment, he almost told her the truth.

Do not worry. You were right. He has no interest in the princess. Only in having his English lands restored. Lady Isabella's virtue is safe.

Would she smile, then? Would her worried frown lift?

No. Or if so, it would be replaced by anger and she would rush to disclose de Coucy's deceit. Once she did, his lands would stay firmly in the grip of King Edward and the two of them would once again be prisoners instead of guests.

'I don't hear you,' the fool called out. 'If you prefer not to tell the lady, you can tell all of us!'

All around them, murmurs. He must think of something to say. Something harmless. She knew nothing of him. Anything he said would be unknown, secret from her.

'I hate parsnips,' he said, quickly, to say something, to say anything except the real secret.

A moment of silence.

And then, Cecily laughed.

Laughed so hard she nearly doubled over, pulling against his arms, almost forcing him to lean back.

Had he ever heard her laugh so? And yet she laughed at him.

'It is not so *comique*.' And yet it was. He near laughed, remembering himself as a petulant five-year-old, pouting at his plate.

She did not answer, but behind him, he heard her coughing as she tried to subdue her laughter.

'You will not be so merry when you must confess to me.' He was eager, somehow, to hear what secret she would share. Only because it might be useful to him. Only because it might help him distract her from Enguerrand. But he knew he lied and he was a man used to telling himself the truth.

'I have nothing to confess,' she said, behind him. Yet the laughter had left her voice.

'Now, ladies. It is your turn.'

'See?' he said, triumphant as a cock. No one dared cross the fool when he reigned.

And the fool, for all the wrinkles lining his face, had more years at court and a greater force of will than most of those in the room. 'First, let go and face each other.'

He hesitated. It had been difficult to share a secret, even when he spoke without seeing her, but to look at her, to see her eyes when she told him…what?

They dropped arms and he turned, slowly and reluctantly. Though she faced him now, her eyes stayed downcast, as if she, too, was reluctant to tell her secrets to his face.

'Now put your arms around each other.'

She looked up, startled, and met his eyes. Both of them were awkward now. When they stood, pressed back to back, they had been protected somehow. But face-to-face again, with her arms around his waist, it was as though their bodies pressed together as lovers' might.

Yet they touched with none of the ease of lovers. She looked away again, and though she clasped her arms around his waist, they were straight and stiff, as if she were trying not to touch him. Uncertain where to put his own arms, he rested them, finally, across her shoulders, the sleeve atop the bare skin, where her neck curved into her shoulder. And it seemed as if he could feel the heat of her through the wool. If he leaned forward, just a bit, her breasts would brush against…

'Now, ladies!' The fool's voice dragged him back. He was in a room full of other people who, fortunately, were looking at their own partners and not at him. 'Tell your partner what you find most attractive about him!'

She lifted her head, dark-green eyes wide with surprise, trapped. Whatever secret she might have shared was lost and he found he regretted it.

'Well?' he said gruffly. 'Do you see something you like?' Disgusted to think that he wanted her to.

'Your hair.'

'My hair?' A man expected to be admired for his strength, his prowess, his bravery, his skill with the sword. Not his hair.

Shocked, he put a hand to it. He had never paid attention to his hair unless he had gone so long without bathing that his scalp itched. Tonight, as he touched it, he was surprised to find it soft on his fingers, but unruly and curving in its own direction. 'What about my hair?'

She shrugged and looked away. 'I had to say something. It was the first thing I saw.'

Something kicked his shin and he looked down to see the fool. 'Put your hand back on her shoulder, where it belongs.'

He lowered it, slowly, forced, this time, to place his palm on the bare skin of her shoulder.

'Now, ladies,' the fool shouted, his voice around Marc's waist, 'put your hand on the part of your partner that you like!'

She flushed and he felt his cheeks go hot as well.

And he held his breath as she lifted her hand to reach for his temple.

Cecily held her breath as her fingers brushed a rogue curl, then tangled in his golden hair. Soft. Perhaps the only soft thing about him.

The heat of his temple warmed her fingers.

Close. Too close. Might not lovers touch so in bed?

She drew her hand away, but her fingers trailed the curve of his cheek bone, then followed the sharp contours of his face, as if by touching him she could see beneath the stubborn jaw and the belligerent lips and glimpse what lay behind the light-brown eyes that pierced her with a glance.

Forced so close, for just this moment, she felt as though they were alone. Did other couples crowd the room? She saw only him.

And if the fool had demanded she tell a secret, she might have even said…

'Now, ladies.' The fool again. His commands as compelling as if he were the hand and she the puppet. 'Lean forward.'

She did. Marc's hand on her neck drew her to him, a touch as intimate as her fingers in his hair.

'Closer.'

And so she came closer. And so did he.

'Close enough to whisper.'

She leaned forward, falling into him. His lips drew near…

'Now whisper what you would like him to do.'

And before she could think, *kiss me* passed her lips.

He did.

Shielded by his arms, warmed by his lips moving hard over hers, she surrendered. He tasted of French wine, as intoxicating as the kiss, and everything else fell away but the two of them, private as lovers.

Or, as she had imagined lovers might be.

Laughter brought her to.

She jerked away and covered her mouth with her hand as if she could erase what they had done. *You would do nothing that would disappoint your parents.* And yet, she had kissed a man, a French hostage, in full view of the court. How many had seen her?

Embarrassed giggles floated in the air and shrieks of laughter echoed off the stone walls, joined by a few masculine growls and belly laughs.

A few quick-witted ladies had ordered their men to hop or laugh or sing, though she had heard none of it. But she saw more than one couple breaking a kiss.

Including, reluctantly, Isabella and Enguerrand.

She looked back at de Marcel. He, too, frowned. Regretful? Angry? So was she. Angry at Isabella and her heedless folly that had forced Cecily into the kiss, into something she would never have done otherwise.

No, no one had seen her kiss. And, she hoped, they had missed that of the princess, too. For it was Yuletide and the world turned upside down, just as she had feared. And not just for Isabella.

The fool's voice again. 'Now step away from each other!'

A suggestion so welcome she did it with a sigh of relief.

Marc did not move. Nor did he take his eyes from her face. What was he thinking?

What was he thinking of her?

His chest rose and fell, as if he had run a long race, but the proud and angry look remained, as if stamped on the shape of his face.

'I'm sorry,' she said. It was true. It must be. Her heart pounded still, but only because she had jumped and twirled.

'I should not...' He shook his head. 'What were you going to say?'

'What?'

'What secret were you going to tell me? Before the fool changed the game.'

That I wanted you to kiss me. What could she say instead? 'I do not like hunting, particularly boar hunting.'

A moment of puzzlement. 'Why?'

Too painful to tell. 'Why do you hate parsnips?'

A question without an answer, but one that broke the spell. He shrugged and, together, they turned to survey the room.

All around them now, couples were by turns moving closer or scurrying away from each other. Happy with the havoc he had created, the fool somersaulted across the floor and the minstrels began to play, signifying the end to the game.

She looked at Isabella and Enguerrand, both smiling, flushed and looking as much shy as aroused. And the look on Isabella's face was one she had not seen before.

If Isabella were to glance her way and de Coucy look at Marc, standing beside her, what, then, would they see?

Things they must not.

For when Marc had kissed her, Cecily had thought no more of the past and grief or future and duty. She had thought only of now. Of this…

No. She had let weak emotion intrude. It was only the Yule foolishness that Lady Isabella had planned. It meant nothing.

And yet… What if it did? For Isabella. For her.

If the fool had not saved her, a fool she might have become. A man such as de Marcel would not stop at a bow or a dance or a kiss. He might not stop until he had taken that which above all things must belong to her husband, whoever he might be.

Chapter Seven

Beside the Lady Cecily, Marc looked out over the room, feeling as if he had been unhorsed.

When he held her in his arms, kissed her, there had been nothing in the world but her.

Dangerous, to be so taken with a woman, particularly this one.

He was here only because of his friend. He had no other reason to even speak to the countess. Best he keep his attention where it belonged.

'And where,' he muttered, 'did the princess put her hand?'

He studied Enguerrand and Lady Isabella, trying to read the connection between them. It kept him from thinking of how close he had come to losing himself in the woman next to him. How much he had wanted the kiss. And more.

Damn the fool and his foolish friend who, he had no doubt, had instigated the frolic.

'More the question,' Lady Cecily answered, 'is where Lord de Coucy placed his.'

The familiar edge had returned to her voice. The one that reminded him they loathed each other. The one that protected him against the pull of her lips, her body, her—

He inhaled, then tightened his lips, as if putting a shield firmly in place. 'We fight each other to defend their honour, while they ignore us and take their own pleasure.'

Her smile, for once, was not reluctant. 'Forgive me. I am not always cruel.'

'Don't believe her.' The voice of the princess floated over his shoulder as Isabella and Enguerrand joined them. 'She has a tongue sharp enough to puncture a chevalier's shield. As I recall, the first thing she said about both of you was at the tournament when she wanted to see you in the mud.'

He remembered that moment, when her hatred had reached across the field. He knew now what bred it. 'Then she was disappointed,' he said.

Relieved, he saw hatred flash across her face again. Easier to handle her hatred than her rare moments of sympathy.

Marc looked to Enguerrand, expecting a smile that would signal his plan was going well. Instead, his friend was smiling at Isabella.

And the princess was chatting again. 'Well, next week, we must all sing for our supper.'

'What do you mean?' Marc asked.

'Each guest must find a way to entertain the court.' Cecily said.

A gay laugh from the princess. 'We have three weeks of amusement to provide. Every guest must do something. Sing, dance, or provide diversion in some other way!'

Bad enough he had to appear and be sociable. Now, they expected him to sing or dance or act the fool. He was a fighting man, not a travelling minstrel.

Isabella turned adoring eyes on Enguerrand. 'I know you sing beautifully.' Then, she turned to Marc, with a glance calculating and sharp. 'What can you do?'

'Yes,' Cecily said. 'What are your talents, other than unhorsing young knights?'

Ah, she did have a sharp tongue when she chose. The familiar edge had definitely returned to her voice. The one that labelled him an enemy to be distrusted. He welcomed it. It reminded him to keep his distance. 'I leave singing to others,' he said, grimly as if he were discussing a battle.

'And we are thankful that you do,' Enguerrand said, with a laugh and a smile and the playfulness that just enough wine and the right woman can bring. 'He has the voice of a frog.'

Marc, who could face swords and arrows without fear, wished he had done as he threatened and stayed in London, chewing bad meat, and leaving Enguerrand to woo the princess alone.

Isabella laughed with the careless cruelty of the royal. 'I'm sure you will think of something.'

Cecily looked Marc up and down, assessing. 'Perhaps a disguising?'

A disguising. To dress up in robes and masques and prance the room. What could be worse? He took a breath to protest, but felt a slight squeeze on his arm. Cecily, warning him to silence.

Lady Isabella clapped her hands in delight. 'Perfect! Father will love it. Remember, Cecily, the year he and your father dressed in monks' robes? Even Mother did not recognise him. And they were both so ribald that when she did figure it out, she gave him a scolding!'

He had not realised her father was so close to the throne. A man so trusted by the king that they could be fools together...

But Cecily, at the mention of her father, stilled, as if the shadow of death had fallen over her.

In the silence, Lady Isabella looked to Enguerrand.

'A disguising, *oui*,' he said, smoothing over the awkward moment. 'What will you do, *mon ami*?'

Cecily, beside him, shrugged off her gloom.

'It will be a surprise.' She waved her hand to heaven, as if to conjure an answer. 'But I promise you, I cannot turn this man into a monk.'

And she laughed, lightly, as if to dismiss both death and kisses.

Lady Isabella looked directly at Marc now, with an arched brow. 'She said she did not care for fair-haired men. I see she has changed her mind.'

Cecily blushed. Deeply. And Marc wished, for a moment, for dark hair.

'See?' Isabella said to Enguerrand. 'She doesn't deny it.'

'Oh, no,' Cecily said. 'I still prefer dark-haired men.' She looked directly at Enguerrand with a smile so forced that even Marc knew she lied.

And by her laughter, Lady Isabella did, too. 'Well, you can't have this one.' She linked her arm in Enguerrand's. 'Come. We must plan our own surprise for the entertainment.'

As soon as they stepped away, Cecily dropped Marc's arm. 'I did not think to give them an excuse to plot in private.'

'What *were* you thinking?' he said, more sharply than he intended.

'I was thinking to save you embarrassment. It seems I should not have bothered.'

Should he be grateful? Too much unknown

and unsaid lay between them. In a battle or tournament, he knew the rules, confident which to
follow and which to ignore. Of this court, this
woman, he knew nothing at all. A stumble threatened every step. 'I will not be paraded like a minstrel's monkey.'

'You will be invisible. Most won't know or
care who hides behind the mask.'

'How am I to conjure up a disguise and a story
in a week?'

'With my help.'

Gentle, simple words. Not at all the sharp-
tongued, brittle woman she had mostly shown
herself to be until now.

He cleared his throat, trying to find a *merci*.
'How long does it need? A costume?' he said,
instead.

'Months. But Isabella is right. The king is
a great lover of disguises. He has prepared at
least one each Yuletide for years. There must
be something left over.' She waved her hand,
gesturing to some unseen storage chamber in
the castle.

At least he would be spared being forced to
sing. *'Je vous remercie.'* He forced the words,
the hardest he had ever spoken.

She shook her head, stiffly. 'Do not thank me
yet. We may still regret this.'

He already did.

* * *

The next morning, in the light of day, Cecily faced Marc and her folly.

'What we must do,' she began, as she surveyed a room stacked with chests, 'is find something here we can stitch a story around.'

She had committed them to both the disguising and the subterfuge and was no longer certain that either had been a good idea.

'All of these?' he asked, looking at the wooden chests staked halfway to the ceiling of the undercroft along the east wall of the upper ward. 'Extra clothes?'

She shook her head. 'Who knows what is here? Isabella thought some of the old ones were packed away, but with all the changes that have been made, she wasn't certain exactly where they were or what was left.'

'They have so much that they do not use?' His voice mixed wonder and disbelief.

She blinked, surprised. 'Do you not?'

He shook his head. 'All I have is what I carry with me.'

And as she looked at his face, she saw the truth of it. A half-opened door. A glimpse of the life of a man who had not lived as she had.

'But a king,' she said, quickly, to drown the twinge of guilt, 'holds wealth and power for all his people. I'm sure King Jean does the same.'

A tight, unfamiliar smile graced his face. 'And I am certain that you, too, have stacks of chests unopened.'

She did. She had left much undone at home. Rooms unvisited since her mother's death. She did not even know what was in some of them. Her parents' possessions, now hers, remained untouched. She could not bear to look at them. And, as he implied, she lived comfortably without them.

'Yes,' she said. 'I do. But they will not help us now, so we will put some of these unneedful things to use.' She pointed to the chest atop the stack before her. 'Help me get that one down.'

He leaned in and reached up, moving the heavy chest with little effort. She sat on the floor in front of it and opened the lid to see gowns and tunics of bright red and green, the very colours reminiscent of childhood.

He crouched down beside her and lifted up a blue cloak and hood, trimmed in white, and emblazoned with a sun, embroidered in gold thread.

She gasped in recognition.

'You know it?' he asked.

'My father wore one like it. The king designed them for a tournament.' Her father had ridden with the king's side in the joust and triumphed. 'The rest of the court wore red and green, but the king's closest wore this.'

Her fingers trailed the velvet, as they had stroked her father's back in a hug before he had mounted. He always rode so close to the king. She had been so proud.

She pulled it from Marc's hands, dropped it back in the chest and let the lid fall. 'We'll find nothing here.' Nothing except memories too painful to revisit. 'Bring me another.'

But instead of moving, his eyes held hers, questioning…

Falling, falling into him again. Too close. Too hard to catch a breath. No one to see them here. If she lifted her hand, touched his hair again—

'When did he die, your father?'

His voice, gentle, but the question cut as sharp as a sword.

Her hand dropped to her lap.

'More than three years ago. Around Easter.' A time that should have meant triumph over death.

'I have heard the English speak of Black Monday. Was it then?'

So had she. Whispered horrors. 'Near that time, I think.' Ashamed, suddenly, that she did not know the day of his death. She had taken the news so badly that her mother had shared none of the details.

'If it happened that day, then I doubt a Frenchman's hand struck your father. More likely, it was the hand of God.'

She shifted, uneasy. King Edward had been heard to speak of the way God had reached out to stop his campaign. Some said the king had ceased his quest for the French throne because he took the dreadful events of Black Monday as a sign of God's will. But she would not desecrate her father's memory by arguing over such details with the Frenchman. 'All death must finally be as God wills,' she said, at last, then pointed to the other side of the room. 'Go. See what you can find over there. I'll look in these chests.'

Slowly, he rose and she did not watch him go.

She should have brought a serving girl, she thought, an hour later. Trunks full of wool and linen. Hose and scraps of silk. Outgrown shoes, forgotten. A few soiled rags. Nothing of value. Silver and gold, goblets and jewellery were held close and accounted for. Here, she found only things left behind, but not let go.

She pulled out a length of wool, large enough to be made into…something, but for a man smaller than de Marcel.

'Look here,' he called, from the other side of the room. He held up two sticks, each with a slightly battered cloth horse-head on one end. 'What are these? A child's trifle?'

The sight brought a smile and she rose to join him. 'They are play horses. For children, yes, but the king has also used them for pageants.' She took one of the sticks and stroked the cloth head. An ear was missing. 'We could do something with these.'

'Horses are used for battle.'

She wanted no reminders of battle. 'No. Not that. We are only two, not a legion.' Evident this man knew nothing but war, which was why she had stepped forward to rescue him. She frowned at the ceiling, trying to think. 'But we could do a mock joust.'

Then, holding her breath, she waited for a frown and a growl. Instead, a determined smile lit his face. 'That is something I know.' Said as if he were ready to unhorse his opponent in a single pass once again.

'But we cannot be serious. The king likes to laugh at Yuletide.' Unless it was a religious pageant, nearly all the season's entertainment was merry.

She knelt before the open chest. He had found a treasure of old robes and discarded masks, including a rabbit's head, large enough to fit over a man's head, with eye holes so the wearer could see out.

'Animals!' she cried. 'We can have a joust between animals.'

Together, they dug to the bottom, discovering

two more heads. Cecily picked up one of them, the hare's head in her other hand. 'Which?'

'I will not be a rabbit.'

She put it aside. 'You must be something.' She held up the final two. 'Choose.'

He looked back and forth between them, his expression serious as if he were assessing a battle field. 'That is a stag, obviously,' he said, pointing to her left hand, which held a brown mask with antlers. 'But what is that?'

She held up the one in her other hand. 'A goat?'

'I refuse to be a rabbit or a goat.' Crossing his arms, unmovable.

She dropped the masks into his lap. 'You are giving the perfect imitation of an ass.'

'An ass is a slow beast that resists commands.'

She raised her eyebrows. 'Just as I said.' She dusted her hands and stood, too angry at him to berate herself for losing her temper. This man, like no other, made her forget who she was. A kiss, a curse—he exposed all the feelings a countess was expected to hide. 'You do not want my help, so be what you will or stand before the court alone and croak like a frog. It matters not to me.'

She turned her back, near running for the door. Every time she was alone with him, she regretted it.

'Wait.'

She did not.

'Wait!' Louder. 'Are you only willing to help if I do things as you wish?'

She whirled around. 'What do you mean?'

'You never even asked my opinion.'

'I did. And you disliked the choices.'

'There must be something else.'

'So late in the day? We have no time. And you've never even done a disguising.'

'No. But I doubt it requires that I be an ass.' A smile, finally. 'Though Enguerrand has accused me of the same on occasion.'

She had to laugh, now. 'Who am I to argue with Lord de Coucy?'

Still sitting on the floor, surrounded by cast-off costumes, he held up the two animal heads, looking from one to the other. 'I shall wear the stag's head,' he said, with a sigh. 'Now, what do we do next?'

An idea. A whisper. Something that would make this all worth doing. She smiled. 'Now we create the play.'

A play, she decided, that would not end the way Marc de Marcel was expecting.

Chapter Eight

$\mathcal{C}\!\!\!\!\sim\!\!\!\sim\!\!\!\mathcal{D}$

As Marc entered the Hall, he was wearing a stag's head, but he felt like an ass.

His only comfort was that with his head fully covered, no one could possibly know who he was.

Lady Cecily had assembled the disguising with a dedication that would have befitted a man at war. The simple horse's head on a stick was now part of a light wood cage in the shape of a destrier. Covered in bright fabric, it resembled a tournament horse in livery. The frame hung from his shoulders and with a hole that hit him about waist high, when he walked, it looked as if he were riding a horse.

They had practised, of course, but the full frame was not complete in time for him to try it. Now, encased, the frame swayed with each step, threatening to bump walls and people. The elaborate one, two, three of the tournament that had seemed manageable when they practised now seemed impossible.

He began to think that singing might have been the better choice.

He squinted through the eyes of the stag's head, barely able to see what was in front of him. Lady Cecily, wearing rabbit ears and a surcoat that disguised her shape, was unrecognisable. A page carrying a flambeau went by, the flame wavering dangerously close to the flopping ears. Marc held his breath, ready to tear off the entire façade and run across the room if she caught fire.

But the moment passed, safely.

He took a step. The 'horse' covering him wobbled uncertainly. Laughter echoed in the Hall. Were they laughing as Cecily had intended, or because he looked the fool? Or, perhaps they were only mirthful with wine and Yuletide spirit and not heeding him at all.

Curse the *roi Anglais* for insisting on entertainment so *ridicule*.

Still, he struggled to do what they had planned, to 'ride' towards each other, feign the expected three passes, then, dip into a mutual, respectful bow.

Across the hall, Cecily started forward, slow and steady.

He took another step. The light wooden cage rocked back and forth, more like a boat than a noble steed, and bumped something, he could not see what. With frustration born of weeks of entrapment, he forced his way ahead, as if at least here, he could break the bonds of captivity.

A crack. Splintered wood. Still, he charged ahead, the dented, drooping corner of the cage trailing fabric behind him.

Now, Cecily came towards him, faster than they had practised, and instead of gracefully riding past, she forced her horse's head into the broken wooden frame, ripping it apart.

Surprised by the strength of the blow, Marc lost his balance, stepped on to the torn fabric and crashed to the floor, felled as completely as if he had been knocked off a real horse on the tournament field.

The stag's head kept his head from being slammed against the floor, but the antlers snapped off.

He raised his head from the wreckage and pulled off the mask.

No question now about the laughter. Or the cheers.

For as his opponent raised his arms in victory and ripped off the rabbit's head, Marc saw not the Countess of Losford, but Sir Gilbert.

Gilbert, who had been given his revenge.

Marc tried to move. His leg was twisted beneath him. Not broken, but with a bruised knee.

Drawing strength from his anger, he straightened it, kicking the broken wood out of the way. He was ready to fight, to jump up with fists flailing and pummel them all.

But he could not even stand.

Gilbert, with a grim, satisfied smile, held out his hand to help. 'We are even now.'

More generous than Marc had expected. Or, probably, deserved.

Forgiveness was easier for the victor. Something he should have remembered when Gilbert had sprawled in the mud of the tournament field.

Marc took the help Gilbert offered, and when he managed to stand they shook hands as the crowd cheered.

'She planned it all, didn't she?' Marc asked, as he limped off the stage. Something, he did not want to call it jealousy, burned in his veins. Lady Cecily's disdain for him ran so deep that she had plotted this elaborate humiliation.

Gilbert looked down, not meeting Marc's eyes. 'I should not have let her.'

And yet, Gilbert had not deserved the humiliation Marc had thrust upon him. Perhaps there was some justice here. He sighed. 'And I should not have treated our joust as if it were a battle.'

'But you were the better man,' the young man said. 'You taught me a lesson. One that may keep me alive some day.'

Marc swallowed. 'I, too, needed a lesson. I am grateful that you forgive me.'

The young man shrugged, then raised his gaze. 'She doesn't.'

Marc followed his gaze to see Cecily across the room, leaving the Hall.

Cecily woke the next morning, weighed down with regret. She had watched the mock joust and laughed, at first, with the rest of them, anticipating the joy of seeing Gilbert vindicated and Marc brought low.

But when he fell, then struggled to rise, she took a step, wanting to be certain he was unhurt. And as she watched him shake hands with Gilbert, instead of glee, she felt shame. In this, he had shown more honour than she. Had she thought that humiliating him would somehow change the outcome of the war?

Would somehow bring her father back?

The honour of the name rests in your care.

And faced with Marc de Marcel, she had once again allowed emotion to trample duty. He was a proud warrior, held captive and she had humiliated him for petty, personal gratification.

He deserved it, of course, for what he had done to Gilbert.

For the kiss.

Yet none of that excused her. Her parents

would have scolded her and if her future husband, whoever he might be, discovered her deceit, he could only wonder whether she were
worthy of the role and title she had been born to.

Wonder, as she wondered every day.

She threw back the bed clothes. Today, she
would keep her promise to Gilbert and request
the sculptor be released to work on her parents'
effigies. In this at least, she must finally do her
duty, no matter how painful. Else, when the king
selected a husband, how would she explain that
she had left the tomb undone?

Her opportunity came later that day, as the
queen had gathered some of the women for an
afternoon's entertainment, listening to a minstrel
tell tales of King Arthur and his court. Cecily left
last, taking a private moment.

'A request, Your Grace, if you would smooth
the way with the king. If the work he came for is
complete, I ask that His Grace release Peter the
Mason to complete my parents' tomb.'

'Ah.' Realisation touched the queen's eyes. She
reached out to Cecily's chin and studied her face.
'And if he is ready, are you?'

The queen's fingers did not allow her to look
away.

She nodded, biting her lip. There would be no
tears allowed.

The queen raised her brows. 'Are you certain, my dear?'

'I still mourn, Your Grace.'

'And so shall you ever. I understand that.' The queen's voice was both strong and gentle. 'But the time to mourn must end.'

Cecily swallowed. 'Yes, Your Grace.' Perhaps her delay had been an effort to stop life so it would change no more. But even if she was not truly ready, just to have asked, to have taken this small step brought a relief she had not expected. 'That is why I must complete their tomb.'

The queen nodded and dropped her hand. 'I will speak to Edward. I expect the sculptor will be able to return to your work as soon as the Yuletide season is over.'

'If he returns to the castle after Twelfth Night, perhaps by spring, by the time of my wedding....' She left the sentence incomplete.

That was where she must put her attention. On her future husband. Perhaps his kisses would leave her as shaken as de Marcel's...

She stopped herself. The French chevalier had no place in her thoughts. And better if her husband raised no such wild emotions, unworthy of a countess. Much better her marriage be of duty only, as her parents' had been. She could not bear to lose someone she loved ever again.

'I'm sorry. I have no news to tell you.' The

queen took her hand. 'Perhaps my daughter is
right and I worry overmuch. Enjoy the season.
The future, and your wedding, will come soon
enough.'

'Yes, Your Grace.' Perhaps she, too, had been
over-worried. Her concern for Isabella, bringing
de Marcel into the picture, all this had only created trouble. Cecily would remember that in the
future. 'And so,' Cecily said, her throat tight on
words reaching for gaiety, 'what is planned for
tomorrow?'

The queen paused. 'A boar hunt.'

The words stole every good intention. She
gripped the queen's hand, afraid her legs might
give way. 'I thought,' she began, sounding ten-
tative even to her own ears, 'there were no more
boar.'

'The huntsman swears he saw one in the park
last week. Now Edward insists we have a boar's
head for the Christmas feast.'

Cecily nodded, but could not speak.

In all things, her mother had been dutiful.
In all except for this one foolhardy pleasure.
Women, of course, rode on stag hunts, but very
few hunted the boar. Fewer still did so with her
mother's reckless passion.

The queen's voice, light and steady, gave Cecily time. 'I, for one, plan to stay warm by the
fire. You'll join me, won't you?'

She had little love for the hunt before her mother's death and had loathed it since. When had she last ridden? She had not even been beside her mother that day.

And now, duty did not require her to ride. No one would think less of her if she huddled around the fire with the queen, listening to sweet music.

No one except Cecily herself.

'I thank you for your invitation, Your Grace. But I will join the hunt.'

'Are you certain?'

'As you said, I must enjoy the season.' Enjoyment, she was certain, was beyond her. But fear was no more acceptable than grief.

Too often, it seemed, thinking about it now, her parents had allowed her to escape her responsibilities. *She's not ready*, her mother would whisper, thinking Cecily could not hear. *Will she ever be ready*? her father would reply.

She must be ready now. And must prove it. To herself.

And to Marc.

She refused to fear any animal.

Or any man.

Especially a French chevalier.

As the men gathered for the hunt in the dim, dawn light, Marc wrapped the extra length of fur-lined cloth over his shoulder. For once, he did not mind rising before the sun.

Here, in the open air, away from the confines of the castle, he felt fully himself again. He had had his fill of courtly games. And of the Countess of Losford.

He had avoided her since the unmasking, two nights before. The Lady Cecily had not forgiven him, young Gilbert said. The sentiment was mutual. He had nothing more to say to her. At least, nothing a chevalier should say to a lady.

He was ready for a day among men, with a weapon in his hand. He could do battle with a boar, much as he could with a man. There was no disguising here, no hidden motives.

Only life. Or death.

And when the foe was a wild boar, well, death was possible. The beast was large and strong, with tusks that could spear a man through.

Beneath his cloak, Marc rubbed his arms for warmth, then mounted his horse, eager to ride. De Coucy, sociable even at this hour, moved among the others, always with a smile.

Lady Isabella was not among them. Thankfully, for this day, both he and de Coucy would be away from the temptation of the women.

The king rode up beside him and pulled his mount to a stop. 'You're de Marcel.'

So surprised that the king would approach and

know him, it took a moment for Marc to locate his tongue. *'Votre Majesté.'* He did not bend his neck, but took the chance to look the king in the eye.

'Honourable. To give young Gilbert his vengeance.'

Marc's cheeks burned despite the cold. 'I must credit Lady Cecily with the idea.'

'Are you as good at hunting boar as you are at the joust?'

At that, he could not help a smile. 'Some say so.'

'Good,' the king said. 'Then ride with me.'

A compliment, even if it came from an enemy king. 'I have ridden to battle beside *le roi*, but not to the hunt.'

'Then you know that the spear of a knight is as deadly as that of a king,' Edward answered.

And for all his hatred of this land and its people, he smiled. He would show this king what the men from Picardy were made of.

So Marc fell into place with the group as King Edward conferred with the huntsmen and set a plan for the day. It gave Marc a new appreciation for the man. If he conducted his campaigns with the vigour that he conducted the hunt, well, his victories were understandable.

This, this would be a good day. A day devoted to the hunt would clear his mind of the countess and kisses and imaginary jousts. That was all he needed. He and Enguerrand both had been confined too long in this world where there was nothing but women's frivolity to pass the time.

He had just convinced himself that he would think no more of Lady Cecily when he saw her.

She was bundled so thoroughly that he could not see the familiar curves, but he recognised her eyes, that same sharp glance that had caught him the day of the tournament, as if the distance between them were no obstacle.

He turned to the king. 'Do your women ride to hunt the boar?' It was one thing for a woman to hunt hare or deer. But at the end of a boar hunt, the hunter must dismount and face the animal with his spear. If he did not strike cleanly and quickly, he would have no second chance.

It was no place for a woman.

The king glanced at the countess and frowned. 'Her mother did. And died doing so. I have not seen Cecily ride to the hunt since.'

Her mother died during a boar hunt.

The very brutality of the image took his breath. He had seen many ugly forms of death on the field of battle. Men came to expect it. But not a woman. Never.

Excusing himself, Marc rode over to Cecily. Fierce determination framed her face and she watched him approach as if daring him to interrupt her.

'You said you did not like the hunt,' he began, 'so why are you here?'

'I do not need your permission.'

'I would not have given it.'

'Do the women of France cower behind their castle walls?' She was again the woman he knew. The one who sparred every sentence with him.

Yet he felt as if she spoke not to him, but to herself, as if sheer force of will could banish her fear. If controlling her fear took that much attention, she would be unable to concentrate on the animal. A dangerous combination.

'The king told me,' he said, 'about your mother.'

She gripped her reins so tightly the horse jerked his head against her hold. 'It has been near a year.' As if time alone could heal her.

Torn, he looked at the king, then back at her. 'You should not ride without someone at your side.'

She smiled, then, with a sweet warmth she had never shown him before. Reward enough for his offer. But as she nodded to an approaching rider, he realised the smile was not meant for him at all.

'Sir Gilbert will be with me.'

Pride gilded Gilbert's grin as he took his place

beside Lady Cecily, as if the brief truce after the disguising was over.

And try as he might, Marc felt, for no good reason, as if the boy had unhorsed him again. 'Take care of her,' he said and whirled his horse away to join the king.

Chapter Nine

As she watched Marc ride away, Cecily took a deep breath, surprised she could do so.

'Are you all right?' Gilbert asked.

She nodded.

Worry bent his brow. 'I was wrong to chide you. Perhaps de Marcel is right. It is too soon. The tomb, this, it can all wait.'

And for a moment, she wanted to agree.

Come, Cecily. Show them the strength of a countess.

She shook her head. 'I am ready.'

Seeing Marc had steadied her, forcing her to feign the courage she lacked. She could not avenge her father's death with a sword, but she could honour her mother's death with her courage. And Marc de Marcel would be a witness. She would prove to him that no English man, or woman, could be bested.

Strengthened, she put a gloved hand on Gilbert's arm. 'Do not worry.' He was kind and sweet to witness her ride, knowing what it cost. For that, for his gentle company, she was grateful. 'I will stay well back.'

They walked the horses towards the others, their hooves beating the snow into mud, their breath turning into puffs in the frigid air.

A small party today. And she, the only woman.

With all of them gathered, she and Gilbert would ride close to the king.

But not as close as Marc. For the king, to her shock, had invited Marc to his inner circle.

'If I had won the joust, I would be the one beside His Grace,' Gilbert muttered.

Seeing Marc favoured, she waited for the familiar resentment to rise and choke her anew. Instead, something quite different welled within her. Pride, coupled with something more earthly, suggesting another of the deadly sins. Now, she could not look at his arms without feeling their strength around her, could not see the curve of his lips without feeling them move hungrily over hers.

And now, his eyes seemed to do the same. Was it anger or desire that lit his gaze?

Marc glared at her, then leaned over to whisper something to the king, who looked back at her, frowning.

'The wind is cold,' the king called out. 'You need not ride today.'

His sentiment? Or Marc's? Either way, it was not the wind that worried them. 'A knight who falls from his horse mounts again, Your Grace. It is time I did the same.'

A pause. A quick nod. And the group headed into Windsor Forest.

As the hours wore on, they kept riding until it seemed they would reach the very limits of the forest before they found the prey. Traitorous relief lifted her spirits. Perhaps, after all, there were no more boar in England. Perhaps, just facing the ride had been courage enough.

But the royal huntsman would not have led them this far unless he was certain, for the king would not be satisfied unless, on Christmas Day, the boar's head, its mouth stuffed with an apple, was held aloft on a golden platter and carried into the Hall.

Yet riding at the rear of the hunters, well shielded, she breathed more easily as the day went on. Gilbert, on the other hand, kept edging himself forward, closer to the king, frustrated that de Marcel had toppled him from the king's favour as well as from his horse. No mock revenge would be enough.

Once, she caught Marc, near swivelled on his horse, looking back at her. She smiled and waved a gloved hand, as if there were nowhere else she would rather be.

But when she heard the distant howls of the bay dogs, she held her breath. The prey spotted. The chase begun. This was the moment her mother had loved. Last year, her mother must have urged her horse forward, riding without hesitation into the chase until—

The hunters galloped ahead, even Gilbert. She tried to force herself to follow, but even the horse could sense her fear, her tight hands on the reins holding him back, and the beast refused to move as the others disappeared into the trees, fading from sight.

Coward. You are not worthy of the title your parents left you.

The sounds of hooves and harness faded, leaving her alone amidst bare trees and trampled snow. For a long time, she stayed in the saddle, listening, until all she could hear was the rattle of branches in the wind.

Discouraged, she dismounted and sank on to a fallen log, pulling her pelt-lined cloak closer.

Gilbert had ridden off without a backward glance and would not miss her until after the kill. She lifted her head and looked behind her. If she followed the tracks they had left, perhaps she could find her way back alone. Inside the castle, the royal ladies would still be gathered by the fire and she could join them, claiming the cold alone had chased her within doors.

Hunching her shoulders against the wind, she looked up. The sky had turned winter white. Snow threatened. And the distant cries of the baying hounds grew alternately soft and loud, as they chased the prey.

She should turn back soon, before the tracks were covered.

Marc heard the howls of the bay hounds, as welcome as a battle horn. He spurred his horse, racing with the king, glad to leave Cecily safely behind with Gilbert.

The chase was long and the beast wily, staying so far ahead that they could not send the catch dogs to corner him for the final kill. In time, they seemed to turn full circle and the huntsman called a pause to confer with the king.

In the lull, Marc looked back for the first time, surprised to see Gilbert on his horse, pausing with the rest of the men.

He squinted, thinking Cecily would be close behind, but he saw only trees edged with snow.

Turning his horse, Marc rode directly to Gilbert. 'Where is she?'

Gilbert looked around, dazed. 'I don't know.'

'What do you mean you don't know? You were to watch out for her.'

'Have you ever tried to tell Lady Cecily what to do?'

Young fool. He had no idea of the dangers that lurked even in this most royal of forests. 'She might have fallen from her horse, or...'

'The king rides again!'

Kicking his horse, Gilbert joined the hunt, leaving Marc behind, forsaken as thoroughly as his duty to Cecily. In the heat of this final chase, no one thought of her.

No one but Marc.

He paused, trying to get his bearings. Clouds now covered the sky. The forest was unfamiliar and with all the turns they had taken, he could not retrace the ride. To search for her alone would only ensure he would be lost as well. By the sound of it, the hunt was near over. As soon as the boar was killed, he would raise a search party. The king, he was certain, would be as troubled as he about her disappearance.

With a final, worried glance at the empty forest, he spurred his horse to catch the others.

He did not have to go far. Finally, they had the boar trapped. The beast was young and powerful, but the chase had sapped his strength. The kill was at hand.

One of the chase dogs got too close and the beast gored his shoulder, sending the pup screeching in pain. The huntsman let lose four catch dogs, who attacked, chomping on the beast's ears and head and legs, holding him fast.

Marc, Enguerrand, Gilbert and the rest watched as the king dismounted and took a spear from the hand of a waiting attendant. The honour of the kill would be his and he approached the pack of screeching, growling animals, looking for an opening. He could spear the shoulders, but the boar's hide was strong there, and the spear might not go deep enough to kill. A surer spot was to spear the throat, but that meant biding his time, waiting for the right moment.

The king crept closer and pulled back to thrust the point home.

And then, the boar, with desperation born of knowing death was near, tossed off the dogs as if they were fleas, charged past the milling horses and men, and disappeared into the forest, back the way he had come.

Where Cecily must be.

Marc, still on his horse, whirled and gave chase.

The distant howls of the baying hounds came closer.

Cecily raised her head, muscles coiled. How long had she been slumped here, searching for the strength to mount? Long enough for silence.

Long enough that she thought the hunt must have ended.

Which direction were they coming from? She tried to listen and that was when she heard, more frightening than the dogs, the snort and the pounding hooves of the boar.

She leapt to her feet. Her horse had wandered out of easy reach, searching for a blade of grass beneath the snow. She tried to run, but her gown and boots, wet from the snow, slowed her steps. Then, the horse, too, heard the sounds. Head lifted, ears flicking back and forth, searching for the source. Then, riderless, he bolted into the trees.

The howls, the hooves, came closer, as if Death itself, inevitable, had finally come for her, too.

And then, louder, faster, a galloping horse, overtaking the boar.

The horse burst into the clearing. Marc hurled himself off the saddle and drew his sword. Before he could speak, the beast crashed through the brush and into the clearing and stopped, looking right at her.

'Don't move,' Marc said.

She could not. She could only stare at the bloodied beast, near exhausted, his breaths pumping his sides and frosting the air.

In the distance, the baying dogs approached.

Knowing he was still chased, the beast summoned his strength and ran towards her.

And between her and the boar, came the point of Marc's sword.

Impaled, the beast staggered, and turned his wrath away from Cecily.

Towards Marc.

The sword was designed to kill a man, not a beast. Stuck firmly in the boar's chest, it would do its deadly work eventually, but now, in the animal's last, desperate moments, anything within reach of his sharp, curved tusks was in jeopardy.

Marc drew his dagger and stepped closer.

Chapter Ten

Later, she could not explain what had happened.

There was a long, endless moment. She, Marc, the wounded boar—none of them moved.

Then, dogs, horses, huntsmen, chaos, invaded the clearing.

The boar, desperate, ran towards Marc.

A quick-thinking attendant raised a spear for the king, but Cecily grabbed it and, with strength that must have come from heaven, thrust it through the beast's chest.

In the throes of death, the beast's movements ripped the staff from her hands, but unlike the sword, it still pierced the boar's body through. With a final lurch, the boar staggered, then dropped to the ground.

Dead.

Now Cecily swayed, afraid she, too, might fall. Whatever mad spirit had fuelled her left as suddenly as it came and she could barely stand.

But there was Marc's strong arm, bracing her.

He led her to the fallen log, let her cling to his hand so she could sit with dignity instead of tumbling to the ground in a heap.

'*Ça va bien?*' Marc's voice, somehow comforting.

Without the strength to speak, she nodded. Looked down at her hands. Wiggled her fingers. Stretched her toes.

Alive. She was alive.

In all her months of grief, first for her father and then for her mother, the thought of her own mortality had never crossed her mind. Only the idea of the long years ahead, uncertain that she could fulfil her parents' expectations.

But today she, too, could have died. As quickly and unexpectedly as her mother.

'I owe you my life,' Marc said. His eyes showed none of the wary cynicism she had come to expect.

She shook her head. 'You risked your life to save me.'

And that realisation violated everything she had believed of him, or wanted to. She had wanted to think of him only as a Frenchman. As one of those who had, or could have, killed her father.

Suddenly she did not know the world she lived

in. And that, in its own way, was as terrifying as the face of death.

An attendant rushed over with wine. Gilbert, ashen, babbled apologies. De Coucy started searching for her missing horse and the king told an attendant to fetch a litter so she could be carried back to the castle.

'No,' Marc said. 'She will ride with me.'

'Can you?' The king's question to her seemed large, important.

She gripped Marc's hand, forcing herself to stand, back straight, head high, feeling for the first time as if she might be worthy of her title. 'Yes.'

And not until she mounted his horse did Marc let go of her hand.

That evening, when Marc entered the Hall, alone, congratulations were forced on him from all sides. Fellow hostages, courtiers, even a few who had not deigned to speak to him before now, all clapped him on the shoulder and lifted a goblet in his direction.

He tried to explain, at first, that they had it all backwards, that Cecily had saved her own life and his besides, but no one wanted to hear. He began to wish she would join them, for he was certain she would never allow him to receive such undeserved praise.

He did not expect to see her tonight. She had not spoken on the ride back and had disappeared without a word as soon as he helped her down from the horse. No doubt she had collapsed on her bed and might not rise until Christmas.

Yet he could still feel the size of her, the way she fit within his arms as he held her snug on the saddle before him. No words. They were not needed. And before he dismounted, he had felt, for one wild moment, that he must keep her close, hold her near, and make certain that harm would never find her again…

And then, as if his thoughts had summoned her, she entered the Hall, trailing fashionable tippets of fur from her sleeves, looking as calm as if she had spent the day before her own hearth. As if the privilege of her rank gave her an ease in facing death as well as moving through life.

Lady Isabella was with her, he noticed, belatedly, and together, they came directly towards him, the crowd giving way for the progress.

'I understand,' the princess began, 'that we all owe you our thanks for saving Lady Cecily. Has she properly conveyed her gratitude?'

Puzzled, he looked at Cecily. She did not meet his gaze, but kept her eyes fixed somewhere beyond his shoulder.

'*C'est moi,*' he said, 'who must make a *merci*. I

tried and failed to slay the beast. It was Lady Cecily's spear that killed him. Did she not tell you?'

Lady Isabella raised a brow. 'Not in every detail. So it seems that you, chevalier, must bow in
thanks to the lady.'

Cecily frowned, yet the princess ignored her
and inclined her head, as if waiting for Marc to
do so.

The courtly insinuations, the turns of language, the suggestions with a wink and a smile
hidden in the words. All these awkward games
came near to dragging feelings too fragile to be
understood into public view.

'A man is always grateful for his life,' he said,
hoping a quick nod of his head would suffice.

'As is a woman,' Cecily answered, finally
meeting his eyes. 'If the chevalier had not bravely
stepped before the beast, I would not be standing here.'

He waited, expecting her to say more. To re-
play the entire drama until everyone knew exactly how close she had come to a death like her
mother's.

She did not. And although she had avoided his
gaze before, now that she looked at him, she did
not take her eyes away. And he, too, felt unable
to move, unable to look away—

'Go. Both of you. Express your thanks away
from prying ears.' Lady Isabella pointed to the

door. 'The fireplace in the gate tower is lit and the room is empty.' She smiled. 'But don't stay too long.'

Cecily started to protest, but the king's daughter had turned her back and left.

Commanded by the princess, they stood, stiff and silent. Cecily no longer looked at him, but at the floor, the room, at anything else. Finally, at the same moment, both took a step, then walked side by side out of the Hall.

He followed her through twisting halls and stairs to a small, welcoming room in the gate tower, warmed by a crackling fire and a floor of bright red-and-yellow tile. The snap of burning wood seemed loud as he waited for her to speak.

She did not.

'I have been commanded,' he said, 'to *encore* say *merci*. And so, *merci*.' Done. His obligation fulfilled.

Did he wish her to say she was glad he had lived? Did he wait to hear her thanks for his effort, too? Did he simply want her to look at him again, as if he were a man?

She did none of these things. Not a word, not a glance. She only stared out of the window, into the dark. And finally, the smallest lift of her shoulders. As if it all were nothing.

He grabbed her arms then, turned her around and forced her to face him, needing something more. 'Your mother died in a hunt,' he said. Blunt words. He knew no others. 'And you nearly lost your life the same way today. Yet you show... nothing.'

The straight spine, always her response. After the first, startled jump at his touch, she had again drawn inward. 'I am the Countess of Losford. What I feel, or do not feel, is not to be trailed before all.'

Especially before you. She might as well have spoken the words aloud.

'Well, I feel—I feel grateful to you and glad to be alive and glad *you* are alive.' He should have let her go, but instead, he moved closer, wanting to see her eyes. Wanting to see *her*. 'Aren't you? Don't you feel any gratitude?'

Regretting the words immediately. Yet at the question, her face transformed, and he saw all the pain and uncertainty he could have wanted.

'Yes,' she said, quietly, meeting his gaze. 'And it seems a betrayal. To be alive because of you. To be alive at all.'

He let her go. Gave her room. 'I have seen more than one man fall at my side in battle from a blow that could have taken me instead. Not one of those men begrudged me my breath.'

'Maybe not. But envied, certainly they envied.' She pursed her lips, a gesture he had learned meant she was holding back more than words. And then, in the warm intimacy of the room, something shifted. 'Do you remember the death of your parents? I mean, were you there when they died?'

A strange turn. He shook his head. 'My father died at Crécy beside Enguerrand's.' At eleven Marc had been too young for battle.

'And your mother?'

'I barely remember her.' She had died in childbirth, along with the babe that would have been his brother.

'I was not there when either of my parents died.' She whispered now and he was not certain whether she spoke to him or to herself. 'Both of them suddenly were just…gone. Other people have stories. Other people can tell you about their last moments with loved ones. Even those taken by the Death, there were a few hours, to prepare. Praying with them, the priest there, ensuring the last rites were said.' She shook her head. 'They would not even let me see her.' A slight shudder.

'It was for your protection.' How much worse would it have been if she had seen the body, seen the pain?

Now, she looked at him, the grief in her green eyes visible behind the steely strength she assumed when she cloaked herself in her rank. 'I have been protected from too much, I think.'

And then he realised, truly, how sheltered she

had been. They had given her no armour against life's constant blows except duty itself.

He took her hands, wishing he might be that buffer, knowing no one could. 'There is no protection from death. Nor from life.'

The grief, the pain, the determination, subtly altered. Her lips softened. And she looked at him, finally, with eyes that saw him as something more than an enemy.

'Nor, Marc de Marcel, from you.'

And the defences, the hate, all the barriers he had built against *les Anglaise*, against her, were suddenly no protection at all.

He wrapped his arms around her, pulled her close, as if that alone would keep her safe from everything that threatened her body and her heart. She leaned into him, resting her head on his chest, where he was certain the thump of his heart was so fast and loud she must hear it.

'Cecile. Je veux t'embrasse. Je peux?'

He was not a man accustomed to asking, but to kiss her now, when she was so fragile, seemed a betrayal larger than the ones she had accused him of. This time, the decision would be hers. She would not be able to say later that he, or the fool, had forced her to submit.

And then, miracle of miracles, she lifted her head, met his eyes and smiled.

His lips met hers, gentle as a benediction.

More than dalliance, less than desire, the kiss said something he could not. Something of—

'Well that seems a very sincere "thank you".' Isabella's voice.

Cecily stiffened. Marc dropped his arms. At the door, Enguerrand and the princess leaned against each other, smiling.

The empty room. The lit fire. *Don't stay long.* He noticed now the waiting wine. The pillowed bench.

'We are finished.' Cecily, speaking as if nothing were wrong, yet so distracted by the interruption that, faced with proof that Isabella and Enguerrand planned their own private Christmas games, she walked out without even frowning at them.

And they did not spare a glance for Marc. As if the room were already empty and theirs, Isabella poured a goblet of wine and lifted it to Enguerrand's lips.

And Marc saw clearly what he should have noticed before. Cecily had complained that his friend had a *tendresse*, but it was not de Coucy's feelings that had worried her. Seeing them together, like this, it was clear.

Lady Isabella was besotted.

Shaken, he stumbled out of the room. Despite Cecily's warning, Marc had counted Enguerrand's guilery a harmless diversion. One that

would keep him amused during their imprisonment. The return of his lands, the prize, a way
of scoring that he had won.

Not something worth dying for.

He felt his own body stir, thinking of Cecily.
The kiss had been gentle, yes. But what if they
had not been interrupted? He could imagine her
hair coming lose, the surcoat sliding to the floor,
her lips hungry and welcoming. Another kiss,
two, three, and he could easily be a man lost in
this woman.

A serving girl might lift her skirts. An unmarried countess, never. And a princess? Un-
imaginable.

A harmless public dalliance was one thing.
Yet what if, some night soon, in a room more se-
cluded than this, the Lady Isabella offered more
than kisses? What if, in a moment of madness,
when the wine was drunk and kisses no longer
satisfied, the princess forgot herself and offered
more?

What man in the throes of passion would say
no?

Not even Lord de Coucy.

And afterwards, after the reckless moment
had passed and the sun rose and they faced each
other would come the realisation that they had
just created a cleft in life itself.

King Edward had been gracious, but that

would change if he discovered his daughter had been dishonoured.

The man who bedded a king's daughter could not be allowed to keep that knowledge as a weapon to be used. There must be no fear that one night, in his cups, a man might spill the secret.

That secret would have to be buried for ever. Along with the man who knew it.

Cecily did not sleep that night.

Visions of death and kisses, of being caught by the princess in Marc's arms, made her thrash and turn. And only later, when she had berated herself once again for her foolishness, did she remember to worry about what had happened after she left that room, leaving Isabella and Enguerrand alone.

But as she faced the princess the next morning, she held her tongue. After last night, she could scarcely criticise Isabella for stealing moments alone with her chevalier.

If she had hopes that Isabella's own *liaison amoureuse* had made her blind to Cecily's, the princess's first words dashed them. 'I'm glad to see you are finally enjoying the season with someone foolish and inappropriate.'

'The way you are?' Her sharp tone was for herself as well as for the princess.

'Are you uneasy about my chevalier or yours?'

'He is not mine.'

'He saved your life! And you saved his! You are a story from the courtly poems come alive!'

The worst thing she could imagine. 'We are no such thing! What if such rumours reach my prospective husband?'

'Then he will think you even more desirable!' Isabella wagged her finger. 'No more sad faces. I want to see you make merry with Marc de Marcel!'

The very thought made Cecily laugh. 'Getting him to be merry is like pushing a boulder uphill.'

'Well, it's a task to keep your mind off the past. Now let that handsome chevalier lift your spirits!'

Cecily waited for the familiar anger and sorrow. It did not come. Marc was a dangerous enemy, yet, now, having bested certain death, this morning she saw the world as sweet and new. Perhaps she had judged herself, and Isabella, too harshly. She had ridden a hunt, killed a beast. And if a handsome chevalier honoured her with a kiss, why should she not take it? As long as she did not let him come too close…

The doubt, the hope, must have shown on her face. Isabella put a hand on her shoulder. 'You have this chance. Don't refuse a sweet when it is offered.'

'A sweet that will be a moment on the tongue and then gone.' Would she even remember the taste, later, of his lips on hers?

'But without it, you will have nothing but a sour taste.' Isabella's tone turned urgent. 'You have only these weeks of Christmas. After that, the chance will be lost.'

Was she trying to convince Cecily, or herself? Yet the argument tempted. Soon, she would be married, locked into duty and away from feelings for the rest of her life. Where she would never see Marc de Marcel again.

The thought was more painful than she had expected. 'It is only a few days.'

'Good.' Isabella smiled again, as if the matter were decided. 'Now go. Find your chevalier. Enguerrand is coming.'

Enguerrand again. 'Here? Again? What will your parents think of...after...' She must ask, but she feared to state the words.

'After my brother's wedding, you mean?'

Cecily nodded. The prince had wed less than two years before, without the church's permission, and it had taken months and a papal intervention before the sins were erased. 'Won't your parents worry?'

Cecily was jealous for a moment that Isabella had parents to worry over her. And she had no doubt that family was more important to the princess than any temporary *tendresse.*

'Mother is still haunted, thinking she should have known something or done something...' Isabella shook her head and then sighed, as if to let go of a painful thought. 'Do not worry on my behalf.' The familiar, light smile returned and she reached for Cecily's hands and squeezed them. 'Now go. Find your chevalier.'

Cecily left, but not to find Marc. No, there was something else she must do first. She had faced a charging boar. It was time to face Peter the Mason.

Chapter Eleven

$$\sim\!\!\mathcal{O}\!\!\curvearrowright\!\!\mathcal{G}\!\!\curvearrowleft\!\!\mathcal{O}\!\!\sim$$

Marc woke before Enguerrand the next morning. A bad sign.

In the aftermath of the previous evening, no word was spoken between them of the princess, of the countess, or of kisses. Every time Marc had tried to frame a question, he could not hammer his thoughts into anything other than a blunt sword.

Does the princess mean more to you than just the land? Do you know the risk if you, if she...?

To even suggest such a thing seemed impossible.

And yet, later that day, as they faced each other over a chessboard borrowed from the Lady Isabella, Enguerrand did nearly that. 'Well, *mon ami,* are you, perhaps, developing a *tendresse* for a certain *femme Anglaise*?'

'What? Who?'

Enguerrand laughed at Marc's clumsy attempt

at denial. 'The lovely countess is a beauty, did I not say?'

'I thought her cold.'

'She did not seem cold to you last night. Last night, she seemed—'

'I'm surprised you could see anything but the princess,' he said, shoving the carved jasper pawn to the next space. He did not want to revisit last night. It raised questions he did not want to answer, not only about Enguerrand. 'I have spent time with the countess only to distract her from your campaign.'

'Ah, I see.'

Marc waited, but Enguerrand said no more.

'She thinks your attention to the princess threatens the woman's heart.'

'Ah.' A move of his carved crystal rook. 'Does it?'

Enguerrand shrugged, not meeting Marc's eyes. 'Who am I to know a woman's heart?'

An honest answer, but not the one he had hoped for. 'But for you. It is only about the land. Nothing more.' He made a statement, yet, he held his breath, waiting for his friend's next words to answer a question.

'*Bien sûr, mon ami.* And a pleasant way to pass the time.'

An answer that came too quickly. 'You're certain? Because the risk, if things go too far—'

'Your suggestion insults both of us.' No easy smile now. Enguerrand slapped his chess piece on the board and scooped Marc's away.

So. There was the answer. The one he had, of course, expected, wanted to hear.

Yet what had he done when de Coucy pressed him about Cecily? Lied. With a denial so transparent Enguerrand made no pretence to believe it. So, now, should he believe or should he—?

'Check!'

He blinked at the board. Enguerrand had him blocked, a move Marc had missed because he was thinking of other things.

And with the victory came the expansive, careless smile he had hoped to see. 'Accept and enjoy life here as you can,' Enguerrand said, clasping Marc's shoulder.

Enjoy. He had never looked at life as something to be enjoyed. Conquered. Vanquished. Triumphed over, yes. But to be given luxury he had not earned felt wrong. 'As a hostage?'

'If it allows you to pass the time with a lovely woman of noble birth, however briefly, then give thanks to God for the blessing. Appreciate the gifts of peace and beauty when they are handed to you. I do.'

Cecily was beautiful, yes, but he hadn't had a moment's peace since he'd met her. 'I would rather be given safe passage home. Wouldn't you?'

If he were Enguerrand, he would. His friend's home was a grand castle high on a rock, near as well defended as this one while Marc's life had been lived in borrowed rooms that belonged to others, fighting their battles, not his own. And yet, that was the life of every chevalier. What would it be like, to defend something of his own? He wondered, sometimes.

'Of course, but here, I am in the company of some of chivalry's flowers. Some of these men will soon leave to go on Crusade. Some day, I may ride beside some of them in this noble endeavour. I cannot hate what represents the finest we strive for.'

Enguerrand, still living the pretence of chivalry in the face of all he had seen. As much of a disguising as wearing the head of a stag.

And yet, when Marc thought of Cecily, he yearned for, even believed in, life as he had never seen it lived.

A friendly blow on the shoulder brought him to. Enguerrand stood, patting his stomach. 'Come. We must not miss dinner. It will be our last before the Christmas Eve fast.'

Reluctantly, he rose. What would Cecily say when she saw him? And what would he say to her?

Better nothing at all.

* * *

Late the next morning, as Cecily watched Peter the Mason enter the room, she realised she had not seen him in months. He was, she could tell, a man whose entire life was devoted to turning stone into sculpture. A short man, it seemed as if he, himself, was made of stone dust. Somehow, it was embedded in the lines in the pads of his fingers, as brass might be beaten into the fine lines of the tombs. Even his hair had turned to the cool white of alabaster.

She took a deep breath. 'It has been a while since we have spoken.'

He nodded. 'Yes, my lady.'

'Your work here at Windsor has gone well. The queen told me the king was pleased.'

A smile touched his lips. Sweet, but still full of pride. 'I am honoured.'

'Since your work is complete, I have permission to ask you to return, to finish my parents'...' she swallowed. To say the word was to pronounce them dead again '...tomb.'

'And have you selected the final details from the drawings?'

Drawings. She could barely remember them.

Designing her father's tomb had been a long, painful process. First, her mother had ordered the stone for the carving, then waited months for the cart to bring it from the north to the coast. Then, more waiting until she could find a mason, the best one, and have the man brought from Nottingham to assess the stone slab that would cover the tomb in the church.

Cecily's mother had excused her from much of this, but insisted that she help select the final effigy design. Even then, Cecily could not look. As if she were a babe instead of a woman grown, she ran to her room, burying her face in her pillow.

That was when her mother had stormed in, judgement, anger and disappointment flashing in her eyes.

You have been raised to be a countess and yet you cower here, indulging in your grief, shirking your duty. You are unworthy of the title you will one day bear.

Yes. Yes, she was. She had behaved as a child, expecting her mother to take care of a daughter's sorrow, not recognising the depths of a wife's mourning would be even more profound.

Dutifully, then, she had followed her mother, looking at the designs, squeezing her eyes shut when her mother could not see. For right beside the carving of her father's body, lying as if asleep, was another roughed-out figure.

Her mother's.

And when Cecily had wept again, her mother, finally despairing of her help, cast her aside and did the work alone. 'Did my mother not choose?'

He nodded. 'For your father, yes. And she had a preference for her own, but you should approve it.'

'Well, I have not looked at the sketches for quite some time.' Even then, she had not really *seen* them. She could remember nothing of them now, not even where she had stored them. 'I will let you know before you return to Dover.'

She ignored his puzzled look as he withdrew.

Where were the sketches? Had she even brought them to court? She should search for them, make a decision, force herself…

But she was not ready for that today.

And then, suddenly, in the midst of all the revelry of a court at play, came Christmas Eve. Instead of playing at dice, or laughing at the fool and his somersaults, the sombre members of the court gathered as a group, and wended their way to the lower ward in the dark of night for the Angel's Mass.

Marc stifled a yawn. He was as religious as the next man. He knew that all was in God's hands and man could only pray for a favourable outcome while trying to be no more of a sinner than was necessary. He knew men who had seen God's hand in the world before their eyes. Some claimed the hailstorm that battered the English army on Black Monday could only have been His work. Cecily had said her father had died near then. Marc wondered whether the man had witnessed it and, if so, what he had thought.

But Marc? What he had seen in life and war suggested more of the devil's power than the Lord's, though he was not one to set himself in judgement. He would observe the expected rites and allow wiser men to make such determinations.

But tonight, all seemed different. Captive under an unfamiliar sky, with air so cold he feared it would shatter like ice, he saw each of God's stars precise and sharp above him. Watching as the angels must have watched the shepherds.

He shifted, uneasy, wondering what they saw.

Give thanks to God, Enguerrand had urged.

One kiss. Now two. And he wanted more. Wanted so fiercely that he was glad he had seen her only from afar since then.

Enguerrand, so facile with courtly games, could dance along the brink, well knowing not to go too far. But Marc was not adept at games. He was a warrior. Winning meant life. Losing meant death, or worse.

As they entered the church dedicated to the patron saint of England, the court's chatter subsided. He had not seen Cecily today, and he found her now, as usual, near the Lady Isabella. Wordless, Enguerrand followed his gaze. Neither of them were thinking, for a moment, of God.

As the chant of the mass began, the Latin words, even with a slightly different accent, washed over him, at once as familiar and incomprehensible as they had been all his life.

Cecily's head was bowed, but even from here, he could see her tremble, then bite her lip and brush her cheeks with shaking fingers.

Tears. She must be crying.

Against his will, his chest tightened. Was she so tender-hearted as to be moved to tears by the thought of Christ's arrival in the world? Or was there something else? Memory. Loss.

You show nothing, he had told her, after the hunt, his words an accusation. But last night, when she had let him glimpse her sorrow, he saw why. A father gone. Then her mother. Even a seasoned warrior would weep.

He had lost his father so long ago that he scarcely remembered him, his mother he remembered not at all. And he had lost brothers-in-arms during battles against the rebellious peasants or the *les goddams*. Loss was inevitable. Unending. He had become hardened to it over the years.

But this woman's heart was still tender. The wound still raw. Protected from too much, she had said. Behind the shield of her straight spine and the smile she wore in company, it seemed that even she grieved and wept and mourned.

And with her family gone, she was as alone as he.

After the service, they prepared again to brave the frigid night, touched with air so cold it could freeze her tears as they fell.

'Come,' Enguerrand whispered, beside him. 'Join us. We are breaking fast.'

Marc's stomach growled. Neither food nor drink had passed his lips this day and the Christmas feast was still hours away. 'I heard nothing of a royal banquet.'

A shake of the head. A slow smile. 'A private party. Isabella. Cecily. A few others.'

The words raised hunger of a different kind.

As the rest of the court returned to their beds, Enguerrand led Marc up the stairs of a tower at the end of the newly completed royal quarters and into a small chamber, gilded and painted like a flower garden.

The princess, Cecily and another dozen or so men and women had gathered already. Intimate indeed. And in this setting, the courtly obediences had been put aside.

As Enguerrand left his side and joined the princess, Cecily looked over and saw him for the first time, her eyes widening in surprise.

He joined her.

'I did not expect you,' she said. Her voice was softer than usual, but her tears had dried.

What should he say now? He knew little of women or their needs. Without a mother or sisters, he had come to the de Coucy castle, a household full of men and thoughts of war. Was she happy to see him? Or not?

What I feel is not to be trailed before all.

He could say the same. Ask of something ordinary, then. Something of the world and not of the heart. 'Do you always spend Christmas at court?' Surprised, he realised he had never thought of her away from here, where the king himself cared about her comfort.

She exhaled, a small sigh of relief. 'We spend, I mean…' She stumbled over the words.

Without intending to, he had again reminded her of loss.

But she shook her head, as if to shake off the sorrow. 'Most of the winter is spent with the court.'

With the court. Far from Losford Castle at Dover. Far from the impregnable guardian of the isle. Invasion would be unlikely when the winter winds blew. Her father the earl could be spared the eternal vigilance for the Christmas season and beyond.

And yet, if Marc had a home, a place of his own, he doubted he would ever leave it.

All of the solemnity of the mass had disappeared as the group gathered about the long table. Food arrived. Fish, baked, grilled, simmered and sauced, yet fish, and so acceptable fare for a day of fast. The room filled with laughter and conversation and he and Cecily sat side by side and no one sent an extra glace their way.

And, if they spoke, he doubted anyone would care what they said. 'You grew up by the sea?' he asked, finally.

As the page passed by with a torch, her face was lit with light and a smile, as if the thought of home had brought happier memories. 'I could see it every day.'

'The Oise River is not so *grand*.' A stupid statement. He was not good at courtly talk.

Yet Cecily seemed to think now of home and not of his failings. 'The sunrise is so beautiful there. You cannot always see it clear, but when you do, it is as if the sun emerges from the sea.'

He gave a grunt of disgust. Sunrise was not something to be rejoiced in, but something to be slept through. 'The only time I wake to see the sun is for battle.'

She smiled at his discomfort. 'You are not an early riser?'

'A man at war learns to sleep when he can.' And he wished he had not said it, for fear he had reminded her of her father again.

But this time, he had not. 'It is beautiful, the sunrise from the battlements of the castle. You should see it.'

'I would like that.'

And then she blushed and looked away and so did he.

She could not have intended to invite him, the enemy, to her home. Could she?

Once again, this man had made her forget everything she should remember. She should not have invited him to see the castle that defended Britain's coast. Inside, looking with a warrior's eye, he would surely learn its secrets, discover its weaknesses, ones she had not even recognised.

For until the king selected her husband, Losford Castle and its protection was in her hands. Yet de Marcel's questions had been about *her*. Not the castle. Not even the countess. For just that moment, she had thought only to share the joy of her home. A mistake. She must turn his attention elsewhere.

'But why speak of Dover?' she said, looking down at her trencher. 'Around you is the most beautiful castle in Christendom.'

He looked up at the walls and ceiling. 'I can see your king builds for beauty as well as strength.'

Had he ever complimented anyone on the island? If so, it was not within her hearing. Perhaps the season had softened both of their tongues. 'You sound surprised.'

'He brought only destruction to my land.'

'Destruction? A strange word to describe a battle.'

'I am not speaking of battles.'

'Then what are you speaking of?' Knowing, even as she asked, that she would not like his answer. But better she think of him as an enemy and not a friend.

He studied her before he spoke, as if assessing how much to say. 'More than once, the English would ride across our lands, not stopping to do battle, but only to burn towns and fields until the earth was scorched and there was nothing left for man or beast.'

She winced. Her father had told her nothing of war, but such wanton destruction did not sound like the way of Christian knights. 'I'm certain my father could not do that.'

Puzzlement in his eyes first. Then pity. 'Ah, my poor countess. You have no idea what life is like beyond your castle walls.'

I have been protected against too much.

Yes, every day she was more certain that she had not learned everything she needed to know. Had she acted as a child for too long? Shirked her duty? Was that the reason her parents had shielded her from the hard work of managing the

household? She had always thought there would
be time. Tomorrow. Next week. Next year.

But she could reveal no weakness to this man.
Not of the castle or of its countess. 'It is you
who do not know how brave and noble the English are.'

She had expected their familiar argument to
begin. Instead, he sighed. 'My people, too, did
not always behave with virtue.'

The sorrow in his words stole her reply.

The meal ended. The guests bowed before the
princess, then took their leave. She and Marc
were the last to leave, save for de Coucy.

She paused, expecting him to join them, but
instead, he called from across the room. '*Mon
ami!* We leave to greet King Jean on Saint Stephen's Day, *oui*?'

As Marc agreed, Cecily gritted her teeth, welcoming the reminder that refreshed her rage.
When the King of France returned, he would be
welcomed and fêted, while her father lay cold
in his tomb. She must cling to that anger and let
it burn away any weakness for Marc de Marcel.

Marc and his friend exchanged a few words,
and then, she found herself walking beside him
through the maze of corridors and stairs.

She looked over her shoulder, but de Coucy
did not follow. 'He lingers with the princess. Can
he be trusted?'

'*Bien sûr.*' Marc's voice carried a touch of indignation.

Her cheeks burned. Had she, unknowing, exposed Isabella's weakness for the man? 'And yet,
you have just admitted your people have not always been honourable.'

'De Coucy is,' he said.

'Then he is alone of your countrymen.'

'No. So is our king.' He spoke in tones of reverence she had never heard from him before.

'You call him honourable, yet he returns because his son was not.'

A deeper frown. 'The Duke d'Anjou shamed
his father when he fled home to French soil. A
man cannot always be proud of his son.'

Or of his daughter. Though she tried—

'And so,' Marc continued, 'the king sacrifices
himself again to set things right. I have seen few
men I admire so much.'

Surprised, she studied him. 'I have not seen
you revere anyone as you do this king of yours.'

'If you had seen him fight that day. At Poitiers.'

Poitiers. That battle so long ago. It had been
a triumph for the English. Her father returned
home that time, full of smiles and ransom rewards. They thought, then, that the war was over
and that peace would last for ever. 'What happened?'

'Your father did not tell you?'

She shook her head. 'A man does not share tales of battle with a twelve-year-old daughter.' Yet another of the many things they had shielded her from knowing.

'Then *I* will tell you, for it is a story everyone should hear.'

They dashed across the Upper Ward, shivering, and entered the tower. At the bottom of the stairs, he paused, as if the story could not be told while walking. As if it deserved his full attention. And hers.

'Here,' he said. 'Sit.'

The stairs were empty. A lone torch on the wall burned low. The others had hurried to bed, knowing they must rise again for mass in only a few hours. She settled on a hard, stone step and waited, reluctantly, for him to begin.

'We had so many more men. Everyone thought the battle would be easy, but we were attacking a well-defended location.'

'And facing a better commander.' All England, all the world knew that, save for his father, the king's son Edward was the greatest warrior in Christendom.

Marc frowned, but she saw the slightest inclination of his head. An acknowledgement?

'At least facing a braver one.' He shook his head. 'The commanders of our flanks, cowards,

held back, then retreated, and left the king un-
protected.'

She had accused the French of many sins, but
she could not imagine any knight doing such a
thing. 'Are you certain? Were you there?'

He nodded and sighed. 'I had just been knighted
and was still brave and foolish. But across the
field, I saw the men protecting the king, even the
fresh troops, start running. I ran towards them,
but it was too far, there were too many of *les goddams*. I could not reach him…'

He looked down so she could not see his eyes,
then cleared his throat. 'The king fought on after
the others deserted him, with no hope of victory, with only his son, little Philippe, by his
side. Barely old enough to be a squire, and yet
he alone did not flinch or run.'

'Worthy of admiration indeed.' Her words,
grudging.

'The enemy swarmed over him, crying for
him to yield or die, as if he were an ordinary
man and not the king. "Where is my cousin?" he
asked them. "Where is the Prince of Wales?" for
it was not right that a king surrender but to one of
a rank worthy of accepting his glove. And yet, *les
goddams* now turned on each other, each wanting to claim the ransom for taking him captive.'

She wanted to tell him he lied. That no English knight would have done such a thing. And

yet, de Marcel had always been as blunt with his speech as with his sword. 'What happened then?'

'Finally, a French knight, exiled and fighting for the English, came to him and promised to lead him to the prince. Only then, when he could surrender with honour, did he hand the man his glove.'

The unsettling image lodged in her mind. A valiant French king and his son beside him. Englishmen falling on him as dogs would snarl over scraps fallen from the table. No wonder her father had protected her from the knowledge of war. 'I see,' she said, 'why he has earned your admiration.'

The very words were an apology.

As his eyes met hers, she saw beneath the shield he kept between himself and the world. Saw, for once, a man who had been disappointed in life. *I know that my people did not always behave as they should.*

And suddenly, she was shamed to think she had imagined no one had ever suffered as she had. 'Perhaps I have been blinded.'

He smiled then, slow and sad, without the satisfaction of victory she had expected to see. 'We just proved that, *n'est-ce pas*?'

Perhaps he had. And perhaps she had been shielded from the truth of the world, the truth which could be so disappointing. Certainly this glimpse of chaos, of life and death, was not what she had expected. Had she been blind to something of her father, too?

No one had told her of her father's death. Why?

Chapter Twelve

And so Cecily did battle with Christmas Day.

There was dawn mass, then midday mass and, finally, fast was broken for the finest feast of the year, full of laughter and memories.

Here were the spiced, baked apples her mother loved so much. Here was the boar's-head song that announced the presentation of the feast, when the king always cajoled her father to raise his voice and sing, the only time of year he ever did so.

She smiled and nodded in response to the laughter around her, but as the candles and songs and feasting continued, grief weighed on her chest and gripped her throat.

This Christmas, for the first time, she was truly alone.

And alone with doubts she hated Marc for raising. It had been difficult before, the wondering whether she was really prepared to rule Los-

ford. But she had kept her head high, surrounded
by those who had known her near since birth,
and shielded her doubts with grief. None of them
had questioned her, or pushed her too quickly.

But this man, this enemy who was only a chevalier and not even a nobleman, had raised new
doubts. For the first time, she realised the world
might be crowded with cowardice, cruelty and
ignoble acts and that war was far from what she
had pictured. Had her parents simply wanted to
shield her until she needed to know? Or did they
think her incapable of facing such truth?

Will she ever be ready?

She did not see much of Marc this day. The
royal family, dressed in their colourful, matching livery, dispensed and received official greet-
ings, so there was none of the cosy intimacy of
the night before and no time alone with Marc.

But the doubts he had sown followed her. For
all that she had mourned her father's death, she
never really knew how her father had died. Perhaps not wished to know.

She did now. And Gilbert must tell her.

Finally, as darkness fell on this short day, she
beckoned Gilbert to her side. He followed her
into the corridor, a wine-coloured smile on his
lips.

It faded when he saw the seriousness on her
face. 'What is wrong?'

'I heard last night about Poitiers. About how we...took the French king in violation of the honour we should have shown him.'

Gilbert looked away. His silence and the sadness on his face confirmed every accusation.

'What about my father? Was he...did he...?'

'No.' Not waiting for her to complete the question. 'Your father remained close to the prince. He was a man of honour, Cecily. Never doubt that.'

A relief, that her father had not been part of that mob. That the man she held in her heart was real.

But that still left a question. 'Tell me about the other battle.'

He blinked, as if coming to. 'Which one?'

So many that he must ask. 'The one that killed my father.'

A moment of what looked like confusion on his face, followed by pain, and then it seemed that scenes she could not see were coming back to him.

'Your father was brave,' he said, finally, as if there was nothing more to be said. As if that were all she needed to know.

Once, it would have been.

'I am certain he was brave,' she said, sharply, though she no longer was. 'I want to know what happened.' Brave, and yet Marc had talked of cowardice. And the way he had described the English victory over the French…had the French been as cruel to her father? 'Did he suffer?'

'Suffer?' He sounded puzzled. She was not certain whether it was from the wine or because it was not a question a warrior would ponder.

'When he died, was it quick? Or did…?' She could barely speak the words. She did not want to think of him, lying wounded on the field for hours. Her mother's death, at least, had been as quick as it was unexpected. At least, that was what they had told her. 'Did God show mercy?'

Questions she had never asked until Marc showed her the real face of war. The conflict had happened across the Channel, out of sight, victory and defeat both softened by the miles.

You have no idea what life is like…

'It was not a battle.'

'What?'

'He did not die in a battle.'

'I don't understand.' No one had suggested this before. All this time she had blamed the French. 'Was it a sickness?'

The look on Gilbert's face was sick with memory. 'It was the hail.'

'What?'

'The storm. Black Monday.'

The very words a chill. She had heard of the storm. Heard the story of how the weather had changed, with the same suddenness as the plagues had rained on Egypt, and how, afterwards, the king seemed to feel that even God wanted him to make peace with France.

But no one had ever said that the storm had killed her father. What else had they hidden?

'Tell me,' she said, in a tone he could not ignore.

He sighed. 'Winter had been hard. The French cowered behind the walls of Paris, refusing to face us so the king decided to take the army back to friendly territory for the summer. Easter was over. It was still spring but it already felt like summer as we marched, warm, sunny. Spirits were lifting, we could see the spires of Chartres ahead of us and then...'

The very joy, the hope he described, doomed. She knew that now. Fists clenched, she held her breath.

'And then,' he said, 'the sky turned dark and cold and angry. As suddenly as when God parted the Red Sea, the heavens opened and hail fell from the sky. Hailstones large as eggs, hard as rocks, hurtled down on us. Many of the men, the archers, those with no armour but their leather jerkins, were struck. Over and over...'

Just those few words and she saw the mayhem. Men stoned to death by frozen rocks from the sky. 'But my father was wearing armour. He was protected.' And yet she knew the story's end. Knew he had—

'He had removed his helmet. When I found him, the hail had pounded so hard, the chainmail was…battered into his skin—'

She shut her eyes against the sight, but Gilbert had given her his memories.

'And was he alive?' she whispered. 'When you found him?'

Gilbert nodded, silent.

'How long?' She gripped his arm and shook it. 'How long did he live?'

His bleak expression said more than words. 'He did not die until the next day.'

She let go. Slumped with the burden of knowing. So he had suffered. Beaten and bloody and waiting for death to take him. Death had not come heroically, as he fought for his king, but it rained down from the sky, as if somehow he had been beaten by a vengeful God. Or, worse, an uncaring one.

A burden her mother had borne alone because her daughter could not even look at a sculptor's drawing with clear eyes. Because her daughter was weak and unworthy of the title she would bear.

You do not know…

Marc was right. She had preconceptions and idealistic notions and no knowledge of the messiness of the life that even her beloved father had lived. Sheltered and cared for, she had expected life and death to unfurl according to plan.

Her father's death, then her mother's, had torn that plan asunder. Lost, angry, she had focused her fury on the French, as if somehow they must pay for her pain. As if that would make the world right and just again.

Instead, she must face a harsher truth. Everything she thought she had known was wrong, or at least, incomplete. Good. Evil. Right. Wrong. All upended. How was she to live? How was she to fulfil her duties, her parents' expectations? How was she to know what to do?

'Was he at peace? At the end? Was there a priest at least, to give him last rites?' Her mother's death, too, had been sudden, but there had been a priest close at hand, so she had the comfort of the church. But Cecily had not thought of these things before when it came to her father's death. Not thought of the possibility of his death at all when he went to war, for how could God allow his warriors to die?

'Yes. He was confessed. Absolved.'

She clung to that comfort. 'And the others? How many others died?' What had he said of those archers without armour?

'Death came to many men and horses, but your father was the only lord who died.'

She felt a fierce kinship with the daughters, wives, mothers of all those nameless men who carried the longbow. Their bodies, no doubt, were laid to rest on enemy soil. No comforting effigy would keep their families company.

Marc was right. She knew nothing of war and even less of war for those who marched instead of rode.

And for that, for that arrogant sureness that he, or his people, had been solely to blame for her father's death, she owed him an apology.

An apology. To a Frenchman. Surely, the world was upside down.

For Marc, the Christmas entertainment seemed unending.

Darkness had fallen, and yet no one sought rest. Cecily was out of reach and without her, the time stretched, wearisome.

Enguerrand, too, seemed ill at ease. The princess had been pressed into royal duties, but instead of singing, dancing and charming the others around him, he sat, watching her from across the room, wearing an expression Marc had never seen before.

Can he be trusted? What had happened, after he and Cecily left last night?

Marc knew him better than any man on earth. Knew when he was putting on a face as a leader.

Knew when he was tired and hungry or angry and holding in his temper.

Now, the way Enguerrand watched this woman, Marc had never seen that face before. Was it yearning? Joy? Happiness? His friend looked different.

And that was dangerous.

Unlike Marc, de Coucy was a leader, not a loner. As skilled with conversation as with the sword, he had a way of getting men to trust him.

Women, too.

But women in general. Not just *one* woman. This, the way he was behaving with Isabella, was different. Others would not notice, for de Coucy had been polite and gracious, singing, dancing, talking to all in the hall.

But he had always come back to Isabella's side.

Marc knew why. Didn't he? Enguerrand had even reassured him there was nothing more than the land and a pleasant disport to interrupt their months in captivity. Calculated. A ruse.

And yet, as Marc watched him, he wondered. It did not seem like that. Not now.

He turned to his friend, only to see him gazing at the princess, with a strange wistfulness.

Marc followed his gaze, wondering what Enguerrand saw. Isabella was beautifully dressed and refined, but she had a rather sallow complexion and, he suspected, in time she would be as plump as her mother. She certainly did not move as gracefully as Cecily did. And she laughed too much, not like…

'Come.'

Cecily's voice. Her hand on his shoulder. She leaned closer. 'I would speak to you alone.'

He glanced at Enguerrand, wondering how to explain his absence, then realised his friend would not even notice.

Marc rose and followed her into the corridor. 'Where are we going?'

'I share a room with two of Isabella's ladies. They are still in the Hall.'

He didn't argue. They walked, silent, down corridors, across the cold Ward, and then up the massive staircase that led to the living quarters of the Round Tower and to a room across the tower from the one he shared with de Coucy.

She closed the door. The air smelled of blanchet powder and rosewater. *Alone* seemed tinged with possibilities, but the tone of her voice did not.

She squared her shoulders and met his eyes. 'I must apologise to you. To all Frenchmen, actually, but you are the one I have most abused.'

He felt his jaw sag in surprise. 'Why so?'

'You were right. My father did not die at the

hand of a Frenchman. Yours or any other's.' Her voice was hard and brittle.

'He fell ill then.' It happened, more often than many would admit.

She shook her head. 'He was bludgeoned to death by frozen rain. God smote him down, for what sin I know not.'

The lifted chin. The determined gaze. All began to crumble. Her lip quivered as tears threatened.

Ah, there was the pain, not only of grief, but of the realisation that war and gallant warriors were not all she had imagined. That the cruelty of men or the world or even God could randomly upset the order of things. That the justice, the rightness, of the world that we believe we see is an illusion and that the reward for a dutiful life could be an unfair death.

Marc knew this. All men in war did. In France, even the women knew it, for in France, battles were everywhere. Castles burned. Goods were stolen. Women dishonoured.

She, so many of them here, had been spared the knowledge of all that. War was over there. Out of sight. And with the impregnable Losford Castle as a bulwark, war did not threaten their homes for more than a fleeting moment.

She had lived here, surrounded by walls and guards and sweet treats and pretty matching costumes, cossetted by her family, protected by the court, and losing her parents was the first thing, really, that had shaken her world.

And he felt a mixture of envy and regret. Regret that she had, finally, discovered the truth.

Envy that she had been spared from it so long.

He had seen only hardness. She, only the soft. And who was to say which of them was more fortunate? Was it the protected lady? Or the warrior with no illusions left?

He put an arm around her shoulder and pulled her to him. 'War is cruel,' he said, knowing words were little comfort.

She shook her head. 'So foolish, to blame you. We were, after all, the ones who crossed the Channel.'

An admission so vast for her that he did not know how to answer.

And yet, the French had tried to invade her island before. They might again. Men were ever seeking wars, though he could not say why except that for him, when he felt the anger, he wanted to strike at something. In battle, he could.

'Does it help? To know how he died?' There was comfort in that, sometimes. A sense of completion.

She looked at him, a bleak hardness in her eyes he had not seen before. 'No.'

He had heard of that day. Seen some of the

aftermath, the carts, abandoned in the field still attached to horses that had frozen to death as they stood. No. A loving daughter would find no comfort in that vision.

'You have not imagined it before. The reality of war.' It was not a question.

Something near a laugh, but only to scoff at herself. 'It is obvious, is it not? Or if I did, I saw a tournament writ large. My father riding at the head of a charge, banners flying...'

So obvious and honourable that she had thought any Frenchman would have known that a red shield with three diamonds belonged to Losford. But that was not what it was like, there, on the battlefield.

'And to discover that instead of honourable combat—' her voice trembled with horror '—he had died like *this*. How can I bear it?'

Her agony was genuine, yet his sympathy soured. Others had suffered and died, yet her grief seemed all for herself. She did not cry for them.

Marc paced the room, unable to stand still. 'You act as if life should stop and the rest of the world should wait for you to recover. You are not the only one to have lost someone. Death is everywhere. Death is every day.' He thought of those days. Not only of battle, but of plague and childbirth and old age and drownings and the threats that hover over all men. 'Everyone loses someone.'

'Did you?'

The question hit him as a blow. He opened his mouth, but could not speak.

And he saw her face change, as if suddenly she saw the truth of him for the first time as a man with pain and passion of his own. He had wanted her to *see*, but not to see *him*.

'Your mother. Your father. Someone more?' she said, finally, near a whisper.

He had thought her selfish for thinking only of her own grief, yet he was reluctant to share his own. Where did he start? How many could he remember? 'A mother, a father, a brother just born. More comrades-in-arms than I can count.' He took a breath, uncertain he could say the words. 'And a woman.'

He could see her face, then. Shock.

'And do you not mourn her?' she said, finally, as if of all of then, she cared to know only of the woman.

'Of course.' Sometimes, as he stood in church, he thought of the woman, alive, and of the babe, up in heaven, he hoped, along with all the rest. Would he be worthy? Would he be good enough to join them there? He was not certain he wanted to know. 'But my life did not end when theirs did.'

'I do not think,' she said, 'that I would have your strength. To survive losing so many.'

He hesitated, then touched her. She flinched. Then turned and met his eyes. 'What was she like? The woman?'

He tried to remember. It had been years. He had been young. Not even knighted, but about to go to war as a squire. He was full of himself and his manhood, ready to battle the world, certain that honour and glory would find him.

As naïve as Cecily.

And into his view came the woman.

'She was fair. With blue eyes.' Rounded. Adoring. And when she looked at him, her eyes, like a mirror, reflected everything that he wanted to see in himself.

Cecily interrupted the silence. 'And did you marry?'

He felt his cheeks go hot, ashamed to confess his weakness. She had offered herself. He had accepted. What warrior would not? There was what was said by the Church, or the chivalric codes, and then, there was what was done. And the difference between those two was never mentioned, never spoken of, never considered surprising or worthy of note.

He cleared his throat. 'She was not of a station for me to wed. And I went to war.'

Still, when after a night, or two, he rode off, he

thought, even expected, that she would be waiting for him when he returned as a knight. He imagined he would see her in the street, passing. Perhaps he would even take her as his mistress.

And if his feelings for her were more about his feelings about himself, he was too young and foolish to know that.

Somehow, he hoped Cecily might understand, so he confessed in words he had never said before. 'But there was a time I thought of her every minute.'

All through that campaign, riding the country, her image stayed with him. In his memory, she became a lady, beautiful, cultured, worthy of fighting for. Every time he remembered her, she became more beautiful. And she had loved him more.

But when the battles were over that time, when the English had triumphed and so many of his fellows had proved themselves cowards, he rode home to find her, this woman who had become bigger in his mind than she had ever been in his arms. He wanted solace, the comfort of seeing himself reflected in her eyes as the man he wanted to be. Hoping her faith, her love would wipe away everything he had seen on the field.

'Did you ever see her again?' Cecily's voice.

'Only once.' He could admit nothing more.

For when he saw her, he saw he had deceived

himself. She was not fair haired and blue eyed, as he had remembered. She did not look at him with admiring glances, nor speak to him in gentle words.

No. She was a miller's daughter, plain, haggard. When he saw her this time, he remembered she had looked at him not with admiration, but with a come-hither hunger. And when she looked at him now, it was with a face of fear.

For while he was away, instead of pining for him as he had imagined, she had married the butcher. And borne a son.

Had she thought he was dead? Had she thought of him at all? Either way, his return threatened to expose her youthful indiscretion. Something he was certain her husband did not know.

Marc must have stared at her for long minutes when he finally recognised her, amazed he had held such a different picture of her in his mind for all these months. Amazed that he had so deceived himself about the truth.

In much the same way Cecily had done.

'And you lost her,' Cecily said. 'And felt as if her going ripped the heart out of your chest.'

Cecily thought she had died, this woman who had never been a real woman, but only his idea of a woman. Well, she was dead to him, along with the illusions he had carried. 'She was not my wife,' he said, once again the hard man she had made him. 'And she was not worth missing.'

'Was there a child?'

Now, he winced. She had held a babe, the butcher's wife. And later, he heard, the babe, blameless, had died. 'Not mine.' He could not stand before Cecily and murmur sorrow for a woman he had not truly loved. 'I thought I knew her. But I only knew what I wanted her to be.'

He waited, expecting Cecily to stare at him in shock and disbelief. Instead, she nodded. 'Maybe I did that, too.' She sighed. 'Saw only what I wanted to see. How impossible, my view of the world.' She shook her head, as if looking at a babe who understood nothing. '*Dieu et mon droit!* God is on our side, so we should always be victorious. And yet, things happen and I can see no reason.'

Despair and freedom mixed in her voice and he could see, finally, how vulnerable she was behind her stern shield. This was the doubt she had hidden, not for him to see until now. And with that glimpse, he saw, he *knew* her. And the feelings she stirred were as raw and vulnerable as her grief.

'Cecily,' he began, his whisper close to her ear, 'I want…'

She turned her eyes to his and he saw his desire reflected there.

He smiled just to see her. When had just the sight of someone brought him such joy? Ever? Perhaps he had been as short-sighted as Cecily, seeing only the bad, when joy and beauty lurked on the edge of his world, tumbled amongst the pain if only he would not be so blind.

Now, in the crack between the horror of war and the pain of captivity, here was the glimmer, no, more than a glimmer, a blinding flash of beautiful sun. Something he did not even know he had hungered for until it was before him.

He cleared his throat. Pushed a stray hair away from her cheek and tried again. 'Life is not easy or simple or fair. But this, this moment, is ours.'

And he *wanted* it. Fiercely.

She smiled, and raised her lips to his.

Cecily could not say how it happened, that she found her lips on his.

When she thought about it, later, she would try to say it was part of the disguising they were playing, but that was a lie, for no one was watching.

Maybe it was a gesture of apology for her treatment of him. Or a search for comfort.

Or maybe, she just wanted to forget.

She refused to think it was because she cared for him.

And then, she did not think at all.

In his arms, with her lips on his, she slipped into a world which held neither sight nor sound but only sensation and safety and yearning for something more.

It was as if all the pent-up hatred had suddenly flared into fire, consumed itself and transformed into something just as strong.

And even more dangerous.

She had tried, tried for so long not to care, not to touch, not to reveal, not to become attached. The need, the hunger, was it for him or for anyone? She wasn't sure. She didn't care.

Did they sink on to her bed? Did his kisses trail down her neck? His fingers seemed to tremble as they tightened on her shoulders. Hard, strong, and yet, a touch intended to be gentle.

Now, she was the one who pushed, who felt that if she kissed him hard enough, held him tightly enough, she could lose herself, lose the memories and the fears and become Cecily instead of a countess.

The weight of him, welcome. His hands, more gentle than she expected, still carried the scars of war. His breath, as ragged as hers, interrupted with fragments.

Je t'aime.

Heat. Pressure. Touch. Hands. Panting. His. Hers. A tingle in the body, her breasts. When had she ever been aware of them? A moment of baring and her skin was touched by air and then his hands. Warm. Exciting. She pushed into him, against him, towards him.

His lips, softer, replaced his fingers. Something stirred between her legs in answer. Was this love? This feeling that if she were not one with him, she would, indeed, prefer death? Worse, worse than she had feared and yet she kissed him again.

Her world shrank to the breadth of his arms and that was world enough. To explore the sharp hollow of his cheek, the waves of his hair. Surrounded by his scent. Something of a soldier—leather and steel—but beneath that, a whiff of something as rich as fine red wine that would only reveal itself over time.

Close to him now, there was no cold, no winter. Only a heat that made her want to shed her hose and her gown, to bare her skin to the warmth of his lips on her throat, her neck, her shoulder, lower, hot on her breast…

And then, he sat up, ripping away the shield of his body, baring her to the world again.

Everything sprang back to life. Chill air, the dress she had left out for washing, a dog barking somewhere in the lower ward.

She blinked. Reached for a breath. Tried to cover her nakedness and swung her feet off the bed and to the floor. He was still there. His touch steadied her and wordless, she studied his eyes, searching for answers. Weeks of anger, days of fighting, moments of trust, but this went beyond a simple truce. It was as if he had accepted her confession and blessed her with his forgiveness.

'I… You…' She had no words.

He did not answer.

She looked away, desperately seeking the world she knew. It was gone. What had been clearly good and bad, black and white, had become confusing, yet rich with possibilities she had never imagined. The wind was still cold, but also bracing. The music still melancholic, but the lilting melody made her want to dance. Christmas held sad memories, but now, new ones.

He was no longer an enemy. What was he?

She fisted her fingers, as if she could cling to the world the way it had been before. All her fears for Isabella and now she had near committed the very act she had tried to prevent.

You would do nothing that would disappoint your parents.

But she had. So many times she had.

Her breathing slowed. In the silence, no longer close enough to touch him, sanity crept over her, along with the memory of who, and what, she was.

She settled her gown back to its proper place and braved his eyes. 'We cannot.'

From Marc, tight lips, a brief nod.

He rose from the bed, adjusted his tunic, and stood, safely out of reach of her hand. 'You were gracious, to explain about your father's death.'

As if that was all she had done. As if nothing else had happened.

'I had wronged you.'

He shook his head. 'This disguising, this game we played for others' sakes, made it too easy to forget…'

'We did not succeed,' Cecily said. 'at what we planned to do.'

He took a breath. 'It is safer that we remain enemies.'

She nodded. 'We will not be alone again.' As if that would be enough. Knowing it wasn't.

'Enguerrand, myself, we leave tomorrow morning. To welcome the king.'

'Enguerrand and Isabella will be apart for some days.'

'As will we.' A sigh. Relief or disappointment? 'And I will return to France shortly after the king returns.'

A blow she had not expected. She had managed to ignore in these days together that he would have to leave. Some day. 'He is bringing the ransom?'

A flicker of a frown. 'That, or the count will return. Or send a substitute.'

'I see.' She nodded, as if it were of no consequence. 'Then tomorrow we will say farewell.'

'Not tomorrow. Tonight. Now.'

The door, closing. The end she should have welcomed.

'Yes, of course. That would be best.'

'I shall not see you again,' he said.

'You do not think…perhaps…in the morning…?'

He shook his head.

'No, of course not.' That would only make it more difficult. She waved her hand vaguely. 'You should go back to the Hall without me.'

He turned his back and opened the door.

'Farewell,' she said, clearly. So he could hear it.

He hesitated, but did not look back.

And then, she heard a whisper. *'Adieu.'*

Chapter Thirteen

Marc did not return to the Hall.

A dream, Marc decided, as he retreated to the room he shared with Enguerrand. He would call it a dream. Passion, tenderness, no more than a night vision to be ignored. Certainly, never trusted.

Something that would fade with the dawn.

The weeks at court that had stretched endless before him were at an end. He should be rejoicing.

Instead, every step away felt like his last.

He approached his door, ready to seek his pallet. Tomorrow, he would rise with the dawn and ride, leaving the court, and Cecily, behind.

He had let himself be caught up in Cecily's fears and the foolish whispers of the court, unable to distinguish disguising from truth. Enguerrand spent time with the king's daughter, true. But he had told Marc why. And at the same time, he was as charming as ever with the other ladies of the court and he spoke of the princess no more than he did of the dance or the food at dinner or the freezing winter cold.

That moment, only a moment, when Enguerrand had seemed too fond, almost jealous... Well, Marc had had his own moments of *folie* during the days of Christmas.

To have thought that he could, or even should, try to control his friend's decisions had only led him to make his own mistakes.

Instead of saving his friend, he had trapped himself. Well, time to put *Angleterre*, and its women, behind them.

Alone in the room, Marc tried to sleep, waking as the infernal clock in the tower struck, hour after hour. It was late, very late, when he heard the door and opened his eyes to see the glimmer of a candle.

Enguerrand crept into the room, wearing a dishevelled shirt and the scent of a woman, heavy and sweet. A farewell Yuletide tumble with a maid, no doubt, except...

The scent. It was one he recognised. Not Cecily's, no, but one he had caught when he was near her. One belonging to...

Isabella.

He sat up, blinking, willing his eyes to adjust

to the dark, trying to see his friend's face, look into his eyes...

'Where have you been?' he said instead. Sharply.

Enguerrand sat on the edge of his bed and set down the candle. 'Saying farewell.'

'To whom?'

'You question me?' Belligerent.

'You've been with her.' Simple. True. And all the worst things he had tried to convince himself would never happen.

And at the words, his friend became no longer a count, but simply a man. He slumped, dropping his head in his hands. No smooth words now. Instead, he alternately nodded his head at the truth of the statement, then, shook it in despair.

No, this was not a man satisfied with a Yuletide fling. This was a man who had seen what he wanted and knew he could not have it.

A feeling Marc knew.

Enguerrand lifted his head. In the dim candle's glow, the empty sadness in his eyes resonated, echoed and magnified Marc's own. 'What are we going to do, *mon ami*?'

We. As if Enguerrand knew it all. Knew everything that Marc had tried to deny, even to himself.

'We will ride out tomorrow to meet the king.

And then, we will return to France as quickly as possible.'

And forget all this ever happened.

The next morning, as Cecily tried not to think about Marc, Peter the Mason appeared at her door. With everything that had happened, she had thought no more of the tomb and the effigies.

'It is not yet Twelfth Night...' she began.

'No, my lady, but they ride for Dover today to greet the king.' He paused when she looked puzzled. 'You do not go with them?'

If she had not been so distracted by Marc, she would have realised. The French king would land, as did everyone who crossed the Channel, at the port of Dover, guarded by Losford Castle. Yet King Edward had not asked her to return to welcome King Jean to England's shore. Did he, too, believe she was not ready for her role? 'I will not be home until...spring.'

'Then, with your permission, I will travel with them and begin work now. It might even be complete when you arrive.'

'I see.' Of course. The plan was one she should have anticipated. The mason could not travel alone and it could be weeks before there would be another chance for an escort. 'Yes, that is wise.'

He paused, as if waiting.

'Yes,' she said again. 'As long as the king has released you, you may leave.'

'But your mother's effigy, my lady. What would you have me do?'

She had not found the sketches. She had not even searched for them. Again, in all these ways, she had proven unworthy of her parents' trust. 'Use the one she was looking at last.'

'But, my lady—'

'You have done this many times. I never have.' A harsh tone. For him, or for herself? She felt as if Marc's scent still clung to her. 'Do as you please.'

He tilted his head, puzzled. 'You do not wish to approve the design?'

No. She did not. She did not want to look at pictures of her parents, already transformed into unmoving rock, looking back at her, judging her for violating every lesson they had taught.

She waved her hands, as if to shoo a fly from her room. 'I'll look at it when I return. In the spring.'

'By then, it will be too late to change.'

'Then it will not be changed.' Her words were clipped. 'You spoke to her about it. I did not. Do what you think represents her wishes.'

Nodding, he mumbled his *yes, my lady* and left.

And only after he was safely out of earshot

did she pound her fist against the table and weep. And she was not certain which loss sparked the tears—her parents, her illusions, or Marc.

Late in the morning of St. Stephen's Day, Marc mounted his horse, ready to leave Windsor, Cecily and all of *Angleterre*.

He and Enguerrand were surrounded by squires and servants, one of the masons who had worked on the palace, another court member he didn't know. And dozens of *Anglais* knights. He wasn't certain whether the number needed was to honour the king or to guard the hostages.

He leaned close to Enguerrand. 'Did you see her?'

Enguerrand shook his head. 'Not since...' *Not since I left her bed.* 'You?'

Marc shook his head. As he intended, he had not seen Cecily and was glad of it. No need to fight that battle again. The next time, he might lose.

Wordless, they mounted and turned the horses towards the gate. Just before they left, Enguerrand looked back over his shoulder and raised his hand in a wave.

Marc gritted his teeth, gripped his reins and kept his eyes on the road ahead. The way home.

Home. The word conjured no vision. His home had been on a horse, in battle. Even the castle of his youth belonged to de Coucy, not to him. Marc was born of a *chevalerie* family, yes, but wealthy in blood only. Everything else had been earned. By his sword. By his strength.

Weakness meant death.

Now, as they rode east towards the sea, he struggled to summon memories of his country. The green of spring, bright enough to burn his eyes. The cliff crowned by de Coucy's castle, high above the river. These things seemed strangely distant now, as if he had left them not when he came to England, but when he went to war.

No, when he said 'home' now, all he could see was Cecily. Someone he intended never to see again.

In the weak sun of the late morning, Cecily and Isabella stole away to the top of the Round Tower, escaping their attendants and the other ladies, to watch the party depart.

As Lord de Coucy, Marc and the rest rode out of the new Lower Ward gatehouse, the French count looked back and waved.

Marc did not.

She glanced at Isabella, who clenched her leather-gloved hands together.

The princess was adept at cloaking her feelings behind a regal smile, but she must be mourning de Coucy's departure as Cecily mourned Marc's. Still, for both of them, this time apart would break the Yuletide spell. When Enguerrand returned with his king, Isabella would have found a new amusement.

And Cecily? She would soon be married. She would force herself to forget.

Yet she stared at the snowy mud churned by the destriers' hooves long after the line of horses had disappeared.

Isabella broke the silence. 'They are gone.'

Cecily nodded.

It was over.

Isabella, silent, turned away as gentle, lazy flakes of snow drifted from the sky. Cecily pulled her cloak closer and followed, searching for something unimportant to say. 'Well, we will have good account of the trip,' she began. 'The queen sent her chronicler with them. Froissart will give us every detail.'

Mindless chatter. And Cecily never chattered.

Not even a nod from Isabella. 'They will be cold,' she said, turning against the wind to gaze in the direction they had ridden.

An echo of her own thoughts. She pictured Marc in cold armour, with a wet cloak, and worried.

'Let us do something gay,' she said, touching Isabella's arm. Isabella had forced her to gaiety. She could return the favour, for both of them. 'Let's find Robert the Fool. He will make us laugh.'

Yet Isabella only shrugged, as if her energy had departed with Enguerrand.

That was not her way. She was always ready to stretch out her hand, and her purse, to fill her life with clothes and jewels, minstrels and dancing.

But not today. Staring back at the gate, she shook her head. 'I don't know what I am going to do.'

'About what?'

Her eyes met Cecily's. Not the eyes of a princess, but of a woman. 'About him.'

'You are going to do nothing.' Cecily shook her arm. 'Remember what you said? The Yule season is short and a time for us to enjoy ourselves. So I played with that surly French hostage, just as you did with Enguerrand. Now, the season is over. We will put it behind us and go on.'

As if saying so could make it possible.

She held her breath, hoping her friend would smile again, shrug off her melancholy and agree. Waited as if for a sign. If Isabella could forget, surely Cecily could, too.

Instead, Isabella shook her head and looked at Cecily with sad, hollow eyes. 'I want to be with him.'

Such simple words. Which meant something impossible.

'You *will* be with him in London.' The court was to be on the move again. In five days, they would all be reunited in London to welcome the French king in royal style. Maybe Marc would not leave immediately. Maybe she would see him again…

'You know that is not what I mean. That is not what *you* want, is it?'

'What *I* want?' Things she could not even speak. Things she certainly did not want Isabella to suspect. Cecily attempted a laugh. 'What do you mean?'

'The time you have spent with him. The way you look at him.'

Was it so obvious to Isabella what she had barely admitted to herself? 'You were the one who told me to be *volage* and giddy with someone who could never be considered a match. It was only a game, for me as well as for you.' As if her insistence could make it so.

Isabella shook her head. 'No. No, it was not. You see, I have…done things…' She pursed her lips and closed her eyes.

I know you would do nothing to disappoint your parents. The queen had said those words to Cecily. And Cecily had assured the queen for herself and for her own daughter. Surely, surely Isabella would not—

'What things? What have you done, Isabella?'

Wide eyes now, meeting hers. 'I have *lain* with him.'

And Cecily's tongue turned to stone, for what she had feared the most, and tried in vain to prevent, had come to pass.

Distracted by Marc, caught up in her own emotions, far from preventing this, she had, no doubt, made it possible.

Taking a breath, she tried to think. What if… 'Are you with…?' How could she even ask? Kings, princes, dukes and earls could father bastards with impunity. Even with admiration. A woman could not. And the daughter of the king? It was beyond thinking. And yet, she must ask. She must know in order to help. 'Child?'

'No. I don't know. I don't think so. It was only last night.'

Last night. While Cecily had wrestled with the same desires, the same feelings, certain that Marc was all in the world she would ever want. No, she could not shame Isabella for sins she herself had nearly shared.

She put an arm around her friend's shoulders, shielding her from the wind. Nothing more could be said once they went inside. Ears were everywhere. 'We will wait then. Wait and see.'

Isabella shook her head, violently. 'Even if I am not, I want to be his wife.'

Cecily opened her mouth to list the objections. *He is a Frenchman. A hostage. Below you in rank.* And then, did not waste the wind. Too late for arguments now, for her or for the princess.

Enguerrand and Isabella will be apart for some days, she had said to Marc. As if absence was a solution. It would be. It must be. 'Your parents? You have said nothing to them, have you?'

'How can I? They have never denied me anything, but this...' She sighed. 'Yet Father has been hospitable, has he not?' She perked up. 'Perhaps in time...'

'But the queen, surely she would...hesitate?' The queen who had never fully recovered from the battle over her son's marriage. Who had begged for Cecily's help. How could Cecily face her now? 'Besides, if you married, you would have to go to France.'

'Father has already agreed to consider restoring de Coucy's English lands,' she said, with a lifted chin. 'We could stay here.'

Only love could be so blind. Certainly Marc wanted only to return home to walk on earth he did not own. De Coucy was one of France's most powerful lords. He ruled his lands from one of the strongest castles in Christendom. No man would exchange that for a few acres in the

trackless north of England. 'And de Coucy?' She
must suggest, gently. 'Does he want the same?'

'Well, I know that with King Jean's return, he
is no longer bound by the treaty to stay. But he
has not said…I haven't asked…'

Cecily sighed. 'Well, there's nothing for us to
do until…later.' Nothing but to pray the princess
was not with child and hope for God's mercy on
both of them.

Isabella nodded, looking miserable. 'Not a
word of this, Cecily. To anyone.'

And yet, as they descended the stairs into
the shelter of the Tower's walls, the one thing
Cecily wanted to do was to tell Marc.

And to thank him.

For she had not saved herself from Isabella's
fate last night. In this, too, she had failed. It had
been Marc who pulled away, and Marc's honour,
honour she had long disdained, that had saved
them both.

Chapter Fourteen

With the end of the Yuletide celebrations, the court moved back to London. King Jean had returned to captivity by making a processional entry to the city, accompanied by two hundred French chevaliers.

And thirty wild boars.

'I'm not certain I can tell the difference,' Cecily said, archly. She had scorned the French so for years. If her words turned hard again, might she hope her heart could do the same?

The other ladies laughed. Isabella did not. And Cecily felt as petty as when she had tricked Marc at the disguising.

The French king settled into the Savoy Palace, and though the Twelve Days of Christmas were over, the royal entertainments continued into frozen January.

Together, Isabella and Cecily counted the days until her woman's time and watched for any signs that she might be with child. And when King Edward hosted his royal 'guest' at Westminster, Isabella, crying, refused to leave her bed, forcing Cecily to concoct a story about her sudden, but not dangerous, illness. De Coucy, it seemed, along with the other noble hostages held to ensure the French king's return, was still in England, for reasons only kings would know. So after the event, Cecily had to recount exactly how Lord de Coucy looked and every syllable of his smoothly worded concern about the princess's health, which, Cecily knew, was asking more than he could say.

She and de Coucy had exchanged not a whisper beyond his polite, public concern. She had not even asked whether Marc de Marcel was still in England. No doubt he had sailed back to France. She was not privy to the conversations of diplomats, so she had heard no details of the coming or going of any individual hostage.

As the days went on, they still could not be certain whether the princess carried de Coucy's child. Isabella still brooded about the man.

Cecily would brood no more. Neither about her parents nor about Marc de Marcel. She was ready to release the past and its griefs and to marry any man the king decreed.

He was still a cipher, this future husband, and somehow, she hoped he would remain so, even after they had wed. It seemed that she had lost, one by one, everyone she had cared for. Perhaps that was the reason her parents had stressed duty and suppressed emotion. They must have been trying to prepare her for the life they had led, the life that would be hers.

And yet, for that short time, someone had looked at her and seen not just a countess, but a woman. Not just a woman, but a person. Seen so much that she had struggled to hide from the world. It had been sweet.

And dreadful.

One cold night in January, the former mayor of London, intent upon his own importance, decided to entertain King Jean. With King Edward's blessing, he planned an extravagant evening in his own house for the Kings of England and France, and their retinues, an illustration of the power of London's merchants, as well as her warriors.

The princess could hide no longer and her preparations were exhaustive, for she must finally face de Coucy again.

'If I see him, what will I say?' Isabella asked.

'You must not worry,' Cecily said, straightening the tippets that dangled from the princess's sleeves. She had hoped Isabella's Yuletide mad-

ness would fade, but here was proof it had not.
'You look beautiful.'

Not an answer, but she had no answers for
her friend.

Cecily, of course, would never have to ask that
question, never see Marc again. But if, in some
far distant, dreamed-of future, she did, what
would she say?

I missed you.

No. He was a French hostage. Someone who
had been useful to her, not someone she cared
about.

Instead, this night, in a house only a fraction
of the size of Windsor's Hall, Cecily spoke pleas-
antly to each of the unmarried lords at court and
even danced with a widowed earl from the West
Country, whose accent was more incomprehensible than that of the French hostages.

*What would it be like to share a bed with this
one?*

She tried to imagine, but instead, Marc's unwelcome image rose before her, along with a
strange sense of regret. Isabella, at least, had a
memory to cherish. While Cecily—

No. She was, truly, thankful for Marc's honour.

As Isabella had expected, Lord de Coucy was
at the evening's event, more ebullient than ever,
singing, dancing, as if making King Jean feel

welcome and entertained was his personal responsibility.

Yet throughout the evening, Isabella and Enguerrand did not dance or sing or even speak together, which meant that both of them were deliberately avoiding each other. Cecily hoped that was not as obvious to the rest of the court as it was to her.

She turned her attention to the rest of the crowd.

This was the first time Cecily had been able to study the French king and she tried to see him through Marc's admiring eyes, a king truly worthy of the title, the most honourable man in Christendom, but she could not picture him besieged by English knights, swinging a sword and shield. With his reddish hair and prominent nose, he looked to her eyes more like a peevish clerk than a royal monarch. King Edward, older, imposing, overshadowed him as they sat side by side.

Her gaze wandered the room, full of newly arrived French chevaliers who had accompanied the king. Despite her sharp remarks at the procession, she no longer saw them as faceless enemies, but now as ordinary men, no better or worse, perhaps, than their English enemies.

Then, across the room, she saw one tall, broad

and blond, standing apart from the others, only pretending to be at ease.

Just as he had weeks before when they first met.

Marc de Marcel.

As Cecily came closer, Marc forced himself to stand rigid. Yet he was more afraid of this delicate, unarmed *femme Anglaise* than of all *les goddams* with swords and arrows.

He had time to prepare, for she did not come directly. No one would suspect that she crossed the room to meet him, for she chatted with one, then another on her way, meandering as a stream might, seemingly without purpose, but inevitably towards the sea.

He marshalled his defences. They had left it behind at Windsor, this thing between them, along with the Christmas season and their ruined plans to separate Enguerrand and Isabella. Now, Lady Cecily was again an English countess. And he, nothing more than a French hostage.

And, even to himself, a lousy liar.

And when she finally stood before him, all he could do was stare at her wide-set eyes and the arched brows that he had seen every night in his dreams. Her dark hair had spilled across his hands. He knew the taste of the pale flesh of her neck. And more—

And as she stood before him, he bowed, deeply.

'I was told once,' he said, the words stumbling over the catch in his throat, 'that it is customary for a knight to acknowledge a lady.'

She bowed her head, slightly. 'I see you have learned much during your time in England.'

'I have learned, Lady Cecily, things that I hoped never to know.' And would never forget.

For once, the sadness of her smile mirrored his. 'As have I, chevalier. As have I.'

Safe. Here among this crowd, they were safe. No one would wonder at a knight and a lady, standing before the fire for a moment's warmth.

'I did not think to see you again,' she said, in lower, more urgent tones.

'Nor I you, Lady Cecily.'

'You did not…' She sounded hesitant. 'I thought you would be already gone.'

'No.' He could not answer the expectant arch of her brow that asked *What happened*?

He was not on his way home. And worse, he did not know why.

From the moment the king stepped ashore, Marc had waited for the words that would mean his freedom. Waited at the port of Dover, but all he heard from the king was gratitude to the English for his royal welcome. Waited all the way to Canterbury, where all he heard was the king's thanks to God and Saint Thomas for his safe journey. Then waited all the way to the gates of London.

And when he heard those gates close behind him, all Londoners' cheers of welcome for King Jean could not disguise the fact that Marc was back in prison, with a wild moment of regret that he had not left honour behind and run when he'd had the chance.

'But I did not see you when the king came to Westminster,' she said. 'Are you not with his household?'

Lord de Coucy had joined King Jean's exiled court at the palace on the river, but there had been no room for Marc there, nor at the Tower, where the rest of the king's men were now housed. 'I am now a permanent guest of our host for the evening, Henri Picard.'

Her eyes widened and she looked towards the table where their host, a prominent wine merchant, was toasting his royal guests with his finest vintages. 'Is he French?'

'Perhaps his family came from Picardy, long ago. Now, he is a merchant who appreciates a few extra shillings in his pocket for housing a hostage.'

She touched his sleeve. 'But why are you not with Lord de Coucy and the others?'

He turned his back on the rest of the room,

creating the illusion of privacy, and covered her hand with his, wishing he could do more. 'Ah, but he is one of the greatest lords of France.' Stark truth, reminding him of all that was impossible. 'I am but a simple chevalier.'

And yet, her eyes met his, her lips parted, and if he moved closer, if they were but alone—

'Ah, Lady Cecily, there you are.' The booming voice of the lady of the house interrupted. 'The Lady Isabella already waits in my chambers, ready for the entertainment. Leave the men to their dicing and join us.'

Her fingers tightened under his. She took a breath and he feared that she would argue. He wanted no unwelcome attention. Not now. For tonight, he and his king were under the same roof.

Tonight, he would confront the man and demand an answer about his future.

A deep bow. Farewell. 'Lady Cecily,' he said. 'Dame Picard has made special plans.' Calm, polite words. False as a disguising.

Her fingers slipped from his arm. She inclined her head, once again acting the countess, and followed the wine merchant's wife up the narrow wooden stairs.

He did not watch them.

'Ah, there you are, *mon ami.*' Enguerrand's voice, one Marc had not heard in days. 'It has been too long.'

A clasp of hands. Backs pounded. As if nothing had changed. And yet, the easy camaraderie they had shared had been shaken.

On the journey to London, he had tried to talk to Enguerrand. About the king. About the princess. About his plans to return to France. And how Marc might do so as well.

His friend's path to freedom was complex. It might take a few weeks to ensure that treaty obligations were met. But Marc? His release should have been a simple matter.

Enguerrand had left all the questions unanswered. And since they had reached the city, they had seen each other not at all.

Was his friend, too, trying to forget? Or was there something more?

'Our host has a fondness for dice and hazard.' Enguerrand nodded towards the other end of the room, where the Kings of England and France were casting die. And, from what he could tell, losing.

'And a talent for it as well.'

'Will you join the game?'

'I am waiting,' Marc said, 'for a chance to speak to King Jean.' He said the words slowly, to be certain Enguerrand heard. 'About my freedom.'

A troubled frown, now. 'Marc, there are things you need to understand. The Treaty, the king—'

He wanted no meaningless excuses. 'I want only what I was promised by the *compte* before I came.' By Easter, the man had said. Barely eight weeks away. 'Do I have your support?'

An answer seemed long in coming. 'What you want is in the hands of kings.' He nodded towards the group in the corner. 'Not mine.'

As if he should join the game and pretend merriment, all the while trying to coax King Jean with honeyed words, the way Enguerrand had coaxed the princess.

And despite it all, Enguerrand had neither his lands nor his happiness. Well, each man had a way, a path that was his own. And close though they might be, de Coucy's was not the way of Marc de Marcel.

'Then it is the king I will ask. Honour should demand he fulfil what was promised. And are you not ready? To leave England?'

A pause. As if de Coucy was not certain what to say.

And then, he nodded his head and backed away. 'I wish you well.'

Marc watched as his friend joined the noisy group in the corner, as much at ease with the English as with his countrymen.

Enguerrand's answers, and his silence, left Marc more uncertain than ever. And yet, the *compte* had promised. And King Jean, of all the world, was a man who upheld honour.

Perhaps he was a fool, expecting the king, the others, to uphold the principles he had seen violated too many times. But he wanted one chance, to put his case before King Jean, clearly and simply. If the king was a man of honour, there could be only one response.

He tried to keep his thoughts in line, but he knew that Cecily was upstairs. She might reappear at any moment, and thoughts that should have been fixed on the king and what he would say kept drifting...

It was another hour before King Jean stepped away and went outside to visit the privy house. As he returned to the house through a small passage, Marc knelt before him.

Though he had journeyed with the group since they landed, he had only seen the king at a distance. Up close, the man looked older than Marc remembered. It had been eight difficult years since Poitiers. The king had been in his prime then and Marc had been newly knighted, bursting with the pride of chivalry.

Things had changed. For them both.

Now, he looked at this king and could not help but compare him to Edward, who ruled with strong, sure grace. His king, now that he looked carefully, seemed troubled, as if he were staring at a jumbled stack of mismatched bricks, uncertain how they were to be fitted together.

What was France like now, with such a ruler? Was it a place to which he wanted to return?

Too late to wonder. He bowed. 'Your Grace.'

'De Marcel? Is that you? I did not know you were here.'

The words said everything he had feared and told him all he needed to know. But his hope, stubborn, refused to be dislodged. 'I was sent as a substitute for the Compte of Oise, Your Grace, with the promise that I would be home by Easter. Did he send the ransom payment with you? Or perhaps a new man to serve in his place?

He held his breath then, hoping, expecting the king to leap forward, to stake his own honour on the promise Marc had been made.

Instead, there was silence. And a shake of the head. The answer he already knew.

So only Enguerrand would be the free man. 'So your return means only the release of those who were held surety for you under the Treaty.'

'I am here, yes, but not as a substitute for the other hostages.'

'But...' Marc's voice splintered like a shield struck too hard.

Treaties and kings, de Coucy had said. No longer the victory or defeat of a simple battle. And here, the strong arm so honoured in war seemed useless, unable to slash through the confusion to reach freedom, either for him or his friend.

Disappointment must have been clear on Marc's face.

'Easter is still before us. There is time yet.' The king put a hand on his shoulder. 'Are you not comfortable? Well treated?'

I'm a prisoner, Marc wanted to yell. Unable to look Cecily in the eye as an equal.

Why should he think of that now? Even if he were free, he never could. She was a countess. He was a *chevalier*, with nothing but a strong arm and the remnants of his honour to offer.

'Why did you return, Your Grace?' He doubted, now, whether honour had been any part of it.

'The terms, the treaty. France's life bleeds away as money is drained by the unending demands of the ransom. I hoped…if Edward and I could talk together, if we could agree…'

To scale back the ruinous ransom. To keep the gold in France's grip. That was the king's concern. Not one lowly chevalier. And not the idle demands of honour.

'And have you?' A question too bold, but what did that matter now?

'Not yet. But I have hope. Soon. Perhaps tomorrow.'

Tomorrow, when there would be another feast and dancing and dicing and the kings would live like kings no matter what the treaty terms. Perhaps the king had returned for no nobler reason than to relish Edward's hospitality.

The king's attention waned and he wandered back to the room. Marc rose from his knees, as weary as if he had spent a day in battle, and climbed the stairs.

But as Marc returned to his small sleeping room, he faced a stark truth he had known and tried to ignore. Hostages had been held for three years and King Jean spoke only of talk and tomorrow. He would see no ransom. There would be no rescue.

He would grow old here, rotting in the clutches of *les Anglais*, abandoned by men to whom honour was only a word.

At once too near and too far from Cecily. Unless…

Unless he, too, decided to violate the laws of chivalry.

After all, if the king's son was willing to escape his captors and dishonour his vows, why shouldn't a chevalier without a *sou* do likewise?

Trapped in Dame Picard's chambers before a fire constantly fed, Cecily wanted only to escape. Marc was here, under this roof. His very nearness had dissolved all her resistance, leaving only the urgent need to see him again.

She did not question why. Or ask herself what would happen when she did.

But Picard's wife was determined that the ladies of the court hear every note of the entire repertoire of the minstrels she had hired for the evening. Music, dense and loud, filled the crowded room. Isabella's fixed smile remained unmoved. Cecily struggled to match her, but she kept glancing at the door, on the other side of the room.

He had said he was going home, and yet, here he was. She wanted an answer for that, at least. Just because she was curious, she told herself, knowing she lied.

Finally, unable to breathe, she whispered to Isabella and rose, all attempts at discretion useless. They would have to assume she needed to visit the privy.

Stepping out of the room, she looked down the empty stairway, thinking to go back to the ground floor, but then, a sound, behind her. She turned to look up the stairs.

And saw Marc.

For a moment, neither moved. And then, she mounted the stairs, her body knowing her intention. He watched her come, and though it was too dark to see his eyes, she knew they held a hunger that matched hers.

And when she reached the landing and stepped inside the small room, she wrapped her arms around him and put her head on his chest.

He hesitated, then, he held her close, his hand on her head, gentle as a caress, but holding her fast as if he would never let her go.

'I thought I would never see you again.' She was unsure whether he could hear her words, spoken into his tunic.

'I did not intend…' And instead of finishing the sentence, he shut the door.

Alone. They were alone.

No hesitation now. No attempts at words. He lifted her chin and kissed her.

Kisses. Nothing but kisses. As if each was a word and they had much to say. Everything else abandoned, as if they were of one mind that wanted them to merge into one body.

He trailed kisses down her throat and she searched, in turn, to find the warmth of his skin beneath his tunic.

He stepped back, never letting her go, stumbled, and in the next moment they were lying on a bed narrow and hard. Nothing more but his body, hers, somehow matched, knowing…

How easy it was, to merge her lips with his,

to caress the bare skin of his back, warm on her palm. Nothing but now and here and...

And then, below them, applause.

Both of them stilled. 'Listen,' he whispered.

Stools and chairs and feet upon wooden boards. Women's laughter and chatter in the stairway. The performance over.

And with that, the madness lifted and she knew again who she was, what she was doing.

And with whom.

He moved first, rolling to his side, standing, shoving a stool in front of the door and then holding a hand to help her rise.

She looked down in horror. One of the braids framing her face swung free. One of her pearl buttons was dangling by a thread and the stitches at the shoulder of her surcoat had pulled away so the skirt dragged uneven on the floor.

If she walked out of this room this way, everyone from the king to the serving girl would know what she had been doing. 'What am I to do?'

Moments before, Marc had been a man in the clutches of love's delirium. Now, he commanded as if he were again a warrior in the midst of battle. 'I found you taken ill and brought you here to rest. I will find a boatman to take you back to Westminster while the others linger here.' He reached for his cloak and covered her with it, settling it on her shoulders, his hands lingering just a moment too long.

She closed her eyes and raised her lips. His hands tightened on her arms…

And then, he let go.

And without a glance or a sweet word, he turned to the door, listening. All attention. Only about the task that faced him.

To save her.

Men's voices, shouts, from the lower floor. He opened the door a crack, peered out, then motioned her to his side. And before she could ask more, he opened the door and lifted her into his arms.

Then he pulled the cloak together to disguise her rumpled gown. 'Now clutch your stomach and moan.'

He stepped into the corridor.

She dared not look around, but kept her chin on her chest, as if too weak to even lift her head. Who was there? Had anyone seen them coming out of Marc's room? If the queen found out…if one of her prospective husbands saw her… Disgrace. The end of all.

And yet, here, held by him, she felt safe.

'What is it? What is wrong?' The merchant's wife, whispering.

Cecily shut her eyes more tightly and moaned.

'I found her collapsed on the stairs,' Marc said, 'clutching her stomach.'

'Not the plague?' in tones so full of horror Cecily almost regretted having to deceive her.

'Perhaps something she ate…' Marc said, with a slight question at the end of his words.

Now the woman gasped. 'But all the food was carefully prepared, I ate it myself. No one else seems ill.'

'If I can just get back to my bed,' Cecily said, her voice weak and low. 'My chambers…'

'Yes, of course,' said Dame Picard. 'My own boatman will take you. This way. We must not disturb the others.'

There must have been stairs directly to the dock on the river, for she felt the sway of them as Marc carried her, then the winter air cut her cheeks and the river's sharp smell told her they were close to the barge.

'I'm so sorry, Lady Cecily,' the woman said, in a voice near tears. 'I can't imagine what it might have been…'

Cecily struggled a bit and Marc set her on her feet, careful that she clutched the cloak around her. 'I'm sure it was nothing you did, Dame Picard. The princess was indisposed a few days ago. Perhaps the same thing…' She held her stomach and coughed a bit.

The woman leaned over to give instructions

to her boatman and Cecily raised her eyes to Marc's face. In the darkness, near impossible to read his expression.

'Will I see you again?' A whisper. It seemed so urgent now, that they not be parted.

He traced the curve of her cheek with cold fingers. 'Soon.'

And then, steadied by his hand, she stepped into the boat. It moved away from the dock and on to the dark river and she looked back. Marc's dark shadow, rimmed in faint light from the house, did not move for as long as she could see it.

Suspended in a rocking boat between Marc and Westminster, she saw herself clearly, as weak and befuddled as she had feared. Another moment, if the applause had not interrupted, lust would surely have triumphed and she would have joined with him.

And that was not the worst. For as the oars bumped against the dock at Westminster and she stepped carefully out of the swaying barge, she admitted that the worst was something even more dangerous.

She had dared dally with this man, knowing that he was totally, completely unavailable. That she was destined to lose him and choosing that, because she imagined she could let him go with no risk of pain or loss.

Instead, she had begun to care for him. Care deeply. Care so much that to lose him would plunge her into the grey, cruel fog of mourning. Again.

As if his feet had frozen to the dock, Marc stood on the edge of the river, watching the boat carry Cecily away until it was swallowed by darkness.

Even then, he could not move.

Too much had happened this night. He was as trapped as he had been in battle when *les goddams* had closed in from all sides, but this time, no strong sword would save him.

The salvation he had expected from the king's arrival had not come. There was no path to freedom. He might live in this hellish limbo for years to come, far from home, and near, but not too near, to Cecily, forced to watch her from afar, forbidden to him, knowing that his hunger for her would only grow stronger, never assuaged.

Yet after holding her again, to think of escape, to leave her deliberately, seemed impossible.

Darkness swallowed the boat, even the sound of the oars disappeared, and he turned back to the house. Inside, he was surprised to see young Gilbert, standing in the small passageway, watching him. How long had he been there? How much had he seen?

Enough, to judge by his frown. 'She will be another man's wife, you know. Soon.'

The bald statement struck like a blow. He knew she could not be his, but he had not, could not, imagine her belonging to someone else.

Another sign of the idiocy that had grabbed him. Did he somehow think they would part and then each pine alone for the rest of their lives?

He had learned the fallacy of that fantasy long ago.

He growled at Gilbert, as if it were the young man's fault. 'Yours?' The colt did not deserve her.

A shake of the head.

'But you know who it will be.'

'Only rumours.'

'Does she know? Who it is?' Did she lie beneath him, kiss him, knowing?

'No one knows except the king. I've heard a few names. Eastham. Northland. Dexter.' Names spoken with pride.

Names that meant little to Marc. 'Are they good men?'

'All close to the king. Trustworthy.'

'I meant will they be good to her?'

Gilbert studied him. 'You do care. I wasn't sure.'

The boy might still be clumsy with a sword, but his words pierced Marc's armour, exposing all the excuses he had given himself. *Just a few weeks. Over soon. It means nothing.*

Lies. It meant everything. 'I care that she will be well treated and taken care of.'

Gilbert nodded, but asked no more. 'The king will be sure of it.'

Instead of comforting him, the words pricked his pride. Another man could do for her things he could not.

Two royal attendants scurried into the passage and out to the dock. One summoned the barge for Westminster, the other the one for the Savoy. The evening was over. Marc turned for the stairway and solitude.

As the guests surged to exit, he felt the grip of Enguerrand's hand on his shoulder. 'Ah, *mon ami*, there you are. I have spoken to the king. I have good news.'

He raised his eyes, knowing he must look as a man who had faced death. '*I* spoke to the king. There is no good news.'

A moment of compassion in de Coucy's gaze. 'I cannot get you home, but I can get you out of the wine merchant's house. I have arranged for you to share my quarters in the king's household. You will be among your own people. With me.' His eyes took in the Picard house entire, so much smaller than the castles he knew. 'And much more comfortable.'

Anger almost refused for him. Days, weeks without a word. And now, so late…?

Enguerrand's smile was sad. 'At least as comfortable as a man can be so close to the fires of hell.'

'The princess? Did she…?' A question he could not ask aloud.

His friend shook his head. But Marc recognised, unspoken, an apology. He had judged Enguerrand harshly. The pincers of love, duty and honour had squeezed them both. A man must be forgiven. 'When?'

'Now. Quickly.'

He had little enough to bring, but as he packed his meagre bag, he wondered whether he would, indeed, be more comfortable with the king's party.

I have not seen you at court.

She would now. Now, he would be tormented with the sight of Cecily day after day.

Chapter Fifteen

A few days later, the Earl of Eastham sent a messenger, asking the countess to join him for a game of chess.

Telling the page she could not answer until she knew whether the princess needed her, Cecily hurried to Isabella's chambers. Did his invitation mean the king had made a decision? She had said all the right words, worn the correct smile, looked in every way as if she were prepared to take on the role she was born for. And yet, beneath the smile, all she could think of was when she might see Marc again.

'Ah, there you are,' Isabella said, looking up from a bench covered with fabrics as Cecily entered the room. The princess seemed near frantic for diversions now. Every day a merchant would appear, tempting her with a new bauble. 'What do you think of this blue for the Easter *gouns*?'

Right now, Cecily could not even pretend to

care. 'Isabella, has the king chosen Eastham?' What could she remember of the man? Widowed. Quiet. Smelling vaguely of onions. 'Is he to be my husband?'

'Nothing has been decided. Another portion of the king's ransom arrived, but they have still barely paid half what is due and the chancellor is harrying Father about expenses. He's had time for naught else. Mother thought you should spend time with some of the men he's considering and let her know if you favour one of them.'

'How kind of her.' And yet, a gesture only. In the end, it would not matter whether Eastham's smile pleased her or whether Northland made her laugh. Or whether she dreamt of a French chevalier while the castle slept. The king would choose a man to match the castle, not to please the bride. 'Then I will say yes, of course.' In words that lacked enthusiasm.

When will I see you again?

Barely a week had passed.

'Mother is more than kind,' Isabella said, holding her hands close to her stomach. 'I spoke to her. About Enguerrand.'

How had she dared? 'How much did you tell her?'

A blush. 'Not all, of course. I mean…' She looked down, as if trying to see if the bump of a babe had appeared. 'I do not yet know…'

She let the words trail, unable to speak the unthinkable. Then, she brightened. 'But after much suasion, she said she would consider the idea that we might be…together.'

'To wed?' Impossible. 'And Enguerrand? Does he want the same?'

A shy smile. 'I think so. But he cannot speak until he knows…until it is safe…'

Of course. To declare himself, to speak of marriage before he knew it would be permitted would be as foolhardy as rushing to battle without knowing how the enemy was arrayed. Yet Isabella's dalliance had been as forbidden as Cecily's dreams. Did the princess suddenly have all within her grasp?

'Nothing is certain. But I have hope.'

Cecily swallowed her envy. Isabella was daughter of a king. Her duty should have been as clear and strong as Cecily's. No hopeless yearning could supplant her father's ambitions. Yet now she spoke of marrying for love. 'I am happy for you.' And yet it made mock of Cecily's duty. She turned to leave. 'I must give Eastham's page my answer.'

'And, Cecily?' Isabella beckoned her back. 'Your chevalier will be at tonight's gathering.'

'He is not my chevalier.' Yet her smile escaped before she could stop it. Soon, he had promised.

Isabella raised a brow. 'But you do like him.'

She could admit nothing when a prospective husband waited for a reply. 'My duty is elsewhere.'

Isabella's folly had made the risks of indiscretion stark and clear. It had only been one time with Enguerrand, she said, and now, she was counting days and watching for signs a child grew. If Cecily, too, had succumbed…she and Marc had come so close…

The princess smiled again, as if she knew a secret she could not wait to share. 'Well, until Father names your husband, you can at least enjoy his company.'

And despite all the danger, that was what she wanted, fiercely, to do for the final few weeks left to her.

Plunged into the court of King Jean in exile, Marc found himself in the midst of an unending season of *Noël*. Today a dinner at the Savoy. Tomorrow, a celebration at Westminster. The river was clogged with barges ferrying the royals and the court from one palace to the other, almost as if these events had become the battles by which the negotiations would be resolved.

So within less than a week, he was back at Westminster, at one of those gatherings Isabella and Enguerrand loved so well, standing at the edge of an alcove, watching Cecily across the room.

She was standing much too close to a burly Englishman.

Marc beat back a streak of jealousy. She was not his. Could never be his. And yet…

Would that man, or whoever the king chose, be good to her?

He must be certain of that. Then, perhaps, he could let her go.

Finally, with subtle grace, she made her way in his direction. She seemed even more beautiful tonight. When he looked at her lips, he remembered the little catch of ecstasy that had escaped when he held her. As fair as her green eyes were, he also knew, now, how they looked, half-closed, when she was overcome with want.

And when she stood before him, it was all he could do to keep his arms at his sides.

He cleared his throat. 'I am glad to see, Countess, that you are recovered from your illness of the other evening.'

'Not fully, I'm afraid.' She did not look at him, but her fingers, clasped before her, tightened. 'It seems this illness…lingers.'

'I understand. I, too, have been touched by that malady. Is there no cure?'

'None that I have found. Even being removed from the source of the infection does not relieve the symptoms.' She lifted her eyes to his. 'I have thought, instead, I should stay close to the source. Perhaps over time, it will lose its power.'

'A few weeks, only,' his words, whispered, drunk on the yearning in her eyes.

She nodded. 'A few weeks more.' She was silent for a moment, then looked over her shoulder before her words dropped to a whisper. 'What happened? I thought, you had expected, when King Jean returned...' She took a breath and looked at him, not as a lady making passing conversation, but with a gaze that tried to burrow into the truth. 'Why did you not go home?'

There had been no time to explain it at Picard's and now he was near as loath to speak of it as he was to bare his feelings. 'The king did not bring my release with him.'

'Nor did he bring his own.' Her voice held an edge of annoyance he shared. 'I feel as if nothing has changed.'

'It seems,' he said, 'that before any hostages are freed, our two kings have many things to negotiate.'

'Do you know what?'

He smiled and shook his head. 'A lowly chevalier is not privy to such things.'

'I know what it is like, to wait for kings.' A sigh.

'Is it that one?' He glared at the man she'd

been with earlier, now telling tales to a man on the other side of the hall. 'The one the king has chosen for you?'

'His name has been mentioned. Along with others.'

He shrugged. 'Does the princess give you no hint of your future?'

She looked at him sharply. 'The princess,' she said, 'has been occupied with other things.'

The edge in her voice jolted him.

You've been with her.

He glanced across the room. Enguerrand and Isabella were standing at a carefully measured distance from each other. Their smiles were strained.

'Has he spoken of her?' Cecily, whispering.

He met her eyes and *knew*, unspoken, that she, too, knew what had passed Christmas night. What had happened since? 'Men keep such things even closer than kings.' Was there a child? The question would be a betrayal. 'But it seems all our efforts accomplished nothing.'

'Nothing except to bring us together.' An outcome worthy of a fool's jest. If they had not tried so hard to keep Enguerrand and Isabella apart, they would not have spent so much time together.

But life was not made of *what if*, but of *what is*.

She glanced over her shoulder. 'The Earl of Northland is expecting me. I must…'

'Of course.' He nodded, quickly.

And yet she did not leave.

He could not hold back the words. 'When will I…'

See you again?

A plea as plaintive as hers had been.

'Soon.' Her smile, gentle with compassion for both of them. 'Lord de Coucy visits often.'

And so, he thought, he and Enguerrand would ride side by side into love, as silently as they had ridden to war. And Marc knew that neither would emerge without wounds.

Held too long within castle walls, Marc needed the release of swinging a sword, even if it were made of wood and the opponent no more than the painted wooden pell, stuck in the ground for pages to practise their strokes. Generous, King Edward had opened his training yard to the hostages, but when Marc hefted a wooden sword and stepped into Westminster Castle's frozen yard on a late January morning, the only other person there was neither page nor squire.

It was young Gilbert.

He was hacking at the motionless pell stake with a familiar zeal, mindless to all but the battle before him. Marc watched, silent, assessing the young man's skill. He had a sure eye and a willingness to work and with the right guidance, and a bit more heft in his shoulders, Sir Gilbert might become a formidable opponent.

If he had the will.

'Lift from your back, not your shoulders.'

Startled, Gilbert stumbled, but he kept his hold on the sword and whirled to face Marc, crouched and ready to strike, both hands firmly on the grip. When he saw who had spoken, he paused, then stood. 'Teach me.'

'What?' A question to allow him time to think.

'Teach me.'

The words were a challenge, not a request, but Marc grinned. 'I taught Lord de Coucy. Do you think to be his equal?'

A lift of the chin, undaunted. 'I think to be yours.'

Words de Coucy might have said, so long ago. Though Marc was only five years older than the young lord, Enguerrand had wanted the comfort and guidance of another male after his father died. And Marc? Perhaps he was looking for a younger brother to replace the one his mother lost.

What was he looking for from this *jeune homme*? Well, if he had to leave Cecily, perhaps he could prepare Gilbert to watch out for her in his stead. 'Then let us begin.'

And so they spent the waning hours of the day, crossing heavy wooden blades, sweating despite the cold. The practice swords could not cut as the real ones did, but they were heavier and so helped a man build strength that would make the metal blades seem light. A few other men drifted into the yard, both his fellows and *les goddams*, calling out a combination of advice and taunts that forced both of them to fight their best.

And when darkness fell and they put the weapons away, he and Gilbert walked into the castle together, speaking of sword and shield makers and how well a man could sleep on hard ground after riding all day.

'How soon can I be ready?' Gilbert asked. 'To join the Crusade?'

And the first word that tempted Marc's lips was *never*.

Oh, a man's body could be trained. Easily. He could build his strength and size and stamina. But it was the spirit that could never be fully prepared, the spirit whose invisible wounds would scar a man as wholly as a spear or a sword.

And he had a moment's regret for what he had lost. And for what this man would, eventually, become.

'Ça depend.' He shrugged. 'We'll see.'

A few days later, Cecily unpacked the last of the chests that had been sent from Windsor to

Westminster with the advance party and found a small box, unfamiliar. 'Is this yours, Isabella?'

'No. What's in it? Some jewels you've forgotten?'

Only Isabella would have so many jewels she could forget some. 'Probably a report from the steward at the castle on the state of the armoury.' One more thing that should have received her attention before now.

No lock held it closed, so she slid the hook away from its clasp and opened the lid. Inside, a stack of parchment sheets. Her hand shook as she lifted them from their little tomb.

The drawings of her father's effigy.

She remembered now. She had last seen them just before her mother died. Her mother had given the mason a few instructions on final changes to her father's figure, then put the drawings safely away, where she could find them.

But what about the drawings of her mother's figure?

'Lord de Coucy will be here after the midday,' Isabella said. 'I must…tell him.'

'Are you certain?' There were no signs she could see. A woman might miss a monthly time, even two, for other reasons.

Yet Isabella, serene as a Madonna, seemed to cup her belly as if she could feel a babe within. 'I can tell.'

Did she know or only wish it to be true? 'But what will you do? Your parents…you can't…'

'I want him to know. We'll speak of the rest… after.'

A servant entered and they fell silent. 'Lady Isabella, Lord de Coucy and Chevalier de Marcel.'

Isabella raised her brows.

'He must have wanted Marc with him,' Cecily said. 'I'll keep him occupied so you can talk to Enguerrand.

The servant left and the men entered. With a warning glance at Cecily, Isabella moved to Enguerrand's side, putting a hand on his arm and leading him to her chamber. 'Come. I've something to tell you.'

Alone, she and Marc looked at each other and then away, suddenly awkward. Had a week passed since she saw him last? It seemed as months.

In the next room, she could hear Isabella's voice, but not her words. 'Here, Marc.' She must be sure he heard nothing. 'Come look'

He came closer, looking over her shoulder. 'What is that?'

'The design for my parents' tomb.'

Without a word of surprise, he picked it up and studied it, as if he were truly interested. 'It honours him. A worthy warrior.'

She warmed at his praise of a man he had never known. An enemy.

But as she looked back at the drawing, the figure wearing armour seemed a stranger to her as well. And when the face was finally sculpted, it, too, would be that of a stranger. The sculptor had not known her father. Only her mother.

Marc pointed to the figure beside him. 'What about your mother?'

Beside him, with no detail, was a shape that was to have represented her mother. But it had not been important, then, what that one looked like. There would be time for that later, or so they had thought.

'She chose something, but...' She leafed through the chest, but found nothing in more detail. 'I don't know what she wanted.'

'So what did you decide?'

She put the drawings back in the box and shut the lid. She had not decided, of course, once again letting her emotions override her duty. 'I told the sculptor to do as he thought best.' And when she returned home, she would be forced to look at their graven images and say farewell all over again. She walked away from the box, as if it were a live thing. 'Just looking at those reminds me they are gone.'

'But if God is good, parents die before their children.'

And yet she had not forgiven God for taking hers. 'Did you think God so good when your parents died?' A cruel and bitter question.

The shock of it reflected in his face. 'No.'

Once again, she had lashed out of her own feelings, forgetting his. She put her fingers on his sleeve, hoping he could sense her regret, and gentled her words. 'Forgive me. I must sound like a witless child. I did not mean to raise old sorrows.'

'I left home when I was seven. I have lived without them for a long time.'

That was the way of men who trained to become knights, but still, she could barely imagine it. Her parents had been a never-ending constant in her world. Or so she imagined they would be. 'So you don't remember them?'

'Of course I do.' A belligerent tone. As if by asking she had accused him. 'My father gave me a sword before I was seven and told me I was strong and brave and must make my way in the world for he was a knight, but held no land. And then he sent me to the Lord de Coucy, Enguerrand's father. He must have believed in me very much to persuade such a great lord to take on my training.'

So many words together. And then he fell silent.

Was that Lord de Coucy's voice coming from

the next room? Steadier than she had expected. She must drown the sound. 'And then you lost him.'

'At Crécy.'

'So your father was killed in a battle with the English. Perhaps even by my father.' She could barely accept the truth. She had hurled countless accusations and *he* was the one who had lost a father to the enemy, not she. 'And all this time, all the things I said…and you said nothing. Why?' A warrior and yet he had never struck back.

He shrugged. 'You had battles enough to fight.'

But instead of fighting her own battles, her inner demons, she had turned her fury on him. And if he had lost his temper, even for a moment, and bludgeoned her with the truth of his own loss instead of letting her discover it in her own time, could she have borne the blow?

'You are good man, Marc de Marcel, though you pretend a lack of honour.'

She had struggled so hard against her own feelings, yet, with a few simple words, this immovable man had shown himself more gentle with such weakness than she had been. She sighed, grateful for the sounds of music and laughter from the other room.

He shook his head. 'When you let go of what has sustained you, the first step is shaky. As is the second, and the third. And just when they become more steady, you will trip over a stone in the path. That is when you must take another step.'

Wisdom learned from a difficult journey. All this time, she had thought him callous. Instead, his silent perseverance was the way he had chosen to meet life. He, at least, had met it, while all this time, she had hidden away, as if by clinging to the past she could make it live again.

'Not only good, but wise.' Wise enough to help de Coucy, though she could not speak of that now. 'I am sorry that I did not realise it earlier.'

If she had expected him to smile, she was mistaken.

'Wise?' He shook his head. 'Perhaps stubborn.'

'And brave. Brave enough to meet life head on.'

He rose and left her side to stare out on the faded winter sky. 'Except for you. I have not been brave with you.'

And suddenly, she felt brave. Brave enough to risk feeling joy, even knowing it would not last. Knowing that this, too, would be torn away. 'Should we be brave together? Just for a few weeks?'

Foolish. Irrational. Any day, perhaps as soon as tomorrow, the king would name the man she must wed. And even if they escaped unscathed and unnoticed, wouldn't it be harder to let him go, after having had…more?

None of those arguments could stop her heart from pounding in her ears as she waited for him to speak.

From the next room, Isabella's laugh.

'They seem to do well enough,' Marc said.

'So could we, as long as we are not…'

'As long as we do not….'

'Exactly.'

'Just until…'

Until she was married or he was ransomed or something they could not control tore them from each other. And if, then, she had to listen again to the endless voices of judgement in her head, she would pay that price. 'Easter?'

They fell silent as Enguerrand and Isabella walked into the room. Nothing more was said, beyond polite farewells.

But, as Marc looked over his shoulder to smile, Cecily counted the scant weeks before Easter and found herself wishing that the whole of winter stretched long and bright before them.

Chapter Sixteen

Days later, Isabella lost the babe.

She had retired to her chambers, weary, complaining again of her stomach, and called Cecily to sit with her as night fell. Later, the aches, the pains, and then the bleeding came. More, heavier than a monthly flow, though later, that was how they explained it.

And after, the princess cried, her face such a mixture of pain, sadness and relief that Cecily was not certain which was the strongest.

'You must go,' she said, exhausted and ready to sleep after the sheets were changed and the morning came. 'Find Enguerrand. Tell him… what happened.'

'Yes, I will.' Murmured words to reassure.

But Isabella gripped her hands. 'Now. You alone. Let no one see you.'

Cecily wanted to protest that was impossible for her to go skulking through the streets alone.

Yet she could have been the one lying in that bed.
If Marc had not been strong...

And so she left the room, knowing that to do
as the princess asked, she must go to the Savoy
not as the countess, but as an ordinary woman.
One who would be unnoticed. Unseen.

And if she was discovered? What would she
say?

Or would it be worse not to be discovered? To
be thought a woman available to any man she
passed on the street?

Fingers trembling, she put on her plainest
wool, covered her hair with a linen kerchief and
her skirt with an apron as the washesters would.
Then, she stuffed a bag with clothes, wrapped a
length of wool to shadow her face, and slipped
out of the castle.

The countess would have called for a boatman to take her to the Savoy, but a laundress
must walk, following the curve of the river between Westminster Palace and the Savoy Palace, and she hurried through the streets, careful
to keep within sight of the river so she would
know where she was. Blessedly, the sun came
out, warming the day and melting the frozen
street, and by the time she reached the home of
the French court, she felt like a laundress indeed.

At the palace, they directed her to the postern gate. Too dangerous to go directly to Lord

de Coucy, and so she asked for the Chevalier de
Marcel, ignoring the ribald comments about the
chevalier's need for a laundress in the middle
of the day.

When they took her to him, he was with Enguerrand. Their frowns replaced by surprise
when they recognised her.

Enguerrand cleared the room of attendants.
Alone with them, she pushed the headcloth away
and set down her sack.

'What are you doing here?' Marc not waiting for his friend to speak. His voice full of surprise. Concern.

She looked at Lord de Coucy, uncertain how
to begin.

His face carried the sharp expression of a fal-
con. As if he knew. As if he had been waiting.
'Isabella.'

It was not a question.

She nodded, glancing at Marc. Did he know?
Did men speak of such things? The secret was
not hers to share with him, yet Isabella had
shared all with her. Had they done the same?

The two men looked at each other, then Enguerrand nodded at her to continue.

She took a deep breath. 'She has lost the babe.'

Suddenly Marc was at her side, as if afraid
she might fall.

Enguerrand's face turned pale. 'But Isabella, is she...?' As if he could not speak his fears.

'She is weak, but will recover.'

Then he did not try to disguise his relief, slumping in the chair as if only force of will had held him upright until now.

'You came alone? Through the streets?' Marc now, his voice rich with concern for her.

'We could trust no one else.'

He nodded and asked no more. Her parents would have judged her. A countess did not disguise herself and walk the streets alone. Yet Marc, a man accustomed to the duties of war, did not question her decision. She had done what was needful.

Yet he did not move from her side. 'You should not go back alone.' He hesitated, looking at Enguerrand, still unmoving.

Cecily tried to read his face. Concern? Relief? Isabella would ask.

Without raising his head, Enguerrand waved them away. 'Go.'

A moment's pause, then they did.

'You knew,' she whispered, when they left the room. Was it an accusation? She wasn't sure.

He nodded. 'Enough.'

Men do not talk of those things, he had said. Yet some things took few words.

'I must thank you again. If not for you, that

night, if you had not been a man of strength and honour…'

I might have been like Isabella. Or worse.

Silent, he cupped her face in his hand, a gesture that said without words, *I cherish you.* 'My mother…died… She and the babe, my brother…'

Such a strong man, and yet, hard for him to speak of the danger that women faced every day. 'I'm sorry.' So many ways to lose a loved one.

He dropped his hand, as if suddenly aware of her sympathy. 'It was long ago. I no longer think of them.'

'Truly?' And for a moment, fierce envy bit her. Would that she could be so strong.

Something flickered across his face. Not quite a smile. 'No more than once a day.'

A confession.

Together, they descended the stairs in silence.

As part of the king's household, Marc had more freedom to come and go, and as they stepped into the streets, Cecily felt strangely free, too. Dressed as she was, walking beside an unknown, ordinary knight, who would know, or care, who she was? Who would judge or condemn her?

The day's unexpected sunshine had brought all manner of Londoners into the streets, lifting their faces to the sun, near giddy with the reminder that the world would not be white and cold for ever.

Cecily had processed through London many times, for ceremonies, on the way to a tournament or travelling between castles. But she had never been in them, part of them. Now, she was eye to eye with people selling firewood or food. No longer on a horse or in a litter, she attracted no special glances. For once, she felt blissfully invisible. No longer wearing the disguising of a countess, but only an ordinary woman, doing things that any woman might.

She touched his sleeve. 'Do we have to return right now?'

'Won't the princess expect you?'

'The night was difficult. She will be sleeping, at least for a while.'

He smiled. A grin as wide as a boy's. 'What would you like to do?'

Be ordinary. 'Be with you.'

And so they turned away from Westminster, and towards the city.

Neither of them knew the way, but she was not afraid because he was there.

And because, today, she was not the countess.

No one gave them more than a glance. No one looked at her, waiting, expecting. So she could gaze at Marc, with a smile as wide as his, brave to feel joy. And to show it.

And when her stomach growled, loud enough that he looked down, they both laughed. And she was certain she had never heard him laugh before.

'But I haven't eaten since the princess...' Her laugh faded. No need to tell the tale again. The night had been dark and long and she had near forgotten that a day could overflow with sunshine.

As if in answer, the cries of 'Hot sausage!', 'Cheese!' and 'Pie!' rang out ahead of them. They could see the stone quays along the river now and food sellers lined the street.

She dug into the purse hanging from her waist. Normally, she would have sent a servant to fetch such food, but she felt strangely powerful as she herself gave the seller a penny, then cupped two warm meat pies in her palms.

'No parsnips,' she said, as she handed one to Marc. 'I promise.'

And he smiled. Smiled as if no one in his life had ever remembered, or cared, that he hated parsnips.

They ate as they walked, and when she was done, Cecily licked her fingers clean.

Clouds had moved over the lowering sun and a gust of wind blew the smell of the river towards the street. 'I should go back,' she said, reluctant.

He nodded. And without words, they turned back towards Westminster, walking so close together that the wind could not slip between them. He took her hand, safely hidden by cloak and skirt, and they slowed their steps. Fewer buildings lined the road near the palace and instead of blending with a crowd, they walked alone.

Far enough from the gate she would not be recognised, she let go his hand and pulled the woollen cloth forward, shadowing her face. 'I must leave you now.'

He looked ahead, at the postern guard. 'They will not let you enter unchallenged.'

'If I could get a message to Isabella.' Foolish idea. Any servant would see her and wonder.

'I have an idea.' He put his arm around her and pulled her close so that her face was hidden against his chest. 'Follow my lead.'

His gait turned uncertain, as if he had drunk too much ale, and she stumbled, keeping up with him. He laughed, then whispered in her ear. 'He will think I have cupped too much and brought back a common woman.'

Her cheeks burned off the last of the cold and her nervous laugh sounded false, but she wrapped him close, as she imagined a whore might do, and did not raise her face from his chest as they came close enough for him to hail the guard.

'Take pity on a man on a cold day,' he called, staggering from one foot to another as if he could barely stand. 'My bed is far away and I need to warm myself with this one.'

Then, he lifted her chin and kissed her. Long, slow and deep as if they had been alone in all of the world.

And she let him. Kissed him in return. Told herself it was only another disguising and knowing she lied. And even forgot for a moment who and where she was and let her hands roam his back as if...

'Come on then.' The guard laughed. 'Get inside before you scare the animals.'

Laughter escaped her throat and her knees gave way. Marc's arm stayed at her back and he swung her up in both arms. Giving the guard thanks and a wicked grin, he carried her inside and out of sight of the man.

Her arms clung to his neck and she dared not raise her head until he said, 'It's safe', and let her down to her feet, which were now truly as unsteady as she had pretended.

They were in a corridor she did not recognise, alone for the moment, her back safely pressed against the wall, with Marc between her and the rest of the world.

'If you see anyone coming,' he whispered, 'start kissing me again.'

She resisted the temptation to kiss him anyway, feeling as if she had been truly as drunk and mad as they had pretended. She took a deep breath, searching for the Countess of Losford.

'I think,' she said, trying to steady herself, 'that this must be one of the worst things I have ever done.'

He smiled, indulgent, kind, as if she were beloved and could do no wrong. 'If this is the worst thing you have done, you must have been a perfect daughter.'

She shook her head. 'Not at all. They were not even certain...'

Will she ever be ready?

She did not want to think of that now. She had only a few more minutes here with Marc in the darkness of day's end. Where she was not the countess, but only Cecily. Only a woman.

She lifted her hand to his golden hair, twirling her fingers through the waves as if she truly were a common woman. Or a wife who had the right. 'What is the worst thing,' she whispered, 'that you have ever done?'

Even in the dim light, she could see the softness leave his face. 'I watched other men do their worst and I let them.'

His memories, dark with horrors she would never know and was afraid to discover.

A noise. Voices. Two men. Squires? Kitchen boys?

Marc took her in his arms, hiding her from their sight, and she clung to him, as if her touch could smooth away his memories and comfort him as he had tried to comfort her.

She closed her ears to the rude remarks. The men passed and they were alone again.

'I must go,' he whispered.

She nodded. But before she let him, she pressed her lips to his once more, no longer pretending to be anything other than herself.

And beginning to realise, as she returned to the life of the countess, just who she might be.

No, she must not risk being alone with Marc de Marcel again. The next time she saw him, they must again be surrounded by members of the court.

Safe.

Cecily had worried, but the princess recovered quickly and was once again herself. Laughing. Full of gaiety. The Isabella of old. Cecily could read nothing behind Enguerrand's expression and when she asked Marc, he had only shrugged.

Men do not talk of those things.

Yet Isabella was once again planning to entertain the court with Lord de Coucy.

'We are preparing a new entertainment, Enguerrand and I!' A flush touched Isabella's check, delicate as a schoolgirl's.

Cecily tried to remember what they had done for the Christmas entertainment. Her attention had been elsewhere that night. 'Will you sing one of Machaut's songs?'

'Not this time, though he sings so beautifully.' There was that silly sigh. And then a smile. 'We have something else planned. This time, we shall perform a scene from the stories of King Arthur.'

Cecily frowned. Isabella's smile gave her a sense of unease. 'Who will you portray?'

'Guinevere.'

Her dismay became a sinking feeling in the pit of her stomach. 'And Enguerrand?'

'Lancelot, of course.'

Guinevere and Lancelot. Ill-fated, adulterous lovers. She was afraid to ask exactly what they would be doing. 'But if you hope to persuade your parents—'

'Mother has given her blessing.'

Shocked, Cecily tried to collect her thoughts. 'You did not tell her! Not about the…' She did not finish the sentence.

'No. But she promised to persuade Father.'

It was the king's approval that was needed and

Edward had always listened to his wife more carefully than most kings. Besides, he had indulged Isabella, his favourite daughter, beyond all reason for most of her life. If he allowed her to break a marriage agreement, why would he not allow her to enter into this one? 'Has she asked him yet?'

Isabella shook her head. 'Mother thought a portrayal from the stories of Arthur might put him in a receptive mood. Father loves the tales of Arthur.'

'I know that,' she retorted. The story of King Arthur had been engrained in the court for as long as she could remember. It motivated the king, she thought, in a direct and personal way that even the Biblical stories did not. But Isabella was being deliberately obtuse. 'But why not Guinevere and Arthur?'

'Because Enguerrand is French, of course.'

And at that, Cecily laughed. Laughed at herself for ever thinking she could stop Isabella from having her way.

And later, when the king saw Guinevere and Lancelot sing and dance with coy smiles, he nodded with satisfaction and leaned over to listen when his wife touched his arm.

So, Cecily thought, unable to meet Marc's gaze, although love had made fools of them all, only Isabella and Enguerrand would reap love's rewards. Her own duty, which had been of such import a few months ago, now seemed a dry, dusty thing, too paltry to sustain her for the rest of her life. And yet she hoped the man of the king's choice would be one she could look on without longing, touch without passion, and lose, if the time ever came, without tears, for she could bear to lose no one else.

Chapter Seventeen

Easter came again, the fourth since her father had died, and with it, the spring.

The snow melted. No cruel hail pounded down from the sky. French and English courts mingled in celebration instead of riding to battle. For Easter, Edward and Jean wore new suits of murray longcloth, making them look like brothers instead of enemies.

Whatever kings spoke of, whatever negotiations dragged on, she knew little but whispers. King Jean had not returned solely as a hostage, it seemed, but to persuade King Edward to reduce the amount England demanded of France by the terms of the treaty. Even Cecily knew King Edward would not agree, but it turned his attention from her marriage and the result was to keep Marc close and the spectre of her husband distant, so she was content. She felt almost whole again.

So when the French king fell ill, just after Easter, it was a cruel reminder. Nothing could last for ever, neither the good, the bad, nor the indeterminate limbo in which she and Marc had existed.

Days passed and King Jean did not rise from his bed. Warmth, life crept into the land. No one noticed. King Edward sent his own physicians to attend *le roi Français*. The French gathered close to their monarch. The court held its breath. Marc, when she did see him, looked grim. Once, when no one was looking, she threaded her fingers in his and squeezed his hand in reassurance.

And they waited for the king to recover.

Marc was with Cecily and the princess when Enguerrand came with the news.

'Le roi et mort.'

'Dead?' His mind fought with his mouth. 'The king is dead?'

Beside him, Cecily turned pale. 'But just a few days ago, he was well. How…?' Her words trailed to nothing.

Marc took her hand. She, of all people, knew the shortness of life and the injustice of death.

His first thought was anger at this accursed country and its cold. He wanted to lash out and blame…who? Cecily was right. The cold was not the fault of her king or her countrymen. Her father had died on his land. Now his king had died on hers.

And despite his admiration of the man, as he had watched him these last few months, he had begun to wonder whether the king was truly honourable or simply clinging stubbornly to a world of his own imaginings. That day at Poitiers, Marc had admired his valiant fight to the end. But if he had retreated, if the battle could have been joined another day, perhaps France would have won after all.

Even his return to England, seen closely, now seemed less a matter of honour than of comfort. Yes, he had tried to persuade Edward to adjust the treaty terms, but he also had spent days and nights enjoying food and drink and music, fêted as much as imprisoned.

Whatever the truth, it had died with him.

'I must go to Father,' Isabella said, gathering her skirts and heading for the door. 'He will be mourning his royal brother. He will need help with arrangements…'

She looked to Enguerrand, but Cecily was the one who came to her side and led her from the room.

The door closed, leaving Marc and his friend alone in the room, and they exchanged glances. 'He mourns for more than that,' Marc muttered. 'He has just lost his most valuable hostage.

De Coucy nodded. 'Why should France pay millions of *écus* for a dead king?'

'Because two kings pledged their honour on the signing.'

'Charles will be king now. His honour is not jeopardized. There are many who opposed the treaty all along. This could allow them to consider it dissolved.'

The words sank into quiet air. Marc's first thoughts had been of the king. Now, he faced a more personal question. He had told himself the king would bring his ransom. And when that failed, he thought that the honour of the king would ensure that the *compte* kept his promise.

But Easter had come and gone. Why should the *compte* come for him now? He, and the new king, had better uses for their coin than to pay for the release of a lowly chevalier.

Enguerrand's hand on his shoulder brought him back. 'But before all that, we must honour him in death. King Edward plans a royal funeral.'

'But he cannot be buried here, on enemy soil.'

'No. He will go home.'

Home. Even in death, the king could return home before Marc de Marcel. Unless…

Two hundred chevaliers had come to England with him. Let some of them stay here for a while. Marc had suffered long enough.

He gripped his friends arm. 'I will go. We can both go. We can take him home.'

The final notes of the French king's funeral mass still echoed in her ears as Cecily hurried through Westminster's corridors on her way to King Edward's chambers.

He has decided.

The past few days had been a blur, with hasty preparations for a grand procession and service for King Jean. The French community had been in mourning and she had seen little of Marc. When she did, he was solemn and silent, grieved, no doubt, by his sovereign's death. She hoped that he had been comforted by King Edward's honours, for the procession and the funeral had been grand, befitting a monarch related by blood and honour and a fellow warrior in Christ.

But as she entered and curtsied before her king, still wearing his black, fur-lined funeral cloak, the cold fear of loss gripped her again. He was older than the dead king. Was there a droop in his shoulders? Could he be taken as quickly as King Jean?

Or her parents?

She had never known a day without King Edward on the throne.

She stood, head high, feeling as if she awaited a death sentence. This was her duty. She knew that. Had always known it. She had no choice but to be ready. And yet…

'A sad day,' the king said, finally.

'Yes, Your Grace.'

'I have selected a husband for you.'

True, then. 'So soon?' All this time. All the waiting, and it seemed as if no time had passed at all.

And all she could think of was Marc.

'Ah, Cecily, you are young. To you, it seems as if life is long.'

The king's death must have reminded King Edward that days were not promised to us. That he should act now. 'Alas, Your Grace, I know it is not.'

'I miss him still.'

'As do I. I miss them both.' And yet, she had attended King Jean's funeral without tears. Perhaps she was healing, finally, after all. Was time the only healer? Or was it also Marc de Marcel?

'Your new husband will help to fill that void.'

Husband. The word came too close to her thoughts of Marc. 'And whom have you chosen, Your Grace?'

'The Earl of Dexter.'

She tried to remember the man. She had not seen him in years. Honourable. Old enough to be her father. Not someone strong and vital, like Marc.

She must not think of Marc.

'Well?' the king asked. 'Have you nothing to say?'

Could she argue with the king? And if she did, what would she say?

I have fallen in love with a French hostage...?

She should speak of nothing but her gratitude, yet she could not form the words. 'He has not been at court, Your Grace. I did not know he was under consideration.'

'He has been with my son Lionel in Ireland, but they are coming home. He should be here within a month. Or less.'

'So soon?' Her voice, faint. She had tried, unsuccessfully, to envision a life beside Eastham and Northland and the others, but she could not even remember Dexter's Christian name.

Just as she had wanted, she would be marrying a man she barely knew and would not care if she lost.

Decision made, the king rose. 'We'll have the banns read as soon as he arrives. You can be married within weeks.'

Weeks. Too soon. She had told herself she needed just a few more days, weeks, months and then she would be ready. She had been telling herself that for years. Telling herself she could do her duty, as her parents would expect, but faced with the truth of it, she knew there was one duty she owed her parents before she wed. 'Your Grace, my parents…the tomb…'

He frowned. 'What about it?'

'The sculptor resumed his work in January. May I have permission to return home and review his progress? All should be complete before my…marriage.'

The past, all of it, well and truly buried before she became a bride.

The king shook his head, no longer even looking at her. 'The funeral procession to accompany King Jean's body leaves tonight. After that, you'll be needed here, to prepare for the wedding. When you and Dexter go home, you can approve the sculptor's work together.' A wave of dismissal.

'Your Grace, before I go—can you tell me his Christian name?'

'Robert. His name is Robert.'

She dipped her farewell.

Wed within weeks. Now it was too late. Too late for everything.

And all she could think of was that she must find Marc.

Preparing himself to leave England to escort King Jean's body back to France, Marc had forced himself to keep his distance from Cecily during the ten days leading up to the funeral.

He no longer trusted himself.

Since the day they had wandered London's streets, Marc had danced by her side in the carol ring, laughed with her as the fool played tricks and ridden beside her to hunt the deer, careful always to stay within sight of the rest of the court. Both knew the risk if they were alone together again. A risk neither could take.

He, of course, was not the only man at her side. Eastham, Northland, others he didn't even know bowed a knee before her, shared a jest with her and boasted of their prowess in war until Marc thought he would go mad with it. Which of them knew the depth of her grief or the height of her courage?

He was discovering he needed new courage of his own. Watching Cecily with one prospective husband, then another, required more bravery than he had ever needed in battle. Each day with her was one day less ahead. Each day chipped away another piece of his heart.

And yet, he did not want it to end.

But now, with farewell close enough to touch, he became a coward, unable to stand at her side and pretend. He would see her just once more, he decided. To say goodbye.

And that would come late in the day. With the funeral and the procession over, the court would accompany the king's body as far as Dartford.

Then, a smaller group would take him on to Canterbury and, finally, to the coast. Within days, Marc would be on a ship, crossing the Channel.

'I have just a few things to gather,' he said to Enguerrand, as they walked out of St Paul's and followed the procession back to the Savoy. 'In less than a fortnight, we'll be home.'

In France. Back at de Coucy's castle. And then…

'No, *mon ami*. We won't.'

'What do you mean? I thought all had been settled. Who must I speak to? Who is making the decision?'

'It has been made. Ten only will be allowed to return with the king. Those names have been chosen and yours—'

'Is not among them.' Disbelief first. Followed by rage. A lowly chevalier. Easy to leave behind. 'And yours?'

He shook his head. 'I will accompany the body only to the port. No further.'

'What?' He studied de Coucy's face, trying to make sense of it all. 'Why?'

'It was my choice. To stay here.' He smiled when he said it.

'The princess?' He could think of no other reason the man would stay.

'Shh!' De Coucy looked around, then lowered his voice. 'That, and other things. The king has given his permission, though we cannot speak of it yet. After the wedding, my lands are to be restored and I will be made an earl. The king has agreed, but no one else knows.'

So, it had come at last, everything his friend had wanted. Sharp envy gnawed. A woman he loved. Respect and land. Ah, de Coucy had, had always had, everything a man could desire in life, so much so that even with his property and land in France, he was content to stay a captive.

Marc was not. He must go home to... To what? France was a broken country, depleted and exhausted and led by an untried king he was not certain he could trust. And without his friend, life would be different. While he might still be a chevalier for the de Coucy family, he would be alone. And if war were to come again, would he and his friend now be on opposite sides?

But all that seemed better than what awaited him if he stayed in England, where he would have to stand by and see Cecily become the wife of another man. And that, despite all the battles he had faced, was the one thing he could not do.

It had become more important to leave England than to go home to France, even if he had nothing to return to. Once there, the memory of Cecily would fade. Surely.

A struggle, for months, but he had kept his

part of the bargain. Despite that, he had been abandoned.

And so the choice he had resisted became clear and inevitable.

He would have to escape.

Chapter Eighteen

In the blur of the gathering of a procession to accompany the king's body on the first stage of its journey home, Marc formulated a plan. He, too, would be bidding England *adieu*.

But first, he wanted to see Cecily.

It was the closest he had been to her in days, yet without having to discuss a plan, they slipped out of the hall and found a quiet alcove with a window that overlooked the Thames. Below them, the river flowed calmly and the sky reflected the golden light of the sunset.

He did not touch her. Any moment, someone could come by, they might be discovered. And yet for a moment, they simply drowned in each other's eyes. He must memorise them. Wide-set, green, tilted up and, tonight, unutterably sad.

'What is wrong?' Thinking, foolishly, that he might fix it.

She lifted her head, once again the countess. 'The king has chosen my husband.'

All this time, he had known this would come, and yet when it did the blow nearly felled him. 'Who?'

'Robert, The Earl of Dexter.'

He searched his mind, trying to place the man.

She shook her head. 'You have not seen him. He has been with the king's son in Ireland.'

'Do you know him?'

'He served with my father. I knew him and his wife.'

His wife. The man must be much older. 'It is better, then,' he said, forcing the words, 'that you will not have to marry a stranger.'

'Or a man I despise.'

'Like me?'

Together, they smiled.

Then, she sighed. 'I know my duty. But I understand now why I was always warned…what happens when feelings become…' She looked away. 'I tried. I tried so hard…'

And so had he. Futile. For both of them.

'If he is in Ireland, the wedding cannot be soon.' As if that might make a difference.

'He returns in weeks and the banns will be read as soon as he arrives.' She looked out of the window, towards the east and Dover. 'I wanted time to go home. I was ready to see the tomb was complete. To finish saying farewell.' Her eyes met his again. 'As you and I must do.'

How certain he had been, when he had whispered to her that he would be escorting King Jean's body home. 'Things…did not go as I expected. I was not chosen. To go home with the king.'

'So you will be in England until the ransom arrives?'

Did he hear the lilt of hope in her voice? Yet he shrugged, as if he would be going home. Some day.

She sighed, and shared a sad smile. 'You and I both—trapped by the schemes of kings.'

Trapped here. And worse torture than his confinement would be to know she was near, and belonged to another man, sharing his bed, night after night—

An idea flickered. 'Unless…'

There *was* a way that he might give her time and himself freedom.

'Cecily, you promised once to help me return to France. Will you still?'

'If I can.'

'What if you could go home to say goodbye? What if I could give that to you?'

'What? How?'

'We can escape together. I can take you hostage and take you home. Tonight.'

* * *

Cecily looked at Marc, waiting for the grip of shock or fear or horror.

Instead, a shiver of excitement rippled through her.

Yes.

She almost said the word aloud. 'But what will happen to you? The king will never let you go without payment of the ransom.'

'There is no ransom. There will be no ransom.'

'What?'

There was something in his expression, as if by telling her this, he had trusted her with a long-hidden, secret shame. 'I was to go home by Easter. Now that the king is dead, not one of my countrymen has any reason to hand over good gold coin to retrieve a simple chevalier.'

'But King Edward…' She had opened her mouth to argue that the king would not agree, but who knew what negotiations would transpire with the new king of France? And if he would not uphold the treaty honourably, the only way to enforce it would be by arms. To start the war anew. 'What about Lord de Coucy?' Had Isabella succeeded?

Hesitation. 'He will accompany the body only as far as the ship. I do not think he wants to leave.'

No. He did not want to leave. The impossible, it seemed, was about to happen. Isabella was going to be allowed to marry for love, a privilege denied the Countess of Losford.

The countess who was about to violate a direct order of the king.

'If I take you hostage,' he said, 'the blame will fall on me. And when the cortège reaches the coast, I will tell them they must let me on the ship or I will harm you. You'll have a few days, before they find us.'

She looked into his eyes again and nodded. 'Yes. Yes.' The man she had thought without honour had arranged all so she would not be dishonoured. 'A few days. That is all I need.'

He nodded. 'To say goodbye.'

And she did not ask whether he meant to her parents or to each other.

In the end, it proved not as difficult as Marc had feared.

King Jean's body was carried out of London that night, accompanied by a mass of mourners, including most of King Edward's court and every Frenchman in England.

Torches, thousands of them, lit the way as the procession passed through the streets of London and into the countryside like a moving creature of light.

At Dartford, before dawn, they paused. Most of the court was to turn back, leaving one of King Edward's trusted knights and Lord de Coucy in charge of the remainder of the journey. From here, they would go on to Canterbury and then Dover. A few selected chevaliers would accompany the body back to France while the rest, those who had been held in lieu of their sovereign, would be here still, their future as uncertain as his.

In the darkness and the confusion, no one was looking closely at Marc de Marcel.

Lady Cecily, on the other hand, was at the princess's right hand.

There had been little time to think. Their whispered plan could easily go awry in this small, dark town, where they were surrounded by hundreds of King Edward's men.

From the shadows, he watched as Cecily, head close to Isabella, waved in the direction of the inn. She needed to pause, to find a privy before they began the trip back to London.

He held his breath, hoping Isabella would not join her.

The princess yawned.

Do not wait for me. That was as she rehearsed it. *I will return with one of the other knights.*

She turned her horse towards the inn.

With a pang of regret, he looked back at En-

guerrand, who would be accompanying the body
of the king as far as the ship. After all the years
together, there would be no farewell. He would
not ask his friend to divide his loyalties. When
they discovered Marc was missing, Enguerrand
would not need to lie. He would know nothing.

He led his horse away, slowly, towards the inn,
and let him drink, along with the other mounts.

Marc gripped the reins, tightly. The waiting
was harder than battle.

The horse, sensing his tenseness, lifted his
head and pulled back. Marc forced his breath
back to an even count and stroked the horse's
neck.

'The horse is *fatigué, oui*?' said one of the
chevaliers who had come to England in January.

Marc, deliberately, yawned. 'It's been a long
night. I'll be glad to get back to London.'

'Though I wonder how long they will let us
stay at the Savoy, now that the king is gone.' He
crossed himself.

Marc shrugged. 'So we must enjoy the time
we have.'

Inconsequential words. Ones that implied he,
too, was looking forward to a soft bed beside the
Thames. Nothing must draw attention. He must
mingle with the others so that they had seen him,
would assume he was there, had ridden back to

London with the rest. Only later would someone notice he was gone.

He mounted and followed the group. The dirt muffled the horses' hoofbeats. The sky lightened behind him. Now was the time. Before it became full light.

He slowed the horse.

A side street. That had been the plan. In full faith that they would both find the same one. But it was dark. The town unfamiliar. And the arrival of hundreds of knights and nobles and the funeral cortège of a king had wakened the entire village. They clogged the roads and opened shutters, gawking.

He could only hope that amidst the multitude of men and horses, no one would notice them slip away.

One of the chevaliers glanced back. Marc raised a hand, then gestured at the horse's leg, as if he needed to remove a stone from its hoof, waving the man ahead, as if he would catch up.

He dismounted and lifted his horse's hoof. Then, as the others rode west, he walked the horse back to the inn and circled it, looking for her.

Around the back, in a little half-street that led nowhere, she was standing beside her horse, waiting.

He had not thought, fully, how much courage

it would take for her to do this. She was wearing what he had come to think of as her 'countess stance', but when she saw him, the relief, the joy on her face said that she had not been sure, quite, whether he would appear or whether she would be left alone in the dark in a strange town.

And though it was mad, in the soft dawn light, he pulled her to him, tightened his arms around her and took her lips with a kiss that was a promise.

Then they mounted and rode away, swinging clear of the road the king's body would travel on its way to Canterbury.

And late in the morning, they paused and looked around. The long, cold, endless winter that had kept the rivers frozen was over. Spring spread across the earth. Green leaves. Pink buds. Everything was fragile and fresh and new.

He felt a crazy sense of hope.

It was April and the sun was shining and they had escaped and for just a few days, who knew how few, he was free.

And they were together.

Chapter Nineteen

As the walls of Losford Castle came into view mid-morning a few days later, Cecily tried to be content.

I have come home, she thought, *to bury them at last.*

But the castle windows stared at Cecily like unblinking eyes, judging her story, knowing it to be an excuse.

You came not for duty, but because of your weakness for this man. You bring the enemy within our walls.

Marc rode beside her, showing no fear and no doubt, as if he had full faith that she would keep him safe here, just as he had done for her these few days on the road.

Because King Jean's procession continued to Canterbury by the main road, Marc and Cecily had swung to the south to avoid them, riding into the downs of Kent. Marc had stashed some extra food into his bag, but they had little else but a silent, shared desire to reach the coast as quickly as possible.

She had not kissed him again, yet she wondered, as the gates opened, whether the steward and the captain of the guard could see what shimmered between them.

If they did, they raised no questions.

Henry, the steward, stepped forward as Marc helped her dismount. 'Welcome home, my lady. We did not expect you.'

Long ago, as a child, she would have hugged him. Now, she gave a gracious, detached smile of recognition, as her mother would have done. 'There are things here I must do before...' *Before my marriage*, though she could not bring herself to say it. To admit that a husband had been chosen, to speak his name, would summon him before them all now. She was not ready for that. 'This is Chevalier Marc de Marcel.' Marc stood tall and close, as if ready to stand between her and any threat.

She said nothing more of who he was or why he had come. As countess, she could not be questioned. Yet as Marc and the steward exchanged words about the horses, she knew his accent must make them wonder.

As the mounts were led away, Henry's brow creased, puzzled. 'You brought nothing more?'

Unheard of, to travel without chest or trunk. 'Does my own home not offer all I need?'

He bowed. 'I will prepare rooms. And send for the mason so you can review his progress.'

In those few words were all the reasons why she had stayed away so long. The tomb where Peter the Mason had worked these last few months seemed to lie in wait, like a monster in a cave, waiting to pounce. She had just vowed to finish it, told herself she was ready, but now...

'No. I do not want to see him yet.'

The steward frowned. 'You do not want to look at his progress?'

Poor Henry. It was his duty to manage her affairs. He should not be punished for her fears. She swallowed and tried again. 'I am weary. Perhaps tomorrow.'

'You have spent a great sum on the work,' Marc whispered, as they followed the steward up the stairs. 'What if it is ill done?'

'If he has cut it wrong, it cannot be fixed.' This was said too sharply. She had told herself she was ready. For her marriage. To face the tomb. Was she so wrong? She sighed. 'I will look in time. First, I have more important things to do.'

He raised his brows. 'What?'

No. He did not believe her lie. 'I must tell the steward of the king's plans so that they can prepare for their new lord. Then, I must meet with the steward and the cook will want to talk about…' Something. Innumerable things she wanted to do before she could face their deaths again.

Just when your steps become more steady, you will trip over a stone in the path. That is when you must take another step.

Coming home was that stone.

'Cecily.'

She turned then, because in the simple syllables of her name he had expressed his total understanding of what she feared. All the courage, suddenly gone again.

What if it is ill done?

Then she would have proof beyond doubt that she had failed her last duty to her parents.

She shook her head. 'Not yet.' Then she lifted her skirt and climbed a safe few steps before him. 'Come. I want to show you.'

Pausing to give the steward instructions on the chambers and their meal, she climbed faster, Marc behind her, until she reached the top of the tower. Stepping on to the roof, she took a deep breath of air tinged with salt.

'Here,' she said, as Marc joined her. 'Look.' She flung her arms wide.

The sea stretched out before them, welcoming her back. To the left, the endless expanse of water. To the right, the sheltered harbour, where a French ship waited peacefully to take King Jean to his final rest. And with a breath of salt air and a view of the water, she was, finally, home.

How had she stayed away so long?

Did he see it as she did? His face showed none of the joy she felt. Instead, he studied the view as he might have a battlefield, then pointed beyond the harbour. In the distance, a ripple of low hills and cliffs formed a wall at the edge of the water. 'And that is France?'

'Yes.' In sight of that land, all her life, inside strong, square stone walls whose sole purpose was to defend against it.

'So close,' he murmured. 'When I came over, I did not realise…'

If it were earth, a man, or an army, could cross it in a day. But water was not so easy.

'What will you do?' The wind battled for her words. 'When you leave?'

His expression turned solemn. 'I will do my best never again to see the shores of England.'

A good reminder. He *would* leave. As soon as next week. And she would be left with the life she had always expected.

And her duty.

Cecily's arrival was unexpected and the staff did not have time to produce a proper meal, so, instead of sitting in an enormous, empty Hall, she and Marc ate cockles and pickled herring alone before the upstairs fire in the forechamber of her rooms.

And instead of having the eyes of the court, or her parents, watching her every move, there was only Marc.

She had expected him to admire the tapestries shielding the stone walls or comment on the size of the hearth, generous for a room so small. Instead, his eyes stayed warm on her.

'It is simpler than court,' he said.

'For now,' she said. It was a relief, in her chambers, to walk without shoes and to let her hair flow down her back without braids or circlets. Inappropriate, to appear so before him, but it seemed a small sin, compared to the rest.

He smiled. She smiled back, wordless, for a moment, content.

The very contentment was a threat.

You cannot become accustomed to him. You cannot get close again. Soon, he will be gone and you will have to explain that he had kept you hostage, forced you to remain silent. You must be able to face the Earl of Dexter without guilt.

She tried to remember what the earl looked like.

'We should plan.' She must keep looking towards the end. 'Isabella will have missed me by now.' Enguerrand, at least, would be riding on with the escort to Dover, unaware that Marc had disappeared. Yet.

'And when she tells the king?'

'He will think I disobeyed him and came home.'

'Will he come after you?'

'I don't know.' Eventually, though, she would have to face his anger. 'But King Jean's party will stop in Canterbury only a few days. Then they will be here, ready to sail, they will come to the castle and then…'

'And then I will show them my knife at your throat and tell them I will release you once I am on the ship. All the blame will be mine.'

'But what if, after that, they decide to punish you?'

'No Frenchman will fault me for wanting to go home.'

Simple. As long as no one looked too closely. 'Then we must act in such a manner that my people would believe such a story.' If they did not, if they accused her of helping a hostage escape, the penalty would be harsh. Even for a countess. 'Will Enguerrand believe you?'

'Even if he does not, he will understand.'

She nodded, hoping he was right. 'So we have a few days.'

Time. Stolen.

'I will stay until…'

Did she hear a touch of longing in his voice? 'Until…?'

Until they were discovered.

Until he left for France.

Until—

A servant knocked. Cecily sat stiff and silent, not looking at Marc, as the man took the food away, then rose and led Marc to the door, making it clear he was leaving her room.

But before he stepped into the corridor, he paused, his eyes on her, pleading. 'Cecily...'

She looked away, shook her head. All the sentences they never finished. The words they would never say. Pretending that to be in sight of each was enough.

'Sleep well,' she said, loud enough so that her voice would echo in the stairs.

He grabbed her hands. Startled, she leaned against him, hovering on the edge of surrender, but he did not kiss her.

'Cecily, there will be much work to do, to bring the castle to rights again.'

She blinked. His words were not what she had expected, but he spoke the truth. She could see already the benign neglect that surrounded her. Not wilful abuse, but after her parents' deaths, Cecily had fled, thinking she could manage her duties from afar. Instead, she had let them drift.

Now that she had returned, she could no longer act as a child, expecting home to be a place of play. Now she was the countess and the castle her responsibility, not her refuge. There were dozens of things to attend to. The kitchen, the tunnels to the sea, the garden, the armoury… She must have them in good order before her marriage, lest her new husband find her wanting.

'I know. But it is what I must do.' What she was born to do. And, finally, eager to do, though the task seemed monumental.

'While I am here, I can help.'

His offer lifted a burden. What could be done in days? More by two than by one. And if they asked, later, what he had been doing…?

She would think of something to say then. 'I would like that.'

'Tomorrow, then.' He nodded and went to his own room. She watched until he closed the door.

He never looked back.

The next morning, Cecily, or the countess, as Marc reminded himself, had meetings with the steward, so he explored the tower and the bailey alone.

Unaccustomed to the room, he had spent a restless night, knowing that just a few steps away, Cecily slept, her hair unbound…

He put the thought out of his mind. Her betrothed was on his way.

And after Marc had gone, her reputation would depend on making their pretence believable so she would claim, later, that he had forced her to come home with him so that he could escape. And that while they had been here, her safety had depended upon not exposing his plan. That meant they should not risk being seen as too friendly.

He vowed to keep himself busy.

So he prowled the castle, looking for things she would not notice, for weaknesses in defence so that he could warn her to set them to rights before the man who was to be her husband arrived. He would not let the man think ill of her, or find her wanting in her duties.

Grey stone walls dotted with towers protected the inner bailey. Strong, straight, square, yet each tower was different. From the land, as they had approached, it looked impregnable, though a small, isolated tower stood guard on the land side, outside the walls. In the other direction, on higher ground towards the sea, stood an older, smaller tower. A watch tower, he thought, perhaps originally with lights to guide friendly ships and guards to warn of an enemy approach. Here, stones had fallen, leaving its shape ragged, as if it were dissolving, slowly. No longer straight and proud, it seemed to lean against the building next to it.

A church.

No mass was in process, so he stepped inside. It was empty except for a small man, smoothing a red-and-gold cloth over a raised stone base.

The tomb.

The man looked up, expectant, but his face fell when he saw only Marc. 'The Lady Cecily. She is not with you?'

Marc's steps echoed as he walked down the aisle. *Not yet*, she had said. The sculptor would wait in vain another day. 'No. Is the work complete?'

The man shook his head. 'It waits only her blessing. I simply look at it each day and polish a portion sometimes.' He touched the stone base with a hand too large for such a small man. 'Do you want to see it?' He reached for the cloth, eager for someone to witness his work.

Without thinking, Marc stayed the man's hand. It seemed wrong, to view it before Cecily did. 'She must be the judge. I did not know the man or his wife.'

'That is not always necessary,' the man said 'to create a likeness.'

A truth. In death, men became idealised versions of themselves, in stories no less than in stone, by those who knew them, as well as by those who didn't. Already, his dead king had been spoken of with reverence befitting a saint. 'You have spent a long time on these.'

The mason shook his head. 'Lady Cecily's mother was confounded when her husband died. Decisions, arrangements all took time. Yet I was near finished with the earl's figure and then she, too, was lost and the Lady Cecily…' He sighed, leaving much unsaid. 'When the king sent a call for stone carvers for Windsor, I was glad of the opportunity.' A proud smile touched his lips. 'You have seen it? Windsor?'

'You did fine work. You and all the others.' Easy now, to acknowledge that the English king had created a beautiful palace. 'And with their likenesses as well, I am sure.'

A smile, but then, he looked back at the tomb with a sigh. 'She must be the judge and she will not even look.'

So the man knew, just as Marc did. 'It has not been easy for her. To approve the work would mean—'

'That they were truly gone.'

'Yes.' And that she was the countess in truth. 'How long ago did you start?'

A crinkle in his forehead. 'Two years? Three? I am ready to go home.'

Poor man. He, too, was a sort of hostage. 'I cannot promise to persuade her, but I will try.'

Perhaps it was the most important thing he could do. Not to prepare the walls of the castle, but to prepare *her* for what was to come.

They had finished supper before Marc raised the subject.

Their first evening meal in her rooms had been a respite after the weeks at court. To have escaped, to be able to look at each other without other eyes on them, had been sweet relief.

Tonight, he was no longer at ease. To be alone together was seductive. Last night, they had resisted. But what about tonight? And tomorrow?

She seemed to have recognised the danger as well. Tonight, her braids still firmly framed her face. A veil, held in place by a circlet, cascaded behind her as her hair had done last night.

Tonight, she was no longer Cecily. She was the countess.

So he listened, silent, as she spoke of her meetings with the steward and the cook. Stories that did not ask for answers. And her eyes, too, cast down at her food, instead of at him.

When the food was taken away and they were alone again, the silence grew long. Awkward.

'We will take our meals in the Hall tomorrow,' Cecily said. A pronouncement, as a countess might make, then rose, as if to dismiss him.

He had waited, all through the meal, not certain how to begin. Every phrase that teased his tongue sounded ill formed. Now, he must speak, despite that. 'I saw the mason.'

She became still. 'Oh?'

No more hint than that. He wished for de Coucy's gentle tongue, but he was a warrior, and knew only that he must advance. 'You must approve his work. And let him go home.'

Only yesterday, she had refused, so he braced himself for her anger. Or tears.

But that was not what came next.

'But I am not...' Grief, still echoing in her voice, she looked away. 'I have not...'

A pause. And he waited, silent.

Then, she turned on him. 'Look at me. Here. Now. Alone with you. I have brought the enemy inside the very castle France must never take. I have violated all their training, all their trust. And their tomb... What if it is ill done because of me? How can I face them again?'

Them. As if the stone would come to life and point accusing fingers.

She did not speak to him. Her words, he thought, were more of a prayer to the dead. For their blessing. For their forgiveness.

Accustomed to war, Marc had not been a man attuned to motives or subtleties. He had not searched for things beneath the surface. Perhaps that was why he had not seen his king's weakness, nor his lover's deception.

But with Cecily, somehow, he *knew*, as clearly as if he could see inside her soul.

'They cannot have expected you to know how to do everything the right way. Not from the beginning,' he said, softly.

'You do not understand.' Now, her straight

back, her lifted chin, trembling. 'I am the Countess of Losford.'

As if the title was a suit of armour that did not fit. And hiding behind it, a child who had been cared for by parents so loving, so demanding, that they had not permitted her to stumble and fall. Had never allowed her to make a mistake and recover, learning in the process that she could. So that now, she believed in duty, in Losford, but not in herself.

He came closer and took her hands. 'Even God does not expect us to be perfect.'

'My parents did. And I failed them.' Nothing but a whisper now. More to herself than to him. She drew her hands from his and went to the window, staring out at angry, red clouds that signalled the day's end.

Nothing he had said had helped her. Why had he thought it would? He only knew one way to comfort and that was to stand between her and danger. To say *I will protect you.* But her family had done the same and it had left her weak instead of strong.

But he had seen her strength. Strength she, and perhaps even her parents, had never believed.

'You did not have to be perfect,' he began, 'to save me from a wild boar.'

A catch in her breath, as if he had taken her by surprise. And though he could not see her face, her shoulders relaxed. A smile, then, as she looked over her shoulder. 'I violated all the rules of the hunt.'

'The boar was just as dead. And I, just as alive.' He took a step closer. 'That is the woman I know. That woman can do anything.'

She turned back to face him. 'Do you believe so strongly?'

Her expression was hard to translate. Had his assurance helped? Was she perplexed?

'In you?' He took her in his arms, pulled her close, and she let him. *'Oui.'*

Her smile… He had never seen her smile that way and he could not believe that something he had said, simple words, had made such a difference. A triumph greater than victory in battle.

And then he kissed her. Not thinking. Not wanting to think. Thinking would only remind him of the future.

Her lips on his were soft, eager. And he wanted more. *Mon Dieu*, he wanted more.

'Cecily,' he said, when he could grasp a breath again. 'We have this night. Perhaps a few more. Do you… Will you…?' He was a man of deeds, not words. But when he looked at her, all he wanted must have shone in his eyes as he waited for her answer.

Chapter Twenty

Yes.

Cecily kissed him, without thought or plan, yet knowing, this, and all that would follow, was what she had wanted for longer than she had been willing to admit.

She had guarded her feelings as Losford guarded the sea, as if she were only a countess and not a woman at all. Feelings had no place where duty must rule.

Yet so certain this man was the enemy, she had allowed her hate to flow without a fence, not noticing until too late that the hate had become its opposite.

Now, it was too late to hold back, too late to pretend. She loved him and he was going to leave.

'I wanted to hate you,' she said, when the kiss was broken.

'Why?' His question, simple.

'So I wouldn't be hurt.' So foolish, when said aloud.

Puzzled, at first. 'I would never hurt you. How could I?'

And in the way he understood it, he wouldn't. But he was a soldier, thinking only of swords and arrows. The wounds she feared were those you could not see. 'Because you must leave.'

And at her words, something invisible, more than his flesh, touched her, as if to protest, to say no, he would not let her go.

She shook her head. She must speak clearly. No more disguises. 'Yes,' she said. 'You must. The time will come, the boat will be ready and you will shove off from the shore and I'll never see you again and I'll never know whether you touched the shores of home or perished beneath the waves, but either way, you'll be gone for ever, and I'll hurt for the rest of my days because I must stay…here.'

Here. As much a part of the castle as its stones and tunnels. She laughed, without mirth, at the thought.

He shook his head, confusion on his brow. *'Ce n'est pas amusant.'*

'No. Because I knew my duty would be to marry and there was no room for feelings that might interfere. But then, I spent time with you. A man I knew I could never love, like, or even tolerate. A man I was certain would never threaten my isolation. A man I knew I would part from without a twinge of sadness.

'And that, you see, is what is funny. Because I tried to avoid caring for anyone I would lose and ended up caring for you.'

'I am here now,' he said. 'And we can create memories instead of regrets. But I must be certain that you want it as well.'

What he suggested was madness. What if there was a child? But her marriage was close, close enough for there to be confusion. And she thought again of the moment she had envied Isabella for having taken Enguerrand to her bed. Her regrets would be deeper if she refused this chance.

Perhaps he had taught her the courage she needed to say yes, even knowing all the pain that would come after. 'And later? Will I be worth missing?'

He winced, as if she had struck a blow. Did he not think she would remember his words about the miller's daughter? And yet he had, finally, forgotten that woman.

Because of this one.

'I will be missing you as I take my last breath.'

They stumbled towards the bed and Marc searched for a way in. A woman's clothes, as impenetrable as armour. Outer garments cut away to show a gown beneath, but no way to reach the gown and her skin. Even her hair, tight in braids, the fashion.

He paused, frustrated. 'What happened to dresses simple as a sack?'

Although she breathed heavily, still, there was a smile. She looked over her shoulder. 'You must play handmaiden. It is not easy to get in and out.'

'Tell me how,' he said, as determined as if the enemy's hill stood before him, ready to be conquered.

And so she tried. Showing him the buttons. Untying the hose. All the elaborateness forcing him to hold back, to restrain himself from ripping it all away to reveal the body he had dreamed of.

But then, he discovered the delight of slow discovery. And while he traced the curve of her bare calf, his anticipation built. And while he let his fingers stroke the bare skin of her neck, shoulder, back, he watched her, tangled in the tippets of her sleeve, becoming as impatient as he.

Finally, she stood before him, one dark braid fallen from her head and lying across her pale shoulder. Speechless, he savoured the sight of her: dark hair, pale shoulders and then the curves below the waist, where the hip flared. Curves suggested, exaggerated by the clothes, but more beautiful, more vulnerable, without the cloth covering.

He still sat on the bed and she stood naked before him, all the hurry slowed. He was still eager, yes, but this sight, this moment, was one to savour.

He had imagined her like this. But imagination was a poor thing compared to what was before him. He had seen her in his dreams, but dreams did not carry the drift of the scent that was Cecily, the sweetness of wild flowers and the tang of the sea that permeated the very air of this place.

Nor had he heard her breath, moving faster, even, than in the dance. And now, as she watched him watch her, the catch of a moan, deep in her throat. A sound that said *I want you* more clearly than words.

And then he touched her.

Cecily felt his touch, more gentle than she had expected from a warrior. And Cecily came to the bed, to lie beneath him and surrender. To him. To desire. And to the truth.

The truth that was she had lied. To him, but mostly, to herself. Pretended hate, then indifference.

And now, she told herself one final lie.

That she would be able to let him go.

But that was not tonight. Tonight, the fullness of him was enough. Of him, filling her arms. Of his tongue, filling her mouth. And, finally, of him between her legs, filling her. Filling all the empty places in her heart.

And if in the incoherent murmurs that lovers make, she nearly said *I love you*, yet carefully, holding that last shield against hurt, she did not.

But somewhere in the rush of words, lips, touches, fingers, some time as she drifted into sleep, safe in his arms, a few words echoed in her dream.

Je t'adore. Toujours.

Cecily rose the next morning, the scent of him still on her skin, and slipped away, thinking he would sleep still, wanting to watch the sun rise and the world turn new again.

As many times as she had done so, this morning, the world really did look new. She had made love with a Frenchman.

No.

She had made love with Marc de Marcel.

She was the one made new this morning. The golden light washed her skin, just as his touch had done. She had battled her weakness for months, fearing that to succumb to her feelings, to him, would be to abandon everything her parents had expected of her. Instead, this morning, she looked out on a Channel clear and calm, free of fog or wind, and with as perfect a sunrise as she had ever seen.

She heard steps behind her and then, he was by her side, yawning. She looked up and smiled. He was not a man who loved the morning. 'I did not think you would wake.'

'You boasted of the sunrise. I thought I should see it.'

Was he, too, a new man, to be rising voluntarily before the sun?

And yet, she could not ask. Everything between them was as delicate as the wash of gold and grey spread across the sky. It would last no more than a breath. Could not be captured, held, or kept from shifting imperceptibly into something else.

So they watched, silent, as the sun lifted itself out of the water and the golden light faded into pale yellow and blue.

'I think the time has come,' he said, when the day had fully arrived, 'for you to see the tomb.'

Tomb. The very word chilled her. She had learned to breathe without tears. To live. Even to love. Had she the courage to confront the inescapable fact of her parents' death? Would she be drawn back to the dark despair and doubt that had held her these past few years? Or would she look, clear-eyed, on the motionless stone out-

lines of their bodies as if she looked at no more
than a rock?

And which would be worse?

Marc's fingers touched her arm. 'I will stand
beside you.'

Simple words that brought quick tears. When
had she been able to lean on anyone at all?

She slipped her hand into his. 'Come. Let us
see the mason's work.'

Cecily sent word that she would come so that
the cloth could be raised and the tomb prepared
for viewing, yet when she entered the church,
she shut her eyes as she took a step.

And stumbled. But Marc's arm was there, at
her waist, not letting her fall. She opened her
eyes and met his.

I will stand beside you.

At the end of the aisle, the square stone block
loomed larger with every step. Beside it, the
short, balding sculptor, stood beside his work,
awaiting her judgement.

When she reached him, unable to speak, she
nodded, then forced herself to look at the effigies.

Images of her parents lay side by side, as stiff
as the stone they were carved from, her father in
his armour, her mother on his other side, hard to
see. A sword, ready, was at his side and a stone

pillow cushioned his head, as if the sculptor had cared for his comfort.

Cecily stepped closer, softly, as if afraid to wake them, as if they might rise from the dead, only to look down on her in disappointment.

The sculptor had carved each individual link of chainmail so that it flowed from her father's helmet, covering his chin and hugging his neck. She stretched out her hand and stroked the alabaster with trembling fingers, surprised to find the stone warmer than she expected.

'It is beautiful work,' she whispered. 'This surpasses anything I could have expected.'

Behind her, he murmured thanks.

But her mother had approved the design for her father's figure. Cecily was the one who had fled her duty. If her mother was portrayed poorly, the blame would be hers.

Barely breathing, she raised her eyes to look.

Here it all was, headdress and gown created in the same, loving detail as the armour. Buttons on the sleeve, stitches down the front. Small flowers carved on the girdle.

And her mother's hand rested gently in her father's, as if even in death, they must be touching each other.

She raised her eyes to the sculptor, speechless.

'You said do what you will, my lady,' he said,

quickly, as if uncertain of her approval. 'And she had looked at this one more than once.'

Silent, she struggled to speak. Duty. Obligation. She had never thought of her parents' marriage as more than that and had never allowed herself to imagine more than that for her own.

But here, this said more loudly than words that duty need not live without love. Could she hope, even expect, such a thing for herself?

And if it came, had she courage enough to grasp it?

'I hope you are content, my lady,'

She nodded, the tears clogging her throat. 'Oh, yes. Yes.' She tried to clear her choked voice. 'You have done work as fine for me as for the king. You may return home with pride.'

'If you want me to work more on her hair I can—'

'C'est tout.' Marc's voice behind her, clearly one of dismissal. 'The countess would like to be alone.'

A murmured farewell, footsteps fading, and the closing of a door.

'Is it so like them?' Marc's voice, as soft as hers had been, but still echoing on the stone.

'Not at all.' The man's face was narrow as all men's were depicted now. Her mother's nose too sharp. Yet that did not matter. 'But this.' She reached across the stone figures to touch the place their hands joined and near burst with smiling.

Then, she turned back to him, barely able to see his face, yet glad to have a witness. 'I had forgotten and he let me see.'

Forgotten. Or perhaps, had never known. For before Marc, she had not understood what another person could be for you. How he could stay beside you, inside you, around you, a constant source of strength you did not know you had.

That was what Marc had given her. And now, she did not know how she would live without it.

Marc watched as Cecily's smiles and tears warred, uncertain what to do. Did she need comfort? Should he reach out to her? Yet she smiled.

He let me see.

'What do you see?'

'Love. I can see their love.' Her face, now radiant, as if she had been touched by it, too. 'When Mother rode to the hunt again, I thought duty had replaced her grief. Now I think...' She looked back at the clasped hands. 'Maybe she just wanted to be with him.'

La faiblesse de la femme. A woman's weakness, something no warrior would know. Certainly when it was time to leave Cecily he would be able to do so, without regret, without—

Too late to pretend his heart was walled from

siege. When he had to leave her, his heart might break as her mother's had.

The church door rattled and they both turned to look. 'My lady.' Henry, the steward, hurried down the aisle. 'The king's representative and Lord de Coucy are here.' He glanced at Marc, as if he would know why. 'They seek food for the horses and some other supplies before boarding the ship to take the body of the king back to France. They sail on the morning tide.'

I will show them my knife at your throat and tell them I will release you once I am on the ship.

And yet, he did not move.

Cecily's eyes met his and they looked at each other for a long, slow moment. Then, she turned to stroke the stone one final time. Finally, she faced the steward, back straight, chin up, in the pose he had seen a hundred times. But this time, she did not don it as a brittle disguise. This time, it seemed, she had truly, finally, become the countess and duty was as much a part of her as her spine-bone.

'Provide them with what they need,' she said. 'But do not tell them that either de Marcel or I am here. Is that clear?'

Henry, brow furrowed, looked from one to the other, then nodded and left the church.

Cecily, straight and silent, started down the aisle. Marc did not know what she was thinking, but he followed her, without questions, out of the church, towards the cliffs and the sea. They left the castle through a little-used gate on the water side and took a path he had not seen before, up the coast, away from the harbour where the ship awaited, until they were atop the cliffs that stretched along the sea.

He had seen them from the ship before he arrived, a white wall of stone, protecting the island. The beach, far below, was too small for a boat to land. The cliffs impossible to scale. So the land protected itself, even before a castle was built.

But this day looked all of peace. Clear sky. Sharp wind. Red poppies scattered the grass, while butterflies, scraps of white or orange, struggled against the breeze.

The path was narrow, precarious in some places, so he let her lead until they were well away from the protection of the walls. Finally, she stopped and turned to gaze towards the castle. The harbour and the ship were barely visible, but beyond, Calais beckoned, a thin stripe atop the waters of the Channel. At the edge of this wild cliff, beyond the reach of eyes and ears, they were, truly, alone.

She gazed out over the water while the wind whipped several strands of hair free from her braid. 'I used to come here as a child,' she began. 'When I wanted to escape.'

He knew now what she had longed to leave. Expectations, as rigid in their own way as his warrior's code. Hovering, looming, as the castle behind them did, high and alone above the town and the sea. Her parents'? Her own? It didn't matter. They had lain in wait and now she must face them.

He took her hand, waiting for her to speak.

'I am ready,' she said, finally. 'Ready to let my parents rest. Ready to be the Countess of Losford, to do my duty. Ready for almost all things…'

For your husband? The very thought, as painful as a blade's thrust. So he waited for her to go on.

She brought her gaze to him. 'But I am not ready to say goodbye.'

His hand touched her hair and smoothed an errant strand from her forehead. What an *imbécile* he had been, thinking he could hold her close and keep his feelings safely walled away. Every castle could be taken. Every wall had a weakness, usually one the commander had overlooked.

Behind him, out of sight, was a ship in the harbour that could take him home. All he had to do was what they had planned. The choice was his.

'I will find another way home.' And he opened his arms to enfold her.

He kissed her, the wind at his back, holding

her so close that the air treated them as one. Together, they stumbled away from the path, away
from the edge of the cliffs, and sank into the
grass.

Kisses, nothing but kisses everywhere lips
could touch. Fast. Unceasing. As if they both
knew, finally, goodbye was inescapable and
close. Too close.

And yet, as they made love, time slowed. Did
the sun travel through the sky? Did noon pass?
Did night fall? He did not notice. Finally, he was
no longer a warrior, coiled for battle and she, no
longer a countess. Only Marc and Cecily.

And when the loving was over, he put his arms
around her. Held her against him because he did
not know what else to do. As long as she was in
his arms, as long as he held her tight and close,
he did not have to meet her eyes.

I will find another way, he had said, pushing
the inevitable into tomorrow or the day after or
the month to come. Yet that did not change one
thing.

There would still be a goodbye.

Chapter Twenty-One

A nd so the king's men received what they needed and left the castle without glimpse or word of Cecily and Marc. The ship sailed for France; de Coucy returned to London, and if Marc thought of either of them again, he did not tell her.

And Cecily began her work as if she had awakened from a long sleep.

She knew, had always known, who she would be and what she must do, but she had always thought she had time and that her parents would be there, to teach her. When she lost them, all she had not learned, all she was not ready to do, had haunted her. And so she had stayed away, blaming grief when it was really fear, foolishly thinking that her parents would rise up and call her not worthy of the title they had left her.

But now, somehow, she felt whole. As if she

had discovered, in these months with Marc, that she was more than just her title. And then, to see that there had been more than duty between her parents. And her mother had chosen to show that for the ages. It gave Cecily faith.

But it did not give her answers.

Still, for now, the castle was *hers* and all the duties she had avoided suddenly seemed urgent, as if they must somehow be complete before her husband arrived.

And before Marc left.

With a sense of wonder, Marc watched Cecily plunge into her duties with a joy he had never seen in her before. Busy, tireless, yet smiling. More, she leaned on him, asked his advice, shared her burdens and accepted his help, as if her love for him had freed her from the past.

So he worked beside her to ready the castle for its new lord, one day and then the next. And as he made the castle better, he forgot to think of it as hers alone and cared for it as if it were his.

What had he ever had that was his? His life beside Enguerrand had been lived in the de Coucy stronghold. Impressive, impregnable. But never, never his. Now, as he helped her build, he thought of the king and Windsor, of a building that would last the ages, that would never be taken.

That would protect her as he would do.

And so one day became the next.

Tomorrow he would prepare a boat. Tomorrow he would lay in supplies to cross the waters for home. Today, he would help her inspect the west wall and the armoury.

And all the while, ignoring that he must leave.

And so they worked, as if each day were their last together, and when the day's duty was done, they found solace in each other. Gradually, the nights became even more important than the days, the nights where he could lie next to her and make love to her and pretend there was nothing in the world beyond the bed in which they lay.

And each morning, he rose early and left her, so the servants would not see. So that later, after he was gone, she could pretend that she had let him stay only because he had threatened her life.

Awake before the gates were opened, he would go to the top of the tower to look out on the scene she had shown him. Some days, fog obscured all—harbour, sea, sky—so he could not even see the ground from the top of the tower. Impossible, on these days, if you walked the cliffs, to know how close you might be to the dangerous edge. Impossible to see an enemy approach, by land or sea.

Impossible to know what lay ahead.

Other days, he saw the promise of light on the horizon, then watched the sun emerge from the sea. On those days, it seemed as if the end of the earth itself was in sight, as sharp and final as the edge of the white cliffs that dropped sharply from land to sea.

When it was that clear, he could turn in the direction of home, close enough that he could see it, reminding himself that he must leave and return to…what?

Ten days later, early in May, a new foal died, the cook burned her hand and Cecily lost her temper with the laundress. She curled up next to Marc that night, near to tears.

'I will never learn all I must. How did my mother do it so easily?'

He hugged her to him. 'By crawling into bed with her husband and moaning of the ills of her day.'

She blinked. She had never thought of her parents…that way. But now, it seemed something she could believe. Even accept.

'Besides,' he continued, 'you did not know your parents when they were young and untried. No knight rides perfectly the first time.'

She sat up, with a sigh, feeling comforted and a bit foolish. 'A countess has much to learn.'

'So does a knight. It takes time. Years.'

'But you learned.'

He shrugged, an attempt to be modest, yet she caught a glimpse of pride in his smile. 'Well enough to teach others.'

'Lord de Coucy?'

'And more. I gave Gilbert better practices than the pell stake at Westminster.'

'Gilbert?' A good man, she had called Marc. Better than she knew. 'And did he improve?' Poor Gilbert. If her father had lived, he could have given Gilbert those final years of training he needed.

Marc grinned. 'One day, he may unhorse me.'

'Today, I feel as if I have been unhorsed.'

He cupped her cheek in his hand. 'Give yourself time.'

And yet, as they drifted to sleep, she knew time with Marc was the one thing she did not have. Soon, he would be gone and she would be wed and eventually, she would teach a daughter, or a son, to be the new ruler of Losford.

Suddenly, that possibility, which had once seemed as distant as her parents' deaths, was near upon her. And instead of thinking of the man the king had chosen, she dreamed of a son with the golden hair and light-brown eyes and broad shoulders of Marc de Marcel.

* * *

As the days went on, Marc thought less of France, shimmering on the distant horizon, and more of Losford and the ground beneath his feet.

The truth was there was little to take him home now. France was a broken country. The coffers were bare. Why was he going back? What had he left behind that was so important? What would greet him when he returned? More battles? There was peace with England, yes, but there was another Crusade being planned. They would need fighting men.

Yet he wondered now, what all the fighting, all the battles had been about. A country? A king?

With the war over, what was there for him to do in France except join one of the companies of knights who ravaged the countryside? Or perhaps he could be a Templar and dedicate his sword to God.

But suddenly, as he looked to what he thought was home, that seemed…not enough. He wanted a place, a person, a home of his own, a family worth fighting for. The rest now seemed to be nothing but empty words and fluttering banners, as hollow as the promises of chivalry.

He himself had not been a chevalier *parfait* and *gentil*. Yet when he had once thought he owed nothing to a code that had forsaken him, to leave now, to dishonour his promise to his king and hers, seemed wrong. It would make him no better a man than all those who had broken their vows while he watched, doing nothing. And he wanted to be better than that. Now.

So as he watched the coming dawn day after day, he realised, gradually, that he must stay.

Oh, he would not have Cecily, no. That could never be. But to leave, to escape, seemed now as if it would dishonour not only himself and his king. It would dishonour her. If his love for her had meaning, then his vows, the promises he had made on the honour of chivalry, must as well.

Otherwise, she could think that this time together meant nothing. Had been no more than flesh meeting flesh.

He did not know how to explain it to her. He was a man of swords and shields, not words. The deed would have to speak for itself. But as he saw the sun appear on the horizon one morning, he knew he had made up his mind.

He would surrender to the king.

A few days later, Cecily woke to a pounding on her door.

She opened her eyes, blinking. Was it still dark?

Next to her, Marc, accustomed to the sudden changes of war, was already out of bed and half-dressed, but there could be no pretence about where he had slept. She pointed under the bed, hoping he would hide, but he had already picked up his sword.

An intrusion at this hour could not be good news.

'My lady. Are you awake?'

She held the sheet to her shoulders, looking frantically for her discarded dress, then called for the steward to enter. She and Marc had been less careful than they should have been and it was too late to fool the servants now.

Henry barely glanced at Marc. 'Sir Gilbert is here, my lady. With a message from the king.'

He had sent for her. She had not expected that. 'The earl has returned from Ireland, then?' To find her in bed with another man?

He shook his head. 'Not yet, my lady.'

She near swooned with relief.

But the man looked at Marc. 'The king is coming for him.'

This, she had not expected. If he had come all this way, the king was angry. There would be no comfortable quarters for a hostage who had tried to escape. There would be prison. Or worse. 'How did he know? How did he know you were here?'

Marc's face looked as it did, she imagined, right before he rode into battle. With death stamped on it. 'Enguerrand. When he found me gone…' A shrug. *'Tout compris.'*

'But even if he did, why would he tell the king?'

'Because of her.'

Isabella. An intimate conversation between them. Whispered speculation. Their loyalty was to each other now. And strangely, she could see how that might be.

The steward interrupted. 'He says, my lady, that the king will be here before we break our fast.'

So she gave the steward hurried instructions and sent him away to tell Gilbert she was on her way.

She had known this moment would come. Had known that she would lose him. Yet every day, she told herself just one more day and she would be ready.

What a fool she had been.

She threw back the covers and swung out of bed, searching for clothes, a comb, a mirror and some sense of the situation.

'You must go,' she said. 'I will tell Gilbert you are coming and then act surprised when you do not. There is a small boat.' One they used occasionally for fishing. 'Take it.' She looked outside, trying to assess the weather. Fog, but a light one. She could only pray the sun would melt it. 'Henry will bring food and water and meet you down on the beach. My people can be trusted. I will keep Gilbert busy. I'll give you time—'

'Cecily.'

His voice commanded her to look. And yet, she could scarcely bear it, to see his face, to know it would be the last time. She had always thought there would be one more time, one more day. And now, there was not even time for a kiss. 'You must hurry.'

'I'm not going.'

'What?'

'I'm not going.' The blackness on his face again. 'I am going to surrender.'

She heard the words, but could not believe she understood. 'But he will lock you away.' *There will be no ransom.* The French would leave him here to grow old, knowing no help would come, until he became a burden on his gaoler and it would be more convenient to have him dead than alive. And all because she had been so greedy as to want a few more days. 'You escaped. This time there will be no parties, no court celebrations.'

A small smile, for he had never been comfortable with the court. 'Then that is as it must be.'

'But why?'

Something in his face, determined, prepared, and yet, at peace. 'I was a hostage. I escaped. I violated my honour. I must make that right.'

'As your king did.'

He nodded.

No, that had not been the plan, but nothing between them had been what they planned.

'Without you,' he said, 'my honour is the only thing left to me.'

She threw herself into his arms then, not wanting to let him go to the sea or to the king. Thinking to hold him, to keep him, to keep this, just a few more moments...

But he was the strong one. He put her away from him, lifted her chin, and kissed her, not with the passion of their nights, but softly and gently and with the finality of farewell. *'Adieu.'*

'No.' She stood, fully a countess now. If he had grown into his honour, she had grown into her strength. 'Please. Give me time. There must be something. There must be another way.'

All she had to do was to think of it.

Letting Cecily think he was heading for a hiding place, Marc dressed and went down to the Hall, hoping for a moment alone with Gilbert before the king arrived.

He would surrender to the young knight, recompense for the wrong he had done months ago. And before he did, he would make certain that the story was firmly planted. He had forced Cecily to bring him here. She was blameless.

Gilbert would believe it. Or pretend he did.

As he entered the Hall, the young man speared him with a glance. 'Where is she? What have you done to her?' The belligerent set of his jaw said he was prepared to ride against Marc all over again.

If so, this time, Marc had no doubt, the boy would cling to his mount for more than one pass.

'I did nothing to harm her.' At once a lie and a truth. 'But I forced her to bring me here and shelter me.'

'Why?'

'So that I could go home.'

Confusion covered his face. 'And yet, you are here.'

'I surrender to you, and to the king, where I will stay until the ransom is paid.'

'And if it isn't?'

He shrugged. 'Then I will die in *Angleterre*.' He wondered how long it would be before he longed for that end.

'For the sake of honour?' As if even an untried knight could not believe the folly of it.

Honour. He had searched for its meaning in kings and in codes, disappointed time after time. Finally, he had found the only meaning of the word that mattered.

'To honour her.'

Some mixture of admiration, resentment, con-

fusion and understanding touched the young
man's face. He would learn some day. Marc
hoped the lesson would be less painful than his
own.

'And does she agree? Is she honoured?'

He smiled, quick and sad. They both cared for
Cecily. Marc hoped she would understand, some
day, what he had done. 'I would not presume to
speak for the countess,' he said, 'but I would ask
you to take me to the king before she appears.'

'You ask too much, Marc de Marcel. And too
late.'

Cecily looked from one guilty face to the
other, uncertain whether passion or fury drove
her. 'You did not wait.'

Yet Marc had not obeyed a king. Why had she
expected him to obey a countess?

Gilbert stepped to her side. 'Did he harm you
when he forced you to bring him here?'

Ah, so Marc had wanted to make sure he told
the story. That she was protected. Well, now, it
would be her turn. 'Is that what he said? The
truth is quite the opposite. I was the one who
compelled him to bring me home.'

Gilbert looked from one to the other, clearly
confused. 'I would have come with you.'

She shook her head. 'The king had ordered

me to stay at court. I could not ask you, or any king's man, to flout him.'

Marc frowned, his expression black with fear for her.

She smiled. *Trust me.* Did he hear her thought?

Beside her, Gilbert still wrestled with his understanding. 'Why was it so important for you to come?'

'There were things I needed to do before my... marriage.' Marriage. A word now near impossible to say. Impossible to imagine surrendering herself to the earl when she belonged to Marc.

'That work,' Marc said, in a voice as gentle as he had used when they were alone, 'is now at an end.' Words that carried the ring of finality.

No. What had ended was any possibility that she could pretend to be another man's wife. She might be ready to be the countess, but she would never be ready to let Marc go.

'And,' Marc continued, speaking to Gilbert, but looking at her, 'when the king arrives, I will surrender myself to be held again.'

'No,' she said. 'I won't allow—'

'My lady!' The steward's voice cut through her words. 'The king!'

Chapter Twenty-Two

Marc watched Cecily turn to face King Edward with the familiar lift of her head and set of her spine he had come to know.

His shoulders squared, matching hers.

The end had come. The king might have admired his skill with a spear, but would mete out no gentler punishment as a result.

He was prepared, as long as Cecily was safe.

The recitation of the king's titles was not complete before the man stormed into the Hall, leaving his men trailing, and stood towering over Cecily.

'Are you unharmed?'

The question more of a loving uncle than an angry sovereign. Marc let go a breath

She smiled and dipped a shallow courtesy. 'Welcome to Losford, Your Grace. I am well and I hope you are the same.' She raised her hand to the steward, just running in from the corridor.

'Henry, please see that the king's men have bread and cheese and ale. I'm certain they are hungry. And then bring some for us. And, Gilbert, please join them to break your fast.'

As the men were shepherded away and Marc and Cecily were left alone with him, the king shook his head, hands on his hips, still looking at her. In the pause, Marc stepped forward, then dropped to one knee before the king. 'I surrender, Your Grace. I am once again your hostage.'

'No!' Cecily reached for him, but he could not look at her, though her hands were on his shoulders, as if willing him to rise.

'And if you rule death as the punishment for my escape, I am prepared.'

The king narrowed his eyes, now fully attending Marc instead of Cecily. 'Why should I kill you and forfeit your ransom?'

Now he must speak truth. 'Under the new king, Your Grace, I do not expect a ransom will come.'

He met the man's eyes and saw understanding. Marc had said aloud what the king must have known, but not admitted. Not only was Marc's ransom at risk. The new king had little reason to hand over good gold coin when he already possessed the king's corpse.

'We speak of honour, of chivalry,' the king said, as if to himself, 'and yet—'

'This man's ransom will be paid,' Cecily said. 'I will pay it.'

Marc was uncertain which face held more shock—his or the king's.

'No!' He stood to protest. 'I won't allow—'

But she pulled him to his feet and laced her fingers in his, not bothering to hide their joined hands. 'And, Your Grace, there is something else you must know. I desire to wed him.'

Had she said it? Did she mean to defy the king? And yet he recognised that slant of her jaw that meant her mind was set. And amidst the certainty that the king would surely strike him dead, he could feel only joy.

The king, at first as stone silent as Marc, now raised his hands…

Marc moved to block a blow. 'You will not harm her.'

'Harm her?' The king's howl was proof she had stirred the royal temper. He flung his arms towards heaven, then started pacing the Hall. 'After telling me for months you were not ready to wed, now you ask this? The Earl of Dexter will be here within days! What will I tell him?'

To go to the devil, Marc thought, but Cecily squeezed his fingers before he could speak.

'You are allowing Isabella to wed the hostage she loves,' Cecily said, in a voice more calm than either he or the king could summon. 'I ask for the same privilege.'

'My daughter does not hold the castle that is the key to England!'

Marc felt her fingers tighten. If the king asked her to give up Losford for him, which would she choose?

Instead, the king turned his eyes to Marc, measuring him. Silent, Marc thought over the past months. What had the king seen of him, after all? A joust. A boar hunt. And too many gatherings at Windsor in which he had stood, silent, at the edge of the company.

Suddenly, he wanted to prove he was worthy. Of Cecily. Of this man.

Of this country.

He dropped to his knees again, this time, for a different kind of surrender. 'I swear, Your Grace, that I will be as loyal to you as to Cecily. And I will defend either of you, and this castle, with my life.'

The king shook his head. 'What am I to do with you women and your men from the Oise Valley?' Exasperation tinged his voice, but laughter lurked at the edges. At least, Marc hoped that was what he heard.

Next to him, Cecily breathed more easily. 'You are to allow us our hearts, Your Grace.'

'Isabella tried to prepare me before I came. She and de Coucy both warned me of this.'

'I will keep my word,' Marc said. 'On my honour.' A vow he finally understood.

'The Earl of Dexter,' the king said, shaking his head, 'is going to be greatly disappointed.'

Epilogue

Windsor Castle—July 27, 1365

'Cecily, you must help me!' Isabella reached up to steady her crown, looking as shy and nervous as a girl.

'Shh,' Cecily said, with a smile. 'Hold still.' The princess and all her ladies were clustered out of sight of those gathered in St George's Chapel.

It was no surprise that Isabella was nervous. It was her wedding day.

The wedding had taken near a year to plan and the nuptials were as lavish as if Isabella were marrying the King of Castile or the Count of Flanders instead of a Lord de Coucy.

'Here,' Cecily said, standing back and surveying the bride. 'You look beautiful. And the crown is *très beau.*'

The crown, only one of the king's many wedding gifts, sparkling with diamonds and sapphires, was as extravagant as if Isabella were assuming a throne.

Cecily, too, had had a wedding, a much quieter affair. She and Marc exchanged vows in the small church at Losford, where her parents, in spirit, could witness it.

Today, all of the nobility of England was here to see the king's daughter wed the French count. They entered the chapel and Cecily smoothed her skirt over her growing stomach. She looked over to where Marc stood and flashed him a smile.

When the ceremony was over, tonight, she would tell her husband the news. Next year, they would be celebrating a christening in the church at Losford Castle.

Marc looked at his friend, ready to be wed, glad their time of estrangement was well behind them.

After all, a man in love could act as one mad. So could a woman. Cecily had, indeed, paid Marc's ransom. If the money ever came from France, she would be recompensed, but in the meantime, as she occasionally reminded him with a smile, Marc belonged to her.

And nothing could have made him happier.

As Marc had expected, France's new king had proved less eager to abide by the treaty terms than his father had been. Some money had crossed the Channel, but less and less as time went on.

With his marriage, Enguerrand was to receive the gift of his freedom. His portion of the ransom was forgiven and once again, the Count, now the Earl of Bedford, was a man free to come and go.

Yes, powerful and strong as this king was, he had a weakness for his children. And, it seemed, for love. In order that Marc have the stature to marry a woman with one of the most powerful titles in England, the king had awarded him an earl's title of his own. Marc felt he had found a new king, worthy of his loyalty.

And a woman worthy of his honour.

* * * * *

Author's Afterword

History does not record when Enguerrand, Lord de Coucy, and Isabella of Woodstock actually met. He arrived in England in 1360 and they married, as I show here, in 1365. The chroniclers do record specifically how charming de Coucy was when King Jean II of France returned to captivity. According to Jean Froissart, recorder of all events of King Edward's reign, '...*the young lord de Coucy shined in dancing and carolling whenever it was his turn. He was in great favour with both the French and English...*'

What woman could help but notice such a man?

I have taken a few liberties with the location of the royal court at any specific time. At this era, the court moved between palaces regularly, often staying only a few days in one place. For simplicity's sake, I have streamlined some of their movements and limited their locations, including those related to the return of King Jean to England.

If you've read *Secrets at Court*, you'll recall Windsor Castle was undergoing extensive re-modelling during this period. Detailed records do not exist for exactly which parts of the castle were completed each year, so I have used my best judgement and information available. If all the rooms I mention were not fully complete and operational during the Yuletide season of 1363, I hope historians will forgive my impulse to show them as Edward had intended.

Cecily's castle is firmly modelled on Dover Castle, but the specifics of her life and family are not those of the Castle's holders. Surpris-ingly, there were very few castles on the English coast at this time. It was not until the reign of Henry VIII that a series of defensive castles was built for protection along the eastern and south-ern coasts of England. Dover, only twenty-one miles across the English Channel from Calais, really did stand alone.

As the 'key to England', Dover was owned by the crown, not an individual family, and the king would then install a trusted associate as a constable. At this time—1361-1364—it was Sir Richard—or Robert—de Herle, also warden of the Cinque Ports and Admiral of the Fleet. And though I invented the Earl of Losford, there was an English lord—Lord Guy Beau-champ—killed in the Black Monday shower of hail, as Cecily's father was.

King Edward did visit Dover Castle in 1364 to consult about a marriage. Alas, it was not the one I described.

As for the story of de Coucy and Isabella, I have tried to adhere to the generally accepted wisdom. Her extravagance and his courtly charm are generally accepted and she was clearly her father's favourite daughter and very attached to home and family. The background of her attempted marriages is accurate. Lord de Coucy's English lands were restored, though that has been variously reported as early as 1363 or not until it was part of the marriage settlement in 1365. He was created the Earl of Bedford by Edward III, to give him an English title to go with the lands, and he was even named a Knight of the Garter. Edward did create such titles several times during his reign, so doing so for Marc de Marcel would have been possible.

For Enguerrand and Isabella, there was no lifelong happy ending. They moved to France, but when Edward III died in 1377, de Coucy gave up his English title and lands and returned his loyalty to the French king. Isabella, who had trav-elled back to England frequently, returned home for good with their two daughters and the couple lived apart for the rest of her life. She died in 1382. After her death, Enguerrand remarried, another Isabelle, this one the daughter of a French duke. They also had a daughter, who did not live to adulthood.

De Coucy spent the rest of his life in wars and fighting, finally dying of the plague in 1396, after being taken prisoner while on Crusade in Turkey. For those who have read my earlier books, Isabella and Enguerrand's second daughter, Philippa, became the wife of Robert de Vere, ninth Earl of Oxford, who plays a prominent role in my book *The Harlot's Daughter*. Philippa appears only offstage.

The situation of the French hostages in England, strange as it may seem to us, was well documented. Chivalry and greed seemed equally mixed and certain among them really did socialise with the court on a regular basis. The party at the ex-mayor's residence is recorded by history. It is sometimes said that four kings, not two, attended, but the best information I could find showed that King David of Scotland and Peter of Cyprus had left London by this time. Even the hospitality of King Edward for King Jean is described in detail in the chronicles, and King Edward gave his fellow monarch a major funeral before sending the body back so that France could do the same.

But King Jean's death in 1364 did, eventually, change the situation of the hostages and of the treaty. Though the last hostage was not released until 1367, King Edward seemed to lose heart and interest, and there were hostages who just disappeared, as Marc tried to do.

As the French historian Édouard Perroy writes in his book *The Hundred Years War*, by this time, 'There remained in London as hostages only the small fry of petty barons and burgesses. Individual measures of clemency set some free, and others married and settled permanently in England...'.

Others, including Lord de Coucy and, perhaps, even someone like Marc de Marcel.

My story ends with England and France at peace, but it did not last. Indeed, as Marc suspected, the death of the King of France unravelled everything. Gradually, fighting began again, and the French king, Charles V, declared the Treaty of Brétigny void in May of 1369. The war resumed, not ending conclusively until the next century. Eventually, it would be known as the Hundred Years War.

A note on word usage: Chaucer did use the term 'princesse' in a manuscript composed in 1385, some twenty years after this story, but it did not appear widely used until the fifteenth century. I have used it here for Isabella because it is likely to have been in use at that time and is more familiar to the modern reader. A count, or *compte* in France, was the same title as an earl in England. However, the female equivalent was countess in both countries.

MILLS & BOON®

The Thirty List

Eva Woods

At thirty, Rachel has slid down every ladder she has ever climbed. Jobless, broke and ditched by her husband, she has to move in with grumpy Patrick and his four-year-old son.

Patrick is also getting divorced, so to cheer themselves up the two decide to draw up bucket lists. Soon they are learning to tango, abseiling, trying stand-up comedy and more. But, as she gets closer to Patrick, Rachel wonders if their relationship is too good to be true…

MILLS & BOON®

Why not subscribe?
Never miss a title and save money too!

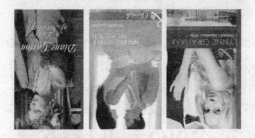

Here's what's available to you if you join the
exclusive **Mills & Boon Book Club** today:

- ✦ *Titles up to a month ahead of the shops*
- ✦ *Amazing discounts*
- ✦ *Free P&P*
- ✦ *Earn Bonus Book points that can be redeemed
  against other titles and gifts*
- ✦ *Choose from monthly or pre-paid plans*

Still want more?
Well, if you join today we'll even give you
50% OFF your first parcel!

So visit **www.millsandboon.co.uk/subs**
or call **Customer Relations on 020 8288 2888**
to be a part of this exclusive Book Club!

MILLS & BOON®

HISTORICAL

AWAKEN THE ROMANCE OF THE PAST

A sneak peek at next month's titles...

In stores from 3rd July 2015:

- **A Rose for Major Flint** – Louise Allen
- **The Duke's Daring Debutante** – Ann Lethbridge
- **Lord Laughraine's Summer Promise** – Elizabeth Beacon
- **Warrior of Ice** – Michelle Willingham
- **A Wager for the Widow** – Elisabeth Hobbes
- **Running Wolf** – Jenna Kernan
